T

T

Mitchell J. Rycus

iUniverse, Inc.
Bloomington

T

iUniverse books may be ordered through booksellers or by contacting:

iUniverse
1663 Liberty Drive
Bloomington, IN 47403
www.iuniverse.com
1-800-Authors (1-800-288-4677)

ISBN: 978-1-4759-7233-7 (sc)
ISBN: 978-1-4759-7234-4 (ebk)

Library of Congress Control Number: 2013901015

Printed in the United States of America

iUniverse rev. date: 01/21/2013

There is only one first principle in planning:

God gets even!

Lovingly dedicated to Carole, Lisa, Saulius, Peter, Meena
and the grandkids Sam, Evan, Tyler and Abe.

PROLOGUE

September 2010

Father Pavlos

It's that time of year when summer starts winding down just before the Labor Day weekend and people are thinking about who will be in the World Series. I'm hoping it's the Detroit Tigers this year, but that probably won't happen. Baseball always reminds me of my childhood. I can almost hear my mother calling me in for dinner, "Pau-leeeey! Pau-leeeey!" as she did in the early 1970s. We lived in the lower flat of a corner duplex house, right across the street from the school playground on the east side of Detroit. Some of the boys from the neighborhood—myself included—would be out there playing ball, or shagging flies if there weren't enough of us to make up teams of at least three on three. And if there were only an odd number of us out there, I'd rather be the umpire or play the catcher position for both sides. You might say that I wasn't very competitive at that time—that may be true. However, I was ambitious, and I still am, even though today I'm the senior priest at Saint Demetrios Greek Orthodox Church in Ypsilanti, Michigan.

People might ask how it is that a priest could think of himself as ambitious when being called to serve our Lord has always been considered a pursuit in humility. In fact, that also reminds me of my mother who would say, "Pauley, if you're always playing baseball, how will you be able to prepare for medical school or, God willing, the priesthood? Have you no ambition?"

My given name is Paul David Kostopoulos, and I was baptized at Annunciation Greek Orthodox Cathedral in downtown Detroit, Michigan, on August 15, 1962. I was three years old at the time, but I can still vividly remember that spiritual awakening. When I was ordained in 1984, I took the name of Father Pavlos after receiving my priestly vestments and returning to

Michigan as a newly appointed assistant priest in a large Orthodox church in Detroit. It was in 1987 that I was called to Ypsilanti, Michigan, as the assistant priest at Saint Demetrios. To me, becoming a priest meant having ambition, almost by definition. And thirteen years ago there was a moment when my ambition made me do something that I think only our Lord himself had the right to do, and I've been penitent for that act to this very day. It all came about because of my participation in some strange—some may even say unworldly—occurrences, and I feel it is my duty, you might even say my calling, to put these experiences in writing not only for my benefit but for the benefit of mankind in general.

That might sound a bit grand on my part, but I honestly think of myself as just an ordinary priest living an unremarkable life in a small midwestern town that is made up of primarily working-class people. Many of my parishioners are employed at the Ford plant and other smaller factories in the area and, for the most part, are not college educated. But they are the best people on the planet for me. Many are first—or, at best, second-generation Americans, their families having emigrated from Greece or some other Eastern European countries where they were raised in an Orthodox environment. They are hard-working, God-loving people devoted to the church and, by association, to me.

I'm actually a first-generation American myself, since both of my parents came over from Greece when they were children. My father was an engineer who worked for Ford in Dearborn, Michigan, and my mother was trained as a nurse, but she never practiced nursing—at least professionally—having married my father shortly after graduating. It was my mother's guidance that got me interested in science and medicine. I was fascinated by botany, and I would enjoy nursing sick animals back to health, frequently using the herbal remedies that I had learned from my botanical science readings.

"Pauley, honey, that robin is too sick for you to be able to help her now. I think it best that you just leave her outside and let God decide her fate," my mother once told me when I brought a very sick robin home.

And so I left the robin outside, but in the morning when I couldn't find the bird, I didn't know whether she had been taken by God or was healed by my treatment. In fact, either way I knew that God had intervened on her behalf. From that experience I knew that I would either be a doctor or a priest. As I grew older, I gradually knew in my heart that it would definitely be the clergy for me.

Indeed, tending to my parishioners is in some sense like a doctor tending to his patients. Only I am interested in healing their spirit through prayer, teaching and practicing the sacraments. My favorite sacrament is the baptismal rite. In our church it requires three complete immersions, and the service can last for more than an hour. I'll never forget my own baptism, even though I was only a very small child at the time. I was so moved by the spirit and gentleness of the priest that even though my head went under water, I had no fear. Because of my baptismal experience, I have always felt that it is my responsibility to conduct that sacrament in the same careful way, knowing the child is frightened to begin with. (I discourage infant baptism, unless the circumstances are extraordinary.) Changing a child's emotion from fear to trust and then filling them with grace is one of the most satisfying parts of my job.

My least favorite job is attending those darn church council meetings. We meet monthly, and I'm really only an ad hoc member, but they know they can't make church policy without my consent. We talk about finances, new deacons, various committees, and all the boring but very important aspects of keeping a church on sound financial and socially responsible ground. Our associate priest is Father Leon, and he's married to a social worker who has been a godsend. She holds the title of secretary on the church council and has taken on all kinds of responsibilities. In some sense I appreciate her more than I do Father Leon. Don't get me wrong—Father Leon has been a great asset to me and helps me out considerably in all our priestly duties, especially since Father Timotheos became emeritus this year. But it's his wife, Zoe, who really has taken over the secular elements of the church.

Zoe runs most of the social programs, such as the Saturday night dances for the over-forty crowd. She teaches in our school and handles many of the youth programs. Since she's a trained social worker, I trust her participation and leadership in many church functions; I don't feel the need to micromanage her responsibilities. I must admit that I'm glad she runs the over-forty dance social, because I've heard that some couples sneak off and do more than dance at these affairs.

Lately the remarkable events of so long ago have been on my mind more than usual. I know that's probably because in a couple of weeks I'll be meeting with two of the players in this saga, and I want to be as thoroughly prepared as possible to address the many issues raised. As I've already said, these unearthly occurrences began thirteen years ago when I came into possession of some strange herbs that were brought back from Indonesia by an engineer and his wife who live in Ann Arbor. The engineer's name was Joseph Gilbert, and when I first met him, he was a tall, clean-cut young man with blond hair, which was lightly streaked with tan. He wore his haircut short in 1997, looking like the professional optical engineer he was trained to be. One almost expected to see a pocket protector for his pens sitting conspicuously in his dress shirt pocket. His tie was worn loosely around his collar, and his sleeve cuffs were casually turned up. His good looks, amplified by his angular face, made him appear mature beyond his years.

Joe's wife, Gabriella, was a stunning woman. She was around five feet, six inches and had black hair, a delicate face, and an exquisite figure. She made me think about my fiancée of many years ago. Maybe it was the black hair, but even after all these years, I still feel some regret for never having married Vicky.

But back to Joe and Gabriella.

Episode 1

APRIL 1997

CHAPTER 1

Joey Gilbert

"You've got incurable cancer," the doctor said, "and I'm not sure how to say it . . . make it sound any easier for you." His eyes were sympathetic when he spoke, but his long surgeon's fingers were moving somewhat erratically. I thought, *How strange for a surgeon to have shaky hands.* His hands didn't actually shake, but after the news he just gave me, I noticed mine were trembling, so why shouldn't his?

I was in Dr. William Kahn's office—an oncologist probably in his midforties—because my internist, Dick Obermeyer, ran some blood tests and other diagnostic procedures on me. Dick had set up the appointment with him after my CT scan. I'd never met Kahn before, but if Dick wanted me to see him, I knew it must be important. After what he just told me, I knew Dick was right.

Those few words nervously spoken by Dr. Kahn in the spring of 1997 started the whole saga off for all of us "survivors of the leaves," as Father Pavlos affectionately called us. I was going on thirty-seven when I got the news of my imminent death.

My wife Gabriella and I were getting ready for our trip, scheduled to leave the next day. Earlier in the week my pain had become unbearable. I'd had some similar pains before but never so severe and never bad enough to make me even think I should see a doctor. After all, I was told that I was in perfect health; why bother when I knew it was only heartburn? So I took the TUMS, but this time the pain didn't go away—it just got worse. We had been planning our trip for a long time; it was a second honeymoon in Bali. Our first honeymoon was a weekend in Niagara Falls, and that was ten years ago. But Bali? *Wow!* I thought.

Gabriella—she hated being called Gabby—had made all the arrangements. We would be staying at Poppies Cottages on Kuta Beach. A little rustic and not at all like the resorts on Nusa Dua where many of the other Americans and Australians stayed, but that's where my wife wanted to be—someplace more remote, more private, less hectic, someplace where you had to walk to the beach down Poppies Lane with coffee shops, souvenir stands, and other local attractions, even a good restaurant or two that most Western tourists had never even heard of. That's what she wanted, that's what she had planned, and now this.

"So what's the prognosis?" I asked, trying not to seem scared by using a little levity. The truth be told, I was terrified.

"Pancreatic cancer. I can help with the pain, but . . ." The doctor appeared less nervous now that he saw I wasn't about to go to pieces in his office. Gabriella wasn't in the examining room then, so Dr. Kahn asked, "Mr. Gilbert, would you like me to call your wife in here?"

I thought about it for a moment and realized she would never forgive me if I didn't fill her in now. I said, "Sure, let's get her in here so we can make arrangements to cancel our trip."

"You're planning a trip? Where are you going?" the doctor asked.

"Bali, Indonesia—our second honeymoon." I choked up a little when I said that.

Dr. Kahn noticed and waited a minute before saying, "If it's for less than a month, why cancel? I think we can control the pain. With some moderation—like don't try to run any marathons—you should still be able to go away for a couple of weeks."

I thought about it for a second and then said, "Why not?"

"I have a friend, Dr. Wayan Setiawan, who's teaching at Udayana University in Denpasar. I'll give you his number in case you experience any trouble, or you can just call him to touch base when you arrive. I'll give you a note to give to him, okay?"

We called Gabriella into the little space and gave her the news. She was crushed, of course, and wouldn't let go of me for about five minutes. Once her sobbing subsided, she seemed to accept the diagnosis, though I knew she didn't believe it.

"Are you sure going to Bali is a good idea?" she asked the doctor through sobs. "What if Joe really gets sick? Can they, uh . . . can they take care of him?" she asked. She meant, "What if he needs to go to the hospital there? Will they have the modern facilities he needs?"

Dr. Kahn answered, "I think it's a great idea. We really can't do much for your husband here right now, but I think this will be a great chance for the two of you to discuss your options without all of the outside pressures of family and friends. You'll have enough of that when you let them all know. This will help you plan without those distractions."

Dr. Kahn assured Gabriella that the hospital in Denpasar could take care of me if needed. We didn't have any children to deal with, and our families would be absolutely panicked about wanting me to get second and third opinions. It was a good idea for the two of us to go off alone for the honeymoon we never really had. If the doctor was wrong about the diagnosis, then that would come out later; and if he was right, well what was the harm?

*   *   *

We arrived at the Denpasar airport around eight in the evening, and the first thing I noticed when we got off the plane, besides the warm ocean air cooling off the evening, was the sweet smell of the frangipani plants and the other tropical flowers that surrounded the tarmac. I had felt a little nauseated on the flight, and I thought it was because I hadn't eaten very much. We had left more than a day before with a night's stopover in Hong Kong. My appetite had not been very good lately, and I had lost some weight in the last few months, but the pressure at work was my excuse for all this discomfort. Now I knew it was the cancer. When we arrived at Poppies, I took some of the pills that Dr. Kahn gave me and decided to contact Dr. Setiawan the next day.

As the evening wore on, I felt a little better as the medicine kicked in. Gabriella and I walked around the grounds, marveling at how peaceful and beautiful that Southeast Asian area was, and I began to resent the fact that I was going to die soon. My anger didn't help in setting a romantic tone for our first evening in Bali. After a fitful night we slept late and woke to the clicking sounds of the geckos that lived with us in our cottage.

*   *   *

"Yes, thank you. I'm looking for Dr. Wayan Setiawan. I was given this number by—"

"One moment, please, while I connect you," the operator said. I had called the number Dr. Kahn had given me in case I wanted to touch base with Dr. Setiawan. It took a little time to find an operator who spoke English, but once I found him I got through quickly.

"Setiawan speaking," I heard on the line.

"Yes, Dr. Setiawan, my name is Joseph Gilbert and my doctor, William Kahn, suggested I call you . . ."

"Bill Kahn, my old roommate at Michigan. How's he doin'? I haven't heard from him in a while. What did you say your name was?"

Dr. Setiawan spoke quickly, but he was friendly and obviously excited about hearing from his old friend and colleague. I explained why I was calling and where I was staying, and after telling me to just call him Setiawan, he said he would come over to Poppies in about an hour to meet us. I didn't expect this to be a social event, but what the hell—we might as well meet the locals, especially when they make house calls.

Setiawan arrived around noon and suggested going for lunch. His looks surprised me a little because he was so much taller than most Balinese men, but his features were definitely of the island. His bronze skin and classic Balinese good looks were unmistakable; it was just his size that was different, giving him an almost regal appearance. The restaurant at Poppies was quite casual, draped in flowering vines and open to the ocean on three sides. It was most delightful for meeting someone for the first time, so we stayed on the grounds. I wasn't hungry and the dull pain in my stomach was beginning to act up again. When we were seated in the restaurant, Setiawan gave our waiter something that looked like marijuana leaves all crumpled up in a plastic bag and explained to the waiter in Balinese (not Bahasa Indonesian—the official language) what to do with them. The waiter brought drinks for Gabriella and Setiawan and a cup of tea for me. Setiawan instructed me to drink the tea while we talked about everything—that is, everything but my cancer. He suggested that I might want to add some honey since the tea might be bitter. He seemed a little disappointed that I really didn't know Dr. Kahn very well. In fact I had just met him the day he diagnosed my incurable disease.

"So how do you feel now?" Setiawan asked after lunch. I had to admit that my pain had subsided and I was able to eat without much discomfort.

"What was in that tea you gave me? Was it some kind of narcotic?" I asked. I wasn't feeling dopey like I had smoked pot or was high on booze, but I did feel a little euphoric.

"I teach homeopathic medicine even though I have a very modern medical degree and a modern practice at the university's hospital," he said, "but every now and then my Balinese training in herbs and natural medicines comes in handy. I left the waiter enough of those herbs to easily last you all week, and even enough to take back with you when you leave. He'll leave the hot tea and honey with your morning bananas on your cottage porch. Call me if for some reason you should need more or you're not feeling good."

When Setiawan left, I was actually feeling in good spirits—even though I knew I was going to die. I hadn't fully accepted that yet and neither had Gabby. (I was the only one who got away with calling her Gabby—but only in private.) We spent the rest of the day exploring our lush surroundings. We went to local shops, walked the beach with its exotic vendors of trinkets and massages, ate martabeks served on banana leaves on the street, and by evening we were glad to be back at Poppies. We decided to have dinner at the restaurant and just relax and plan out the rest of our vacation.

Our usual waiter—well, for at least that day—was there to take care of us. "How you feeling this evening, Mr. Gilbert? Hope morning tea was good for you," he said. He was one of those beautiful Bali boys world famous for their looks and charm. His smile was infectious.

"Feeling fine, uh, Madé," I said, reading his name on his shiny brass name tag. "Do you know Dr. Setiawan?"

"Everyone know Setiawan. He has many patients all over Bali. He has, you say . . . clinics for villages everywhere. He is good doctor. Much loved." There was little doubt that Madé revered Setiawan.

Gabriella and I ordered dinner and tried to talk about how we would deal with the future: who we would we tell, and how we would tell them; redoing the will; quitting work; and all the other things one needs to do when one knows, or rather has been told, that one is going to die soon. It was somewhat reassuring talking about all these things, even though we found ourselves crying frequently. It was good to know that we could get things settled. The waiter noticed our situation and stayed discreetly in the background, only coming over when he saw us smile or laugh. Some things were funny, like telling our neighbor he could have the lawnmower he was always borrowing. In between crying and laughing sprees we somehow got through dinner and even a couple of after-dinner drinks.

Walking on the grounds back to our cottage, we once again noticed the serenity of the place. The fragrances of the tropics and feeling the soft sea breeze blowing over the incredibly green grass made me think that maybe I should die there. Or just maybe, I thought, *I'm not going to die at all!*

The bed had been turned down, and the geckos were either fast asleep or eating the mosquitoes, so they were quiet. We undressed and got in bed, and although we were still feeling melancholy, as we snuggled up we became sexually aroused.

"Are you sure you feel well enough?" Gabriella asked.

I kissed her gently and then deeply as I rubbed my naked body between her legs. "Does that answer your question?" I said somewhat breathlessly as I proceeded to enter her. We made love for a long time, both of us experiencing the pleasure of each other over and over again.

"What the fuck do you think was in that tea Setiawan gave me?" I said afterward, giggling.

"I have no idea, but I hope you can get more of it when we get home," Gabriella said with a smile in her voice.

We lay there for a long time, and as we drifted off, I tried not to think about my cancer, but that was impossible.

* * *

The next morning there were two thermos bottles on our porch table, decorated with traditional Balinese symbols, and a basket of bananas. I could tell by the aroma which thermos had Setiawan's tea in it; the other had simply plain Indonesian, or Indian, tea. There was also a small jar of honey and a couple of spoons and two mugs for us. The porch of our thatched-roof cottage was very small, but the small, rustic bamboo table and the two matching chairs fit nicely on it. The table was covered with a washed-out black-and-white checkered cloth, and some paper napkins were in the banana basket.

"Want some tea, hon?" I asked Gabriella as I poured myself some of Setiawan's tea. "These bananas are great. Do you think they have aphrodisiac powers?" I said with an impish grin on my face.

"Gee, I hope not. I don't know if I could take another night like last night," Gabriella answered with a mocked look of pain on her face. Then she took a banana, made an obscene gesture with it, and bit off a large hunk, smiling at me all the time she was chewing it. We finished our tea, planned our day, made love again, showered, dressed, and left for an island adventure.

All day long I couldn't get over how good I felt—no nausea, no pain, my appetite had returned, and that yellowish hue in my complexion seemed to be turning into a nice Bali tan. For the rest of the week we thoroughly enjoyed ourselves—for the most part making love almost every night and morning. However, there were the ups and downs with crying, laughing, and angry outbursts (which I understand is part of the dying process). Mostly we went about our day in as normal a way as we possibly could.

I dreaded the week ending and going back to work. I was sure that once I started working again my discomfort would return. Then again if I was dying, why should I even have to go back to work? *If I'm dying*, I thought again. Why would I think the doctors were wrong? Setiawan didn't even examine me, so how would he know? My own doctor, Dr. Obermeyer, didn't say anything before recommending Kahn, so I only had Kahn's diagnosis. In some sense I felt relieved that maybe I wasn't dying after all, and in another I felt tense about having to face work again. Who would have thought that going back to work would be a more stressful activity than facing eminent death?

"You know what, honey?" Gabriella said one day, her gentle, loving eyes looking into me. "When we get home, ask for a leave of absence from work. Then go back to Dick Obermeyer and have him check you out thoroughly for the cancer. Maybe you just had a touch of jaundice or some other type of hepatitis that mimicked the cancer and now it's gone. This will give us time to rethink our options, and either way we've done a lot of serious planning that can only work for us down the line. What do you say?"

"Sounds like a plan to me."

In a way I didn't want to go back to my doctor; I just wanted to believe for a while longer that I wasn't going to die. I felt great, so why not simply enjoy it for as long as I could and keep the hope that I was all right—*I'm not dying!*

"When we get back on Saturday, I'll try to get hold of Glen and tell him what's going on and ask him for a leave of absence."

I worked for an electro-optical products development company, Benson Engineering. We made devices that used lasers and sophisticated optics for things like the UPC scanners you see at all the check-out counters around the world. I'm their chief engineer and my boss, Glen Masden, and I have been working together for some time now. Glen was an MBA and the project manager on all our company products; he keeps me very busy writing proposals, meeting deadlines, and worrying me half to death all the time about how the company was in desperate need of new contracts or it will go under. Gabriella felt Glen was using me, and she was angry with him—and me—because she felt I spent more time with the company and worrying about Benson Engineering than I did with her and worrying about our relationship. She had told me more than once to quit.

"With your skills you can get a job anywhere you want for twice what they're paying you at Benson's, and with less aggravation and more interesting work for you. Why don't you try looking for something else? It won't hurt to look," she kept telling me.

When I mentioned asking Glen about a leave of absence, her response was quick. "He's a shithead; he could care less if you're dying. All he thinks about is getting those damn contracts, and you're the only one that can do the work. You gotta call Benson directly—skip Glen." Gabriella's anger was noticeably reflected in her voice.

The owner of the company, Roger Benson, was a kind, old man, who she thought would be more sympathetic. Roger would probably tell me to clear it through Glen anyway, so I said, "Okay, let's wait till we get home to make that decision. On Monday I'll call Dick Obermeyer and make an appointment. He's probably heard from Kahn by now, so he might even be expecting me to call."

Gabriella always got antsy and unsettled when preparing to go home after a trip, so I thought it best not to push about calling Glen now and wait till she was in a better mood.

We started to pack up for our trip home. We would be leaving the next morning for Hong Kong, and then we would go back to Detroit Metro from there. We checked out the drawers and closets for any items we might have forgotten to pack. While doing this, I told Gabriella, "Madé gave me the tea leaves that Setiawan left for me; there's still a lot here." I noticed the plastic bag with about a pound of the leaves still left in it. "Do you think I can get these through customs?"

"Just put it in your suitcase. They won't bother you about it if it's packed away," Gabriella proclaimed tersely. She was still testy, so I figured that I best not bother her about anymore decisions. I wanted to say something like, "That's not the way to talk to a dying man," but thought better of it.

*   *   *

After our morning tea and bananas—both of us had only regular tea—Madé came over to tell us that our transport to the airport was waiting. He brought a porter along with him, and the two of them took our luggage out to the van. I tipped Madé generously, we said our good-byes and, Gabriella and I left for the Denpasar airport.

10

Our flight to Hong Kong and back to the States was uneventful. We talked little during the flights. I think the feeling that this would probably be our last trip together put a damper on the journey back home. We didn't talk about death or illness but just mundane stuff like, "We should stop at Kroger's for bread and milk." However, there was an underlying feeling of anger in both of us, and unfortunately we were taking it out on each other.

I've been told that anger is one of the five stages of grief that a person goes through when they are told they're going to die. I didn't know that one's spouse went through the same stages, but there was little doubt that Gabriella was also going through all the stages with me. We hadn't finished the denial stage yet, and here we were into anger. I suspected that she might even be angry at me for dying on her while she was still so young or even angry at God for this cruel turn of events, but whatever it was, both of us were feeling it. However, I must admit that my anger had significantly decreased over the last few days, and I wasn't sure why. Maybe I was still going through the denial stage and hadn't fully accepted the fact that I was dying, or maybe I was skipping some stages and just going straight to acceptance. Whatever the reason, poor Gabriella was still apparently angry while I was feeling pretty good. That is, until we landed and went through customs.

It was raining on that April day when we reached Detroit. On the plane I filled out that customs form and stupidly mentioned I was bringing back some tea with me. I guess I was worried that if their food-sniffing dogs did find the bag and I hadn't said anything, I'd be in deep shit because it looked so much like grass. I wrote it in without telling Gabriella. When going through customs, the agent made me open my suitcase to show him the tea. He took one look and said it had to be left with him because it was opened and not sealed. He pointed out that bringing open food back from Indonesia was not allowed. He just took it and threw it in a cardboard box with other food like oranges, cookies, and what looked like a box of Cheerios. I could tell by the way he looked first at it and then at me, and even after he quickly smelled it, that he thought for sure it was marijuana.

Gabriella jumped in by saying, "That's actually a medical infusion prescribed by a licensed doctor, so may we have it back, please?"

"Do you have a copy of the prescription and a receipt for the purchase?" the customs agent asked. Gabriella gave some exasperated answer about Indonesia being a tiny, third-world nation and things didn't happen that way there.

"I'm sorry I can't return it to you, but it will be kept here at our office for two weeks, and if you can come back with proper medical and customs documentation, then you can have it back." He was very polite even though I'm sure he had heard this same story many times before and no one ever came back for their "medicine."

"Why did you list the tea on the customs form?" Gabriella asked me as we were driving home. She had cooled down enough to sound reasonable.

"I just didn't want to take any chances with all this concern over drugs and everything; I only wanted to play it safe. I'll have Kahn get us more from Setiawan. It's no big deal. It's only tea," I said. However, both of us knew that it was that tea that had caused those remarkable physical changes in me, and I should probably have kept a better handle on it than I did.

*   *   *

"Hi, Mr. Benson, it's me, Joey Gilbert . . . Yes, we got back a few hours ago. Bali was wonderful."

I was talking on the phone to my boss shortly after we landed. I asked him about taking a leave of absence for a couple of months, explaining that my doctor felt I needed the rest. After listening to Benson explain to me why I needed to call Glen Masden, I simply said, "Okay, I'll call him now. Thanks. Good night."

"I take it he wants you to call that asshole, Masden," Gabriella said in a disgusted manner. "Well, good luck with that!"

I dialed Glen's number. "Glen, it's me Joe . . . Yeah, we just got back a few hours ago. Look, there's something I have to ask you."

I told him what I said to Benson about needing a leave of absence. Glen sounded very upset and asked to come over. I said, "Yeah, sure, if you want. I'm a little tired, so let's not make it long. See you in a bit."

"What was that all about?" Gabriella asked.

"He wants to come over and talk with me. He sounded concerned. What could I say? So I told him to come over."

"Are you going to tell him now?" she asked. She was concerned how I might handle it.

"I don't know. I'll play it by ear and see what happens. Well, we have to start with someone, so why not Glen. It may be hard for you to believe, but at one time we were really good friends and worked well together."

And that was true. When Glen came to Benson's place more than ten years ago, I was just another engineer and he was coming in to push for new product development. For one reason or another we hit it off, and the two of us, as a team, were very successful. Glen had a nose for what products would sell, and he would push me to come up with the technical know-how to develop them, like holographic product identifiers that couldn't be copied by the Chinese.

We rose up the company ladder together, and we're now at the top of our game. But Glen does have a knack for turning people off, and at times he's tried pushing me a little too far with his own personal agenda. He was more concerned with trying to make as much money as possible in the shortest possible time than quality and public safety. Gabriella had sensed this and didn't trust him, let alone like him. But I've been able to keep Glen in check, and even though he could stress me out, I owed my success at the company to him—or at least that's how I felt.

About fifteen minutes later the doorbell rang, and Glen walked in without waiting for me to answer the door. Glen was a lean man, around five feet, ten inches, with an unremarkable face. He was not homely, but you wouldn't say he was good looking either—I guess the word plain describes him best. He had straight, washed-out brown hair that he wore low on his forehead, making him look a little like a caveman. And he was always moving his eyes; he never seemed to focus on anything for very long. I think it was because of his eyes that Gabriella distrusted him so much.

"So what's going on?" Glen asked even before he got his coat off. He looked very nervous and was not his usual hyperactive self. "It just seems strange to me that you would ask for leave now. I did notice you weren't looking so well these last couple of months, and I wanted to talk to you about that."

"How about a drink?" I asked as he sat down. Gabriella had gone into the bedroom to leave the two of us alone. "I'm going to have a scotch. Join me?"

"Sure, why not." Glen was definitely tense and seemed to be on the verge of divulging some deep dark secret to me. I poured us both long Glenfiddichs—neat with just two drops of cold water in each.

* * *

We had been talking for more than an hour when Gabriella quietly walked in from the bedroom. She apologized for disturbing us and pointed out, "I hadn't heard anything from the front room for a while, so I thought I should see if everything was all right."

"That's okay, honey," I said. "We were just about ready to wrap this up anyway. Come on in."

"How ya doin', Gabriella?" Glen asked, with obvious concern in his voice.

Gabriella could see that both of us had red eyes and swollen faces, and I guess she knew just by our mannerisms that I must have told Glen about my cancer. One thing about Glen that she did like was that he always called her Gabriella, not Gabby or, even worse, Gabe. She seemed to feel sorry for Glen; he looked so desperately sad.

"I'm hanging in there. We're going to be all right," she said with a thin smile on her face. She seemed to feel that Glen needed more cheering up than she did. "Can I freshen your drinks?"

"No, no, we're done here and I'm really getting tired. Jet lag and all," I said, meaning that I was emotionally drained and needed a break.

"Yep, it's time for me to go too," said Glen. "I've got to go in over the weekend and work on that proposal so that we can get it out on Monday. I'll talk to you later. You know I really love you guys, even if I don't always show it." His eyes were welling up again, and they glistened in the dark room lit only by a single lamp.

He put his coat on silently and left, leaving Gabriella and me to talk about our emotional conversation. "I see you told him. He seems to be taking it much worse than I expected," Gabriella said.

"Yeah, I told him, but you won't believe why we were so broken up. I don't know how . . ." I started to say but hesitated for a moment, and then continued. "When he came in here, he could see that something was wrong and asked right away, 'What's the matter?' I told him about getting the cancer verdict."

"He must have shit himself right there, knowing he needed you for that damn proposal," Gabriella said.

"No, no, that wasn't it at all. Yes, he did break down immediately and we both sat there crying like babies—but not because he needed me for the fuckin' proposal," I explained. I told Gabriella that Glen had been planning for more than a year—though he never mentioned it to me—to break away from Benson Engineering to start *our* own company. I would be a full partner heading the engineering, and he would head the business end. He had all the details worked out, even the company name—Gilbert and Masden Digital Optics, Inc.—the location, all the financials, everything. He even had a promise of a fat contract.

Gabriella looked stunned; eyes wide open, mouth a little agape. "How much did he want from you?"

"Nothing! Just the commitment. I would be getting stock initially, and so would he. But all other expenses—setting up the corporation, leasing the space, hiring staff—would be covered by a group of investors that he already had put together! Can you believe that?"

"Wow! Your bombshell must have really sent him reeling. I actually feel sorry for the guy. So what are you going to do?"

"The surprising thing is that he still wants me to commit. We agreed that neither one of us knows how long I have or how long I could work—two months, two years—but whatever it is he wants it. Even if I do nothing more than set up the engineering department, that's okay with him. No matter what the outcome, the stock I'll receive initially will help you out later." I paused here to catch my breath and hold back the emotion, and then I continued. "He intends to finish that last proposal for Benson, get it in on Monday and then give him notice. He was certain I would join him after hearing about all the groundwork he'd done, and then we would give Benson a reasonable time to reorganize. After all, Benson has been good to us, even though the company will soon be outdated under his leadership. That's why Glen started planning our new company."

Gabriella and I sat there in silence for a while. I started to cry again. Gabriella was holding me, comforting me, rocking me back and forth, and gently kissing my cheeks.

*   *   *

It was 9:00 a.m. Monday morning, and Dr. Obermeyer wanted to see me as soon as I could get there. He explained to me why he had wanted Kahn to see me when I went in earlier in the month, complaining of stomach problems and other issues. After seeing my lab results, he had suspected cancer. He wanted Kahn to see if surgery was possible, but without a CT scan he knew the surgeon couldn't be sure. That was why he had scheduled the CT scan under emergency orders and sent me to Kahn. Kahn saw the tumor and the lab work and knew from experience that I was too far gone for surgery.

"I must say you certainly are looking much better than when I saw you more than a week ago," Dr. Obermeyer said. "Bali must have been good for you. How are you feeling? Any pain or discomfort in general?" Obermeyer asked.

"You know, Dick, I must admit that I feel great. No pain, appetite back, no nausea, and my coloring is much better. But that's probably from the Bali sun," I answered.

"I had your blood sent out and asked the pathologist to look at it stat and get back to me," Dr. Obermeyer said. "Once I get the results I'll get back to you. Also I've set up another appointment with Dr. Kahn and another CT scan just to be sure. I know it's only been a week or so, but because of your current condition I thought it wise to follow up on it, okay?"

Later on Monday evening, Dr. Obermeyer called me at home.

"Joe, I just got your preliminary lab results, and I couldn't believe it but your bilirubin level is apparently normal now. But even stranger, a marker we sometimes use for estimating tumor size is, for all practical purposes, gone, whereas before it was at a significantly high level. I'll need a few days to confirm all this, but right now I can't explain what happened. I'll have the final results sent to Dr. Kahn before your appointment."

"So does that mean I don't have pancreatic cancer?" I asked.

"I don't know what it means right now. But don't get your hopes up too high. We've seen apparent remissions like this before that turned out to be false, okay?"

"Okay, no false hopes. I'm anxious to see what Kahn says after my CT scan," I said.

Gabriella had been in the room listening to the conversation. "What was that 'no pancreatic cancer' bit you and Dr. Obermeyer were talking about?"

I related my conversation with Dr. Obermeyer and couldn't get over the anxious look on Gabriella's face when I finished. There was no doubt that she had been terrified over my dying and any hope—false or otherwise—was emotionally explosive for her. It was still raining as it had been for the last few days, and the gloomy weather didn't do much for peace of mind. She burst into tears.

"Oh, God, please, God, let it be true!" she pleaded.

I held her tight. "It's gonna be okay, it's gonna be okay," I kept saying.

*   *   *

"Look here at the two scans side by side," Dr. Kahn said to us. He had set the CT scans up on his viewing screen so we could compare one to the other. "See how large that growth is back there, and here it's gone. I mean completely gone! I've never seen anything like this. Of course I can't be sure without doing a biopsy, but with your blood work and the scan, I'd say you're cancer free."

"Well, what do you think I should do? Get a biopsy or do other tests?" I asked.

"It's pretty much up to you. I would suggest we just wait a little while and repeat the blood work and scan again, say in a month? As I've said, I've never seen this kind of remission before, but I've heard that it has happened without any explanation. You say you started feeling better right after drinking Setiawan's home brew. Do you have any left?"

"No, the bastards confiscated it at customs coming back into the country. Do you think you could get it out of customs for me?" I asked Dr. Kahn.

"I doubt it. It will be easier for me to ask Setiawan to send me some. I'll give him a call. I haven't talked to him in months, so it's time I got in touch with him."

All the way home on that marvelous sun-shiny day in late April, Gabriella and I were smiling. The sky was blue and the temperature was in the low sixties. We stopped off at Gallup Park and walked the Furstenberg nature trail, stopping occasionally to hug and kiss.

"I'm calling Glen to tell him the news. I really want to start our business. I'm so psyched about all this." I paused and then said, "I'm not a fool though. I know that in a month it can all easily change back, but I'm grabbing what I can now. You with me?" I asked Gabriella.

"Of course I am. Call Glen and invite him for dinner. I'll cook up a feast for you and your new business partner."

And that's how it ended—or I should say started. Glen and I became partners. Subsequent tests for the cancer were negative, and as far as I know, Setiawan never sent Kahn any tea. I have no idea what cured my cancer, or even if I had cancer, but I still believe it was the tea that changed everything.

I'm not a very religious man, but I am a believer, and I think of myself as a good Christian. If I didn't know any better, I might have been tempted to think that God had given me a second chance on life for some reason by administering those leaves. I also thought that maybe the leaves were put here just for my benefit and that's why God had the customs people destroy them after I was through using them.

I wondered what other things the tea might have been capable of treating and how many other people could have been helped had they not been destroyed. But I knew it wasn't for me to decide who should get the leaves and who shouldn't. However, because of a strange twist to the story, I soon found out who did get the leaves and what happened to them. It was something totally unexpected, and something that shocked both Gabriella and me when we learned the entire story.

CHAPTER 2

Connie Sarbanes

I was talking to my housemate, Albert Mancini (known to his friends as Al the Man). Al and I shared a modest two-bedroom apartment on Cloverlane Drive in Ypsilanti, Michigan. Cloverlane was south of the expressway and on the western edge of town. It was a quiet neighborhood and an easy hop for me to get on I-94 to the airport.

"I've been a US customs agent for more than ten years and I've heard it all," I told Al, "'That's medicine', or 'that's not food, its ointment,' or some other cockamamie reason why I shouldn't be confiscating their shit. But as far as I'm concerned, I'm just protecting them and other citizens from foreign diseases and harm."

My Greek Orthodox baptismal certificate listed my name as Konstantinos Georgios Sarbanes, however on my Saint Joseph Hospital birth certificate, I was Constantine George. Everyone called me Connie, of course, which was fine by me. Ypsilanti was located just east of Ann Arbor, and a short eighteen miles to my job at Detroit Metro. I could have lived a little closer to work, but I grew up in Ypsi, as we locals called it, and felt comfortable living here. I liked the people, many of them having southern roots going back to WWII when their grandfathers moved up from the South to work in the defense plants. It was then that Ypsi got its nickname, Ypsi-tucky. Some folks are offended by that, but us natives don't mind it at all—it says who we were, and that's fine with me.

I held up the bag for Al to see and continued. "But I have to admit, this stuff interested me. It didn't smell like pot, but I was sure it was some kind of dope. Maybe it was my experience with dopesters that convinced me, but a young, college-educated couple like that, dressed somewhat like hippies in April—well, that's a classic example of folks who bring home dope they bought from some guy on a foreign beach."

"So what are your gonna do with it, Connie? And if you think it's dope, then why did you bring it home?" Al asked.

"I'm not sure just yet. But you know the eye doctor told me I have this eye disease, glaucoma. It's just starting, and it's going to get worse."

I had heard that marijuana could help treat the disease, but I didn't want to risk my job trying to find that out by getting it from a dope peddler. I thought that I would smoke some of the leaves I just got to see what would happen. Who knew—if it worked, then maybe I wouldn't have to take a medical pension or go blind. I felt indecisive about experimenting with it, but by the same token I almost felt compelled to try it.

"It's your life, Connie, but supposin' it can harm you or you get caught with it. Then you'll lose your job and your pension," Al said.

"I don't know exactly what I'm gonna do yet, so let's not jump to any conclusions."

Al was a good guy. We'd been roommates and now housemates since after high school. I went into government service while still enrolled at Washtenaw Community College were we met. Al was in the building apprentice program and was now a licensed carpenter. The apartment we shared was a little small, but it was all we needed and the rent was reasonable. Neither of us ever married but there was still hope—that is if I didn't go blind. In my bedroom there was a Greek cross hanging over my bed; it was called a tau cross because it looked like the Greek letter tau. I'm not very religious, but I grew up in a Greek Orthodox house and we had taus hung up over everyone's bed. My mother told me it was for good luck. I guess luck was what I'd need now if I didn't want to go blind.

I had some old cigarette papers that I once confiscated at the airport. I don't know why I took them home, just like I don't know why I took this tea home, but here they were in my bedroom, and maybe it was fate that brought them together. I fell asleep that night thinking about dope, cigarettes, taus, and going blind.

*   *   *

I didn't work that Saturday and just hung around the apartment. Al had an indoor job he was working on. Spring was here and the higher-paying outdoor work would soon be coming in for him, but when he worked on Saturdays, he got a weekend premium, which made up for his lower winter income. I sat on the bed in my room for a long time, looking at the papers and the tea leaves before I tried rolling a cigarette.

The kids I hung around with in high school never tried dope. The dopesters, or greasers, were an entirely different set of kids, and I didn't have much to do with them. As a customs agent, though, I knew what cannabis leaves looked like, but I also knew they came in many varieties and you couldn't always tell by just looking at them or smelling them. They called the cigarettes joints, and they were harder to roll than it looked. It was a good thing I practiced over some newspaper because most of it spilled out. Once I got one to hold together, it looked pretty bad—fat in the middle, skinny on the ends, and all wet with spit. What a mess.

I made sure my door was closed and the window slightly open in my room. I also made sure no one was outside, because I knew that if someone smelled it they'd know it was coming from my room. It was raining again, so I really didn't have to worry about people hanging around outside. I nervously put one of the skinny ends in my mouth (a lot of the leaves came out and onto my tongue) and then lit the other end. The joint burned quickly down to the fat part and then started to smoke just like a real cigarette. I took a big drag, held it in my lungs for a long time, like I'd seen on TV, and then exhaled. I coughed as my eyes watered and my lungs burned. But I did it again and again, until I couldn't hold the joint anymore. My coughing stopped. Nothing! No high, no happy feeling, nothing! *Well, that was a waste of time,* I thought. I looked at my red eyes in the mirror, all teary from the dope, or tea, or whatever that shit was—the red was still there and the dull pain was there as well.

*   *   *

"What's that smell in here? You cooking something Greek again?" Al said when he came home later in the day. I noticed that the odor of my joint was more like burning autumn leaves and not at all like the pot smell I had some familiarity with because of my job. I acted blasé about the slight remnant of odor when Al asked me.

"Must be someone burning leaves and stuff outside. I haven't cooked all day. You want to share a pizza tonight?" I asked, thinking how lame my response about burning leaves was since it had been raining all day.

"Okay by me. Call it in. Put pepperoni and anchovies on my side. I can eat early. Get a salad too. We got any pop in the house?"

After our pizza dinner I started to clean up the kitchen, and I told Al about the leaves. "I smoked some of that tea today. Didn't do a thing for me. Probably was just tea after all."

"I thought you looked different when I came in. Let's see. It's your eyes—they're not as red as they usually are. You have new eye drops?"

I was surprised to hear Al say that, because they were so red earlier in the day. I went into the bathroom and looked in the mirror. My eyes looked clear; the whites were white, not red and blood shot. The dull pain I had had was gone as well. *Maybe that stuff was dope and it's now curing my glaucoma,* I thought. *But not that fast—how can that be?* I wondered.

"Al, that shit worked! I think it actually worked," I said with some excitement as I came out of the bathroom. I knew it was probably just a temporary thing since nothing could work that fast, and maybe I was just being overly hopeful that I might have stumbled on a cure for my glaucoma. Even Al knew that I had been a bit too optimistic about saying I was cured.

"That fast?" Al said. "I don't know. Sounds a bit hokey to me. But, hey, if you feel better and your eyes don't bother you, then go for it."

I couldn't help but smile as I finished cleaning up the dinner dishes. We were going to my church dance that night—Al wasn't Greek, but he liked the Greek ladies—so we got dressed and left for the evening.

Saint Demetrios, the Greek Orthodox church I attend faithfully on Christmas Eve but seldom during the rest of the year, was an elegant old church with a good Saturday evening social program for the forty-plus crowd. I was actually baptized in the church, so I felt very comfortable there. Our associate priest, Father Pavlos, seemed like a nice guy, though I must admit I didn't see him very often. Maybe I was more comfortable with him because we looked like brothers—both of us were around six feet tall, a little on the stocky side, had that black, wavy Greek hair, and our noses were not the least bit small. However, I thought my facial features were more youthful than his. In addition he reminded me, not surprisingly, of my father; although I would say we were about the same age. But he was one person I had no problem with calling Father—he just looked like he could be someone's father. When I was at services last Christmas, I had a strange feeling that I would soon become more drawn into the church with Father Pavlos, but I couldn't say why. I thought that maybe it was time, after so many years, to come to confession again, not that I had much to confess.

When I was a kid, I attended Sunday school at Saint Demetrios as well; in fact the school was in the basement social area where the Saturday dances were held. There were a lot of little rooms for classes and socializing in the area, and if you got lucky, you could take your date to one of those rooms (if you knew your way around like I did) for a quickie.

* * *

"Well, look what the cat dragged in, Connie and his boyfriend, Al the Man," Sally Ann Bemis loudly proclaimed when we arrived. The music, arranged and played on CDs by a volunteer church social worker, had already started. The crowd was mostly single women—divorcees, widows, and women who had never been, or ever would be, married. The few men who showed up without dates stood around talking and drinking punch most of the time, occasionally glancing over at the women. Many of the women danced together, but a few male-female couples were on the floor as well. I learned long ago that if you ever wanted to meet a girl, you could always find one at a church social.

"Hey, Sal, what's shakin'?" I said with a broad smile on my face. I liked Sally even though she loved to tease me and Al. She knew we had been roommates for years, and on more than one occasion she had made remarks about us living together. It was all in fun, and if nothing else, it made it that much easier for the two of us to get it on. Al, as usual, went over to the group of men while Sally and I socialized. We danced a couple of dances and then headed off to the school area and found a dark, little study room that was unlocked.

After the usual brief, but very satisfying, tryst on the couch, she said with a warm smile on her face, "Gee, I didn't know you gay guys could make love like that. Maybe after all these months I'm finally straightening you out."

"Yeah, you're right. Al is not nearly as much fun as you are," I retorted.

Sally gave me a love tap on my shoulder and the crude teasing ended. We went back to the dance before people started asking questions; those who knew what was going on when they saw a couple leave the room never really brought it up. Of course we weren't the only couples who disappeared for a while. Many of the women still lived at home or with relatives and could never take a man back to their place without some heavy chaperoning. It was also not surprising that many of the men still lived with their mothers and in no way could they bring another woman home. The social area in the church basement was a nice place to hook up.

23

"So how about a movie tomorrow?" I asked Sally. "I'd like to see that *Star Wars* remake. There's a two o'clock showing. Want to go with me?"

"If you swing for the tickets, I'll treat you to hamburgers after the show," she said.

We had dated like that on a number of occasions over the last year or so—Saturday night dance, a little sex, and a movie on Sunday. Sally and I went to high school together. She was still a nice-looking woman after all these years, raising a family and all. She hadn't let herself go—that is, get fat—and she still had a very trim figure. She had a classic Greek face, almost like it was chiseled from stone, and it fascinated me, especially when we made love. Her maiden name was Remis and her family also attended Saint Demetrios. She dated Johnny Bemis, and they married right out of high school—from Remis to Bemis, not much of a change there. After twenty years of marriage—two children, twin girls who were away at college—they divorced. Johnny found someone younger.

Sally started coming to the church dances about once a month shortly after her divorce, and we'd get together when the chance arose. I found out that she was a receptionist for an ophthalmologist—beady-eyed Bennet we called him—and I told her about my recent diagnosis of glaucoma. She was concerned and wanted to know who my doctor was, what my treatments were, and everything else. It was nice to find a caring woman who had apparently liked me even way back in high school.

In some sense her caring reminded me of my mother. I was a sickly kid—although you wouldn't know it by looking at me today. My mother always nursed me back to health from the colds, earaches, and other infections I came home from school with. She was the only person I ever knew that really cared for me that way, and now here was Sally acting like she cared for me—I liked that.

*   *   *

Sunday morning after a quick breakfast, I asked Al, "You want to smoke some of that tea with me? I actually think that it helped me. Look," I said, leaning close to Al and pointing to my eyes. "They're not red anymore and no pains. Also, I haven't seen a halo since I smoked that stuff yesterday. Now that's a first!"

Al looked into both my eyes and said, "They do look a lot clearer, but they always look a little clearer after you've taken your medicine. Did you take it today?"

"Yeah, of course. I'm not stupid. But believe me, they looked this clear even before I took the drops."

Al nodded and declined my invitation to smoke the tea. He hadn't smoked in a couple of years and was afraid he might get hooked on cigarettes again if he smoked anything.

I went into my room, pulled out the bag of tea and a cigarette paper, and rolled a joint. It was a little better than yesterday's but still very amateurish. I was worried that someone might find the stuff—the cleaning lady, a repairman, or who knows who—so I took a black Magic Marker and wrote a big "T" on the bag for tea. Writing on a plastic bag mostly filled with leaves and twigs made the "T" look more like a "τ" the Greek letter tau. *I hope no one will think I'm being disrespectful,* I thought, referring to the tau cross. Then again, who was going to see it? I put the bag of leaves in one place and the papers in another, just to play it safe and so that the two items, if discovered, wouldn't be found together.

After smoking the joint and going back into our kitchen, Al asked, "So, feeling good?"

"Same as yesterday—no effect on my mind or attitude like I understand that taking dope can cause. Hey, I have nothing to lose trying, right?"

"Your eyes look a little red to me now. Maybe that stuff is hurting you," Al said.

"They're just a little red from the smoke. You watch, that'll be gone in a minute or so," I said with a lot of wishful thinking on my part.

I got cleaned up and left to pick up Sally for the afternoon movie. Before leaving I checked the mirror, and my eyes weren't red. Also no discomfort and no halos . . . so far today.

*   *   *

"That was probably the best movie I've seen in a long time," Sally was saying at the Robin Hood diner. We went there after seeing *The Empire Strikes Back*, a twenty-year rerelease of the 1977 movie. It was still raining, and the cloudy sky was getting even darker as evening approached. We talked about the movie, and I mentioned that I thought the modern visuals were like eye candy to me.

"Speaking of eye candy, how are your eyes?" Sally asked. "A few months ago you told me you had been diagnosed with glaucoma. You must be responding to your treatment because your eyes look clear to me." I hesitated for a minute, and Sally, detecting my uncertainty, stopped eating and stared intently at me. "What's the problem? Nothing more serious, I hope," she said with real concern in her voice, like when I had first told her about my condition.

"No, no, nothing more serious. I still have glaucoma, I think, but I'm responding well, um . . . to some new treatment that seems to be helpful."

Sally never smoked marijuana in high school—or at least that's what I thought—and I was a little worried as to how she might take my trying dope to cure the glaucoma.

"Are you smoking pot?" she asked in a very nonjudgmental way.

It caught me by surprise, but I had to ask, "Have you heard or do you know if dope cures glaucoma?"

"I know it helps with the pain and nausea for folks in advanced stages, but I don't think anyone has ever been cured by it. So answer me, are you smoking pot?"

I filled her in on the whole story about the bag of tea and how I had made and smoked two joints. She had to laugh about my clumsy attempt at rolling joints. "Why didn't you just make tea with the stuff and drink it. Why did you think you had to smoke it?"

"I don't know. I guess I was influenced by TV. I thought that was the only way you got the stuff you needed out of pot."

"Looking at your eyes," she said leaning close to me, "I'm not a doctor, but they look just fine to me. I see glaucoma patients every day, and their eyes look different than yours. You should go back to your doctor and get reexamined. They do make mistakes, you know." She started eating again. "After all, you're just forty-one, and that's on the early side for glaucoma patients."

"Yeah, I was thinking the same thing. I'll call tomorrow for an appointment. It's a little soon for my checkup, but I'll make some excuse to see him."

"Well, if he won't see you, let me know and I'll get you in with old beady-eyed. He's a good guy and good doctor. Also, if you want, let me have some of that tea and I'll get it checked out for you with our lab. I'll have no problem having them check it since medical marijuana is legal in some states. I'll just say some guy from Alaska brought it in, and they can handle that."

All of a sudden I felt like a real load was lifted from my shoulders. The guilt I was feeling seemed to disappear now that Sally was helping me. *I think I'm falling in love—either that or I miss my mother,* I thought.

*   *   *

"Well, it seems to me that something very strange is going on here," my doctor told me. "Your IOP—that's the pressure on your optic nerve—is about half of what it was when you were last here. Also, your peripheral vision is normal. I'm not certain yet, but it would appear to me that you don't have glaucoma!"

I was sitting in an examining chair in his office. He had just finished looking at my dilated eyes and testing my vision. "Could we have been mistaken about the diagnosis?" I asked.

"I don't know. You've been examined . . . let me see here . . ." The doctor was reading his notes. "Yeah, I've seen you three times since your first diagnosis almost a year ago, and in all three cases your IOP was high enough, along with the other tests we did, to warrant a glaucoma diagnosis. But now . . ." He kept looking at the file and shaking his head. "I'm going to ask some of my colleagues to look at all this and then I'll get back to you. In the mean time continue taking your medication. Let's also schedule you to come in again in the next couple of weeks, okay?" He had a sheepish smile on his face, like he was afraid I might sue him if it was true that I didn't have glaucoma.

"Have people been cured of this condition?" I asked. "I mean has it ever happened that it just goes away?"

"Not in my experience, but I suppose it's happened. I'll have to check it out. As I said, let me see what Dr. Epstein thinks of all this—he's the senior guy here—and I'll get back to you."

I felt great leaving the doctor's office. I couldn't wait to tell Sally. I had given her some of the tea leaves in a small baggy, and she was supposed to call me today and let me know what the stuff was. I could hardly wait to tell her. I had taken a sick day for the exam, so I wasn't going to work, and it was still very early in the afternoon when I got home. I had rolled some joints earlier and decided to have one. I tried brewing tea from the stuff, but it didn't taste very good, even with sugar, so I decided just to smoke it. Sally said it could also be made into brownies, but I wasn't hot on that idea.

When the phone rang, my new caller ID told me it was Sally's office phone. "So what is that stuff? Is it dope?" I asked excitedly.

"Relax!" Sally said. "According to the tech the stuff you gave me has no THC—that's the chemical in pot that supposedly does the trick. He said they did some kind of mass spec analysis—I'm not sure exactly what that is—and the stuff you're smoking is mostly like tea."

"So it is tea!" I said, "But how can tea lower my IOP like the doctor just told me?"

"Your IOP is down? Wow! I've heard that pot does lower the IOP in older patients."

"Not just down, actually normal he said. Also, all my other symptoms are gone! He's going to check it out with their senior guy, but when I left the office, his head was shaking. He said he's never seen anything like it."

"Strange," Sally said. "You know the tech didn't say that it was actually normal tea leaves. He said it was a bunch of different stuff, but much of it resembled lightly processed tea leaves or green tea. He said it would be too expensive to try to determine everything in the mix, but it definitely does not contain THC, and that's all they really looked for," Sally explained.

"I wonder what it would cost to find out exactly what it is," I said, almost as a question to myself rather than Sally.

"More than you or I could afford; thousands of dollars I would guess. This lab stuff doesn't come cheap. In any case, you can smoke it, drink it, or eat it, and you won't be doing anything illegal. You might kill yourself with that stuff, but it's not a controlled substance, or so we think. So how's that?"

When I hung up, I wondered what the couple who I confiscated the tea from had been using it for. She said it was a medicinal infusion, which sounded so bogus at the time; maybe I should have let them keep it. I hoped neither of them was taking it for a permanent disability like I had—or thought I had. I thought about that for a while, and the more I thought about it, the more I realized I had to take the leaves back. I decided that I would just slip the bag back in the storage cage just in case that couple came back. I really hadn't taken that much, and with the few joints I made, you wouldn't even know there was any missing. *In any case, I'm cured!* I thought—or hoped.

*   *   *

The sun was shining that Friday when I brought the tea back. I was looking forward to Saturday night when Sally and I would be getting together again. All of a sudden my life seemed to be turning around—no glaucoma and a new, or newly refurbished, friendship with a woman I really liked, or even loved. Whatever that tea was needed for, I just hoped the young couple would come back for it.

When I returned to work on Monday, I noticed that the tea was gone from the cage. I casually asked around if anybody knew where it had gone, but nobody knew or cared. There was so much crap in that cage that if we didn't shit-can it every two weeks, we wouldn't have room for our own stuff. I checked the ledger where people were supposed to report anything that was either returned to passengers—which is very rare—or turned over to other authorities. A clerk entered all the details on a computer file once or twice a week, but in this case the tea was not listed anyplace. I had filled out a form for it and attached it to the bag, and that too should have been put in a file with the disposition status entered, but the disposition form wasn't there either.

Since the bag was in my possession for more than a week, I decided not to push it. It was not unusual for things to disappear from the cage, especially a bag that looked like dope but was not marked as probable dope. My poorly written "τ" on the bag must have peaked somebody's curiosity. Or the couple came back with proper paperwork and claimed it. The date and time on the form would be about all they needed to identify the bag. Whoever gave it back was just too lazy to do the paperwork, so it was gone. I certainly hoped that's what had happened, but I guessed at that time that I would never know.

*   *   *

I called Sally and told her about my returning to work and finding that the bag of tea was gone.

"I hope it went to those folks you took it from in the first place," she said. "I don't know why, but I feel that stuff might be important, and I would hate to think that it ended up in the wrong hands."

"Why? What'd you think could happen if it did?" I asked.

"I don't know." Sally had some somberness in her voice. "All I know is the tech who tested the stuff sounded a bit strange about it. He said something to the effect that he had never seen a combination of materials like that before and that we should take care of them. He was from India originally, and East Indians have some strange religious notions about herbs and such."

"He said that *we* should take care of them? Was he suggesting that *we* should get together or somethin'?"

Being on the phone made it easier for me to talk like this to Sally than when we were actually together. I had never been very comfortable talking about my feelings with women. Maybe that was why I never got married, although I must admit I hadn't had much experience with other women. With the exception of some teenage romances and an occasional one night stand, Sally was my first real love affair with a grown woman. At work I'm known as Mr. Nice Guy. It seems I can get along with anybody and never lose my cool, and that's why I can do my job without raising a lot of fuss when I have to take something away from people. But Sally was changing me—I felt I could say what I wanted and not worry that I was offending someone or being too personal. I also felt I could take a chance letting Sally know how I honestly felt about her.

"What are you trying to say, Connie?"

"Maybe he's right—maybe we should get together. What'a ya think?" I asked nervously.

"Well, if that's what he meant, then I think he has a point. That's what I think."

"Then let's make it soon, okay? I've got a lot of catching up to do. Oh, Sally?" I paused, and with a break in my voice like a thirteen-year-old kid, I said, "I love you."

"Me too, Connie, me too," she said with a smile in her voice.

*   *   *

Sally and I got married in July and Al was the best man. Sally's twins were both maids of honor. I also got promoted. I no longer had to search suitcases; I'd be supervising the agents who did. And best of all, my glaucoma seemed to be gone. The doctors wouldn't tell me how or why it happened but just say I'm in remission—if there is such a thing for glaucoma. But I know it was the tea that cured me, and maybe my putting the Greek cross on the bag, even if it was an accident, might have had something to do with it. But I still wanted to know what happened to the bag of tea—who got it and what did they do with it?

It wasn't long after Sally and I decided to get married that I found all that out. It didn't surprise me to learn that the leaves did have powers to cure, and I was anxious to see to it that the couple got them back. And because of a bizarre coincidence at a Saturday night church dance, I was able to reunite with the leaves once again and get them back to their owner.

CHAPTER 3

Nando Garcia

We lived in a nice, two-bedroom apartment on West Forest Avenue that was walking distance from the Eastern Michigan University campus. I was enrolled at EMU and working on my degree in elementary education. There were a number of student families living in the complex, so there was much camaraderie among the tenants. We were all working and going to school, so money was tight and there was a lot of sharing and socializing among the tenants.

I was thirty-two then, and in order to afford my college expenses, I worked as a janitor at Detroit Metro airport, which was almost twenty miles away. I had been at the airport for less than two years, and I took the job because it paid much better than the other service jobs I'd held in Ypsi while going back to school. We never planned to move closer to the airport while my daughter was in school, and while I was finishing up my degree. I was to start my student teaching next year, so moving made no sense. We liked living in Ypsi with the college campus and the diversity of the city. The proximity to Ann Arbor afforded us many opportunities to take advantage of the various cultural activities, like the Latin Music Festival.

It was late Sunday morning and I was in the kitchen getting ready to start working on my homework. I was looking at a bag of leaves that I had brought home from work and talking with my wife, Maribel.

"While I was working last night, cleaning up in the storage room at the custom's facility, I saw this bag." I showed her the plastic bag with the letter on it. "It's marked with a Greek cross and that made me curious. Why would somebody put a cross on a bag of leaves, I wondered."

"Maybe it's holy things, like holy water. Stuff that the Greeks use in their ceremonies," Maribel suggested. "But why did you take it, Nando? You know you can be fired for stealing and go to jail, or even be deported back to Mexico. Why would you risk our safety for something like that?"

My name was Fernando Garcia, but Maribel always called me by my boyhood nickname, Nando. "Relax, relax, nobody's going to jail. Even if they knew I took it, nobody is going to say anything. And I'm not gonna be deported—we're citizens now. That place is so loose, the last thing they want people to know is how easy it is to take things out of there. I checked the form and it was out for more than a week before it showed up. Sarbanes—that's the agent's name who signed the confiscation form—probably had it, so I'm sure he won't be asking any questions."

I put the bag on the table and sat down looking at it suspiciously. I wondered if it was just some herbal stuff that people often tried to bring home from overseas. "People take food stuff from there—the storage cage—all the time before it's incinerated, so the missing bag of 'whatever that shit is' is no big issue. And I know it isn't dope or something else illegal, or it would have been tagged that way on the form."

"So what are you going to do with it, Nando? Even if it is some Greek thing, how is it going to benefit us?" Maribel asked.

"I don't know just yet. I'm going to do some research for my comparative religion class and see if there is something in the Orthodox Christian religions about herbs. Maybe I'll write my term paper on it. I think it might be incense, so maybe I'll just burn a little of it and see what it smells like. I don't know . . . I don't know what I'll do with it yet," I said with some irritation. I knew Maribel was right, but something had made me feel that I needed to have the stuff when I saw it on the shelf in the storage cage.

"And what about Maria Elena? Her First Communion is in a week. Are you ready for that?"

"Yeah, I'm ready, I'm ready. Stop nagging me about it. I'll carry her through the whole ceremony. She's light as a feather."

Our daughter, Maria Elena, had MD, muscular dystrophy, or specifically, Duchenne muscular dystrophy. She was diagnosed almost as soon as she was able to walk; that was seven years ago. She spent most of her time in a wheelchair, but she had insisted that for her First Communion she would not be pushed in her wheelchair down the aisle. I promised to carry her to the rail in her brand new, white satin communion dress and kneel with her when she received the Eucharist. She looked so gorgeous in that white dress, with her big, deep brown eyes and beautiful brown skin. We loved her so much.

"Stop your daydreaming and do your studying. I don't want you coming to bed at one in the morning again. Then you're too tired to get up to go to work," Maribel scolded.

"I'm studying, I'm studying . . . stop nagging me. I have enough to worry about right now without you nagging me." I loved my wife dearly, but at times she could be a real pain in the ass. She only wanted the best for me and our family. When we came from Mexico almost ten years ago, we had such high hopes. I had been teaching for a year and thought I would be able to teach here when our visas were issued. But it didn't turn out that way. So now I was studying part-time, and had been for almost six years, in order to get my teaching certificate in the United States. It was a lot of work, and there was much apprehension on our part, but I'd persevere no matter what. I was determined to be a teacher again.

*   *   *

One of my coworkers, Dwayne, greeted me as I walked in early Monday morning. "Hey, taco man, how's it goin'?" It was his usual way of greeting me. I didn't like it, but after a while I knew he meant nothing by it, so I just ignored him. We usually worked in two-man crews around the airport and received different assignments two or three times a week, so as not to get bored or sloppy in our jobs. Some of my fellow cleaning staff didn't like that—they preferred to be doing the same thing every day. Others, like me, found the change in routine better to deal with because the work itself was pretty monotonous. And some jobs, like cleaning the restrooms, were just too gross to have to be doing it all the time.

"Did you bring any good Mexee food for lunch?" Dwayne asked.

"Yes, I did, but none for you, my lazy-ass friend. Make your own lunches, or better yet, have your mama make it for you," I retorted.

"Now you know my mama don't make me no lunches—no time. You should share with me. We partners, right?" he teased.

Most of my coworkers were African American, and some of them resented the fact that a Mexican American had a relatively high-paying job. They felt it belonged to them. What I found even more interesting was that because of my Afro-Cuban roots I was actually darker than many of the guys; yet they still considered me to be just another white man taking a good-paying black man's job. I had a lot of hazing the first few months, but I put up with it and eventually it stopped. However, "taco man" became my nickname because they thought Fernando was just too fancy sounding. Our supervisor never interfered with the workers' personal problems unless it became a work problem. My coworkers were careful not to call me taco man in front of her. They called me Mr. T, when she was around, like that guy that used to be on TV. She never questioned it and no one ever explained it to her, and I, of course, never complained.

"So you still goin' to school, right?" Dwayne, asked me. "Someone told me you already got a college degree, so why you goin' twice?"

I explained to Dwayne that my degree was from a small Catholic college in Veracruz and was not fully recognized by Michigan. I had to get a diploma from an accredited university, do my student teaching, and take certain courses about Michigan history in order to get certified; that was why I had to do it twice. He was just being friendly and not trying to be a wiseass.

"That's gotta be tough—going to school to better yourself and then having to go again. Sounds like someone changed the rules on you just 'cause you black," he said in a serious way. "You know they fucked me over too 'cause I'm black. After I got out of the army, I was supposed to get a good job or go to school, or even re-up with a bonus, but I got shit."

"What did you do in the army?" I asked, mostly to make light conversation that would help pass the time. I was pleased when I realized that for the first time that Dwayne thought of me as an equal.

"Man, I was a radioman. I had to learn all that alpha-bravo shit and Morse code and how to operate any AN/PRC—that's military radio—devices out there. But do you think that would get me a good job? Well, hell no! I'm still shoveling shit like before I went in," he said to me as we worked along in the waiting areas.

And then it hit me, when he said he was a radioman. "You were the asshole that painted that dash on my locker, weren't you?" I said.

"Yeah," he said, surprised I knew it was him. "But that was a long time ago. I was just kidding with that. Nobody knew what it meant. It was all in fun—we all kid each other. Are you still sore about that?" he asked.

When I had first started working at the airport, someone painted a dash on my locker. Just a dash, that was all. It was months later that I found out while studying for my communication class what it meant. It was Morse code for a T—Mr. T, my nickname.

"No, man, I'm not pissed anymore. But how would you like it if I put a dash-dot on your locker?" I asked him.

"Huh? Dash-dot—oh, man . . . that's code for N. That would no way be funny. You wouldn't do that shit, would you?"

I just smiled and let him think about it for a while.

"Hey, we still friends, right? You're a good guy, Freddy. I'm sorry I fucked with you that way, but like I said, that was a long time ago. So we all right?"

Freddy, I thought, *well that's a start.* We worked the rest of the shift pretty much in silence, just speaking when we had to.

*   *   *

"Max, what is the purpose of burning incense? I found that many religions and cultures use it, not just the Greek Orthodox," I asked my comparative religion instructor in class that evening.

"It has different meanings, symbols, and practices depending on the culture, but basically it's used for purification—both spiritually and physically," he said. Then continuing along the topic of incense, and now speaking to the whole class, he said, "They often use little pieces of charcoal to keep the fire going and add all kinds of aromatic stuff: oil, leaves, plant roots, and the like. Quite frequently it involves some kind of ritualistic action, like swinging it back and forth over the four sides of the altar in the Greek tradition. Did you find that part interesting in your reading on various religious rituals?" he asked, turning back to me.

"Yes, I did. It just amazed me that it had Jewish roots but is now practiced mainly by Christians. Also, I found that Buddhists and other Eastern religion practitioners burn incense as well. And you say it's all for the same reason? I just find that fascinating."

"No more so than the fact that all those diverse religions believe in a godlike being and a form of prayer. The burning of incense is just one more thing that demonstrates our similarities as opposed to playing up our differences." Again turning to the whole class—most of them did not participate in this discussion—he continued. "By the way, it would appear that a marriage ceremony and a death ceremony, or ritual, also seem to be a part of all religions. Next week we'll start discussing the various differences in religions and how they might have originated. Turn in your last short paper for the semester by tomorrow. I'll have them back to you next week."

I hung around class for a while after the recitation period to talk with Max. I would finally be starting my student teaching next semester and be on my way to certification. Max had been my mentor for the six years it was taking me to complete my degree working part-time, and we had become friends.

"So, Max, where do you think I'll be doing my student teaching?" I asked. "Do you think I could get my daughter's school?"

"Not likely, Nando. You'll probably be doing your first semester at the high school, like most first-time teachers."

"But I've already taught before, so maybe they'll give me a break this one time and put me into an elementary school. That's where I want to teach," I said.

It seemed that no matter what I said about my previous education and experience it fell on deaf ears. I was still treated like a kid going through the process for the first time. In any case, I did a lot of home-schooling with Maria Elena because of her MD; she had to be in a special school program that didn't cover nearly enough academic topics for her to get a well-rounded education. As soon as I got my BA in elementary education, I'd start on my master's degree in special ed, working with kids like Maria Elena. But I had to be patient, going through the hoops and keeping my mouth shut. I was too close to the end, or I should say the beginning, to inadvertently delay it anymore.

"Okay, whatever you say, Max. You're my man. Fun stuff today—I really enjoy this class."

And with that I headed home for a late supper and some quality time with Maria Elena before bed. Living where I did, so near to campus, made it much easier for me to take evening classes and still be home at a reasonable time.

Walking down West Cross Avenue on the way home, I stopped by a Chinese food market to pick up some things that Maribel wanted and noticed they had small home censers for sale. They were made of brass and quite reasonably priced, so I bought one, along with some unscented charcoal just to see what it was all about.

It had been sunny today, the first day without rain in some time, so it was nice to be able to walk without my umbrella. There were a lot of little stores typical of a college town—bookstores, drugstores, coffee shops—on West Cross, as well as a magnificent old Greek Orthodox church that I occasionally walked by while running errands or walking to school. By the time I got home I was feeling good and ready for one of Maribel's great fish dinners.

After dinner I propped Maria Elena up on our bed so that the two of us could study together. This way I could help her if she needed it, and it would give Maribel a little break from her daily routine of caring for her. Since it had rained a lot recently, the room was damp and smelled a little musty, even though it had been a dry day. I thought, *Why not try that incense I brought home, just to take the damp smell out of the room?* I put some charcoal in the censer and lit it. Once it started smoldering I added some of the leaves and watched them smoke as they lay on the burning coal. It was a nice smell—not like the sweet smell of incense I expected but more like the burning leaves of autumn.

"What's that nice leaf smell, Papi?" Maria Elena asked.

"Just some stuff I found at work. I think the Greek Orthodox church uses it in their incense burning ceremony," I answered. I went on to tell Maria Elena all that I had learned in class about incense burning, and she was fascinated.

It was getting on to nine o'clock when I said, "Okay, it's late. Have you finished your reading?" She nodded yes and yawned. "Then let's get ready for bed." As I picked her up to carry her to the bathroom, I noticed something strange. She was moving her legs! Not in a stilted, jerky fashion, but in an almost normal manner like she was walking—first one and then the other. She hadn't done that on her own in some time. I had to ask, "Sweetheart, when were you able to do that movement with your legs again?"

"I don't know, Papi. It just seemed to be the thing to do," she answered. "Do you think on Sunday that I'll be able to walk down the aisle for communion?"

"Maybe, honey, we'll just have to wait, but I would love to carry you down the aisle and kneel with you when you receive the Eucharist. Won't that be fun?" I never discouraged her from thinking about walking again. I knew it probably would never happen, but you never knew. Her type of MD disorder was rare in girls, and the only effective (although somewhat short-term) treatment for boys had been some steroid therapy. She was put on it about a month ago with the caveat that it had not been shown to be effective for girls, but we said we wanted to try it anyway. *Now maybe that stuff is working. Thanks to God,* I thought.

*   *   *

When we got up the next morning for work and school, Maribel hollered out to me just as I was turning over to catch another five minutes of sleep. "Nando, come in here quick and look at our daughter!" she cried. I ran into Maria Elena's room, and there she was, standing there in her jammies with a big grin on her face.

"Look, Papi, I can stand all by myself now," she said, just beaming with delight. "And I don't feel dizzy or like maybe I'm gonna fall," she said, looking from one foot to the other. "Want to see me walk?" she asked.

"You bet I do, but wait, let me help you, okay?" I said as I hurried to her side to hold her hand and keep her from falling. But she didn't need me. She started walking—a little unsteady and slow, but she was able to do it all by herself. Maribel and I stood there with tears streaming down our cheeks. "Honey, how do you feel?" I asked.

"I feel good, Papi. My body is not so funny feeling anymore. Can I go into the regular school now?" she pleaded.

"We'll see, sweetheart, we'll see." I did not want to give her any false hope. *I'm sure the steroid shots must finally be kicking in,* I thought. Even though we had been told that the steroid fix wasn't permanent, it was hope, and we desperately wanted hope.

I called into work and said I would be coming in late, and then I called Maria Elena's school to say that she had a doctor's appointment and wouldn't be in. At the doctor's office we had to wait because she didn't have a scheduled appointment, but they said they'd squeeze her in when they could.

"Hi there, and how's our beautiful Maria Elena today?" the doctor asked with his usual warm, friendly smile. He had been treating her for a few years now, and we knew he was fond of her. "And look how straight you're sitting there."

"Watch this, Dr. Flores. Mami let me do this," Maria Elena said as she slid off the chair to show the doctor how she could walk. The doctor wanted to grab her at first, but he wasn't quick enough. He watched in utter amazement as she first stood all by herself and then determinedly walked over to him to grab his hand.

"What's going on here?" I asked almost in a whisper. I was a little afraid that he might say it was an aberration—a short-term phenomenon caused by the medicine—and would soon fade. When Maria Elena reached Dr. Flores, he picked her up and spun her around with such a hug that I was afraid he'd hurt her. She was still so delicate.

"That was marvelous, just marvelous," Dr. Flores said as he swung her around, holding her close to him. He was just beaming, and Maria Elena was squealing in delight. I think he even had tears in his eyes.

"Now, let's see," he said as he put her down carefully and watched her walk slowly back to her chair and sit down. He was shaking his head. "She had the ten-shot series of prednisolone about a month ago and was scheduled to start again in a few days, right?" He was looking at her records. "I've never seen such a rapid recovery like that, even in the boys we've treated.

I'm going to do some blood work and schedule some other tests, and then we'll try to see what this is all about—but in the meantime enjoy! Let her do whatever she can tolerate, but be reasonable. Don't overdo anything. Keep the same regimen until I get back to you and keep exercising those tiny muscles. If she's going to walk she'll need to fatten them up a little more. And remember, this steroid treatment we're doing is still considered to be experimental."

Dr. Flores looked over at Maria Elena, and seeing the smile on her face, he broke into a broad grin, "Well, my little friend, we've had quite an accomplishment here. Let's keep it up, and we'll have you dancing again real soon." He seemed so sure of himself. I was afraid of raising false hopes, but seeing the doctor like this made Maribel and me feel like we could finally celebrate Maria Elena's victory. That's what it was—a victory over some bad happening that was about to change and, hopefully, forever.

*   *   *

We got the doctor's report a few days later when he told us that Maria Elena's tests were completely negative for DMD. Dr. Flores told me, "Her genetic test showed she still has the defect, but maybe now, like most girls that have it, she is just a carrier and will remain asymptomatic for the rest of her life." He didn't know if the treatment she received did it or if it was just a case of spontaneous remission. In any case we embraced the news and watched in joy as Maria Elena became even more normal as the week progressed.

On that lovely, sunshiny Sunday in late April, Maribel and I watched, through both tears and smiles, as our little girl walked down the aisle and received her First Communion. My heart was beating so hard I thought my chest would break. Whatever cured her—God, the incense, the steroids—was not our concern. Our only concern was that she was now cured and she would remain a healthy little girl.

After services Maribel couldn't resist giving Maria Elena a giant hug and kiss on the church walk while the other parishioners looked on with smiles on their faces. Seeing Maribel hugging our daughter, I was much taken by Maria Elena's resemblance to her mother—not that it was strange, but I couldn't help noticing it this time.

I had met Maribel when I was in school. I was studying to be a teacher, and she was studying to get her certification in English so she could get a higher-paying government job. Maribel was also of Afro-Cuban ancestry, and our families were descendants of fishermen from the villages along the southeastern coast of Mexico. Our parents worked very hard for us to be able to go to school, and we both appreciated the sacrifices they had made. Not many of our cousins or friends had the opportunity to go to college. But most important to our families after we married and finished school was Maria Elena. They hoped that she would have a better chance for a good life in the United States. We were determined to see that happen, in spite of her MD, and now that she was cured there would be no stopping her from reaching the moon if she wanted to.

During the following week, after Maria Elena's First Communion, we continued to study in my bedroom together, and I continued to burn a little incense until the weather changed. Somehow I felt that the Greek Orthodox incense was, in part, responsible for her healing. "To purify both spiritually and physically," Max had told me, and so maybe it did.

* * *

I felt obligated to share the incense with the world just on the chance that it did have the purification powers that Max said incense users believed in. Early Monday afternoon, before going to work, I decided to take the bag full of incense—we had hardly used any at all—to Saint Demetrios, the Greek Orthodox church near me, where I asked to meet with one of the priests. I was led by a church deacon to a small office with the name plate of "Father Pavlos, M Div." on the door. The office was in the lower level of the church, where the school and social halls were located. In a few minutes Father Pavlos walked in and greeted me.

"Good afternoon, I'm Father Pavlos, and I've been told you wanted to see me. How can I help you, my son?" he said in a solid and friendly voice that reflected his divinity school training. He was a tall man, maybe six feet, which was tall for me. His olive-complexioned face, although still young, was friendly and mature. He was dressed in a simple black cassock with his white clerical collar barely showing through in the front. The office itself had a small conference table and two chairs in front of the father's desk. The sparsely decorated space was nicely appointed, however, and looked like a comfortable place to work and visit. I knew immediately that I could get along with this priest as I sat down in one of the chairs as he motioned me to do so.

"I'm not sure, Father, but I think that these leaves are used in your censers because someone wrote a Greek cross on the bag. Either way I would like you to have them in case they are your incense leaves."

I handed the bag of leaves over to Father Pavlos, who after briefly examining the contents of the bag and sifting some of the leaves through his fingers, said, "Where did you get these, my son?"

"I found them where I work. I'm a janitor at the airport. They were probably brought in by a tourist from Greece, and because they were in an unsealed package, they had to be confiscated. I brought them home before they were to be incinerated, thinking that someone might find them useful." I didn't tell him the whole story about Maria Elena, hopefully just enough about her remission to get him interested.

"Well, that was very thoughtful of you . . . Alfredo?" the priest said.

"It's Fernando, Father, but that's all right," I gently said.

"Fernando, yes, sorry. Yes, that was thoughtful indeed. I'll put them with our other incense materials. The Greek cross, or tau, drawn on the package is interesting. I'm certain there's a fascinating story here. Thank you again, Fernando, for thinking of us."

I could tell by the way Father Pavlos examined the leaves—rubbing them between his fingers and then gingerly smelling the residue—that he knew that they weren't incense leaves, at least not the kind that were used in Greek Orthodox ceremonies. He told me that he was a trained herbalist, and although he didn't say anything about marijuana, it was apparent that he knew they weren't cannabis leaves. I'm guessing that at this point he didn't know what they were, but maybe my brief story about Maria Elena led him to believe in my earnestness to do right by them. Rather than embarrass me, I think Father Pavlos decided that it would be best to keep them for now.

*   *   *

Maria Elena continued to improve over the semester. We were informed, after a few consultations with the principal and letters from Dr. Flores, that she would go into the regular school program in the fall. I also found out that I would start my student teaching at her school.

"Do you think you'll be in my class, Papi?" Maria Elena asked me.

"I don't think they'll do that, honey, but I'll be there in the school somewhere if you should need me, okay?"

And as far as the doctors were concerned, Maria Elena was in complete remission brought on by the steroid treatments she had received late in March. They wanted to follow up closely with her because there were journal articles they needed to consider, so that others might benefit from the treatment. However, I didn't think the others would benefit as much without the incense remedy too—but I didn't tell them that.

How the leaves could have cured Maria Elena, I'd never know, but I suspected it had something to do with our faith. It all began to happen so close to Easter at the end of March, and Maria Elena's First Communion was also on the Greek Orthodox Easter. It was her very first communion that she was able to walk and receive the sacraments. As I learned in class, most religions had more similarities than differences. In particular, the Abrahamic religions all had the same God, so it was not unusual that as good Catholics we should also benefit from Orthodox beliefs as well.

In any case we were grateful to God for lending us the leaves and only hoped that others would benefit from them as well when they breathed in their mystical, purifying strength. It was not long after that I did find out about the others and was pleased that someone else was also blessed with good health. But I must admit that on occasion we found ourselves holding our breath—afraid that maybe it was only a temporary thing and Maria Elena's illness would come back again.

CHAPTER 4

Mitch Foley

I had been working with the Orthodox priest, Father Pavlos, for a few weeks now, serving on his ecumenical committee. They were concerned with some hate crimes—derogatory and even racist graffiti spray-painted on walls in the business area around campus. My full name is Kevin Mitchell Foley, but everyone called me Mitch. As an Ypsilanti police officer assigned to the Youth Bureau, I was familiar with gang-related crimes in the area, so it was logical that Father Pavlos would ask me to be on his committee. Nevertheless, I had had my own problems related to anger issues for some time now. I received a notice—you might say an ultimatum—that if I didn't attend anger management classes and do something to control my temper, I'd be off the force. It turned out that the priest, Father Pavlos, gave those classes, and that was how we met.

I'd been going to the classes weekly for a couple of months now, and we worked in a small group setting, a lot like Alcoholics Anonymous. Father Pavlos and I had hit it off right away, even though I wasn't Greek—I'm an Irish cop, as you might have guessed by my name. I liked his methods and his apparent trust in me getting through the anger management program successfully. Maybe that was why he had asked me to serve on his ecumenical committee as a special resource person.

It was a gray, drizzly day at the end of April, and we were cruising in the squad car. I was talking to my partner, Gerry Patterson, about the bag of leaves the father had given me. "Father Pavlos gave them to me. He thinks they might be gang related, and he asked me to look into it. He thinks that some guys are making joints with this harmless stuff and then selling it as dope to kids who don't know any better."

"Kids today know better, Mitch. They could spot a scam like that faster than we can," Gerry said.

"Yeah, you're right, but I told him I'd look into it anyway."

Gerry and I were one of the few two-man squad-car teams left in the department. That was because we specialized in gang-related activities and could be dispatched at any time to anywhere in the city. But when we weren't working on a case, we did regular patrol duty.

"You know the father is also helping me with my anger management issue." I said, shaking my hands and head. "You know I had to go, or they would have canned me. It's a bum rap, but I'll put up with that shit if it gets me to retirement."

"What do you mean bum rap?" Gerry said. "You beat the shit out of that guy, Louie, remember? I was there for Christ's sake. If I hadn't stopped you, you might have killed him."

"Yeah, yeah, but do you also remember what that motherfucker called me? He called me a Nazi. Me—a Nazi! Hey, baby, I'm as liberal as they come. I'm no Nazi."

"Whatever he called you, you shouldn't have beat him that way, Mitch, and you know it. So stop your bitchin'. It's me, Gerry. I've been you're partner for eight years—I know you."

Gerry was right; we'd been partners and friends a long time. We worked well together and had saved each other's asses many times. He was like a brother to me.

My own problems started around a year ago—after the divorce. I was so angry at her, at him (the guy she ran off with), and everybody else that I had to take it out on somebody, so why not the perps? They at least deserved it. Our lieutenant gave me a choice: either anger management classes or early retirement. I chose the classes with Father Pavlos. So far it was working out for me—I hadn't hurt anyone. Well, actually, I hadn't really had the chance to hurt anyone in a while.

"Hey, Gerry, you wanna smoke some of this shit to see if it does work?" I joked as I ran some of the leaves over my hand. Looking at the marking on the bag I said, "I've never seen this symbol before on any gang-related items. And a bag this big would never carry a gang sign." I examined the package of leaves and continued. "That is a strange symbol; Father Pavlos said it looks like a Greek cross. But then again, you never know what those assholes will do today. The next time we get a chance, I'll ask Louie if he knows what's goin' on with this stuff."

"Are you nuts or somethin'? You know you can't talk to Louie since you beat him up. I mean, for Christ's sake, Mitch, I think he'd be glad to put you away for good," Gerry said.

"Nah, he's okay with me now. He knows that the little roughhousing was just that one time, and he's probably anxious to show me he really is on our side again. And by the way, that beating he took gave him a lot of street cred, so I think he might even be grateful."

Louie the Snitch was a greasy informant who worked both sides of the law. He was a user and would do anything for a fix—or anything it took to stay out of jail. I hadn't seen him in months and our Loo told me to keep away from him. But this was an exception, and it tied into my anger management classes and my volunteer work as well. Loo should understand that.

*   *   *

"No, and that's final! It's just been four months, and you still haven't finished your classes with Father Pavlos. Don't you go anywhere near him. And that's an order," our lieutenant told me.

"But, Loo—," I started to say.

"No buts! If it's that important to you, and you think it really is part of bigger crime situation, then have Gerry do it alone," the lieutenant told us.

"I can do that," Gerry said. "I've known Louie a long time, and he still trusts me. He's no threat, so there's no need for both of us to go. It's just a friendly interview, that's all."

"Okay, I'm cool with that," I said, deciding it was better to cool down the situation. I was already in enough trouble, so there was no need to make matters worse. "Gerry can fill me in afterward, and then we can tell Father Pavlos if anything falls out. I want to give that stuff back to him anyway. I don't know why, but I feel some kind of responsibility for it. The father said that someone gave it to him because the sign on the bag that the stuff was in looked like a Greek letter. He said it was a Hispanic man, so maybe it came from one of the Hispanic gangs, but I doubt that."

"If you guys are all right with leaving it at that—letting Gerry interview Louie—then that's what we'll do." Looking at Gerry, Loo continued. "Just you alone, Gerry. You got that?" Gerry nodded, and the two of us left his office.

*   *   *

The next day Gerry made a call to Louie and set up a time and place to meet with him. He dropped me off at one of our coffee shop hangouts near where his appointment with Louie was to take place and said he'd be back in less than an hour. I planned on reading the paper while I waited for Gerry to return.

I left my personal communication radio on just in case Gerry needed to contact me, and in less than ten minutes, I heard the call: "Officer down! Officer down!"

I jumped up and started to run out of the shop, screaming into my radio, "Where? Where?" But I knew it was Gerry's voice, and I knew he was at Louie's apartment just three blocks away. I could hear sirens in the distance and figured someone else was also responding to Gerry's call.

I was out of breath when I arrived, but mostly from fear of what I might find. As I ran into the apartment, I saw some people running out. I grabbed one of them—it was Louie the Snitch.

"It wasn't me, Mitch! Honest, it wasn't me!" Louie was screaming.

"Where's Gerry? Where is Gerry?" I screamed back.

"He's in the apartment—he took a hit," Louie said with absolute terror in his eyes.

I dragged Louie along with me and made him show me which apartment Gerry was in. As we entered the open door, I saw Gerry on the floor in a pool of blood. The place was empty. I had my weapon drawn going in, but seeing Gerry on the floor, I started to attend to him immediately.

"Don't move, partner. I'm here, I'm here. Everything will be okay now. Where'd they get you? Gerry, can you hear me? Can you hear me?" I was crying uncontrollably when two other officers arrived and started to assist. "Arrest that asshole, and don't let him get out of your sight. Either he did it or he knows who did it. Arrest him!" I screamed, pointing my gun at Louie, whose eyes were so wide with fear that I thought they were going to pop out of his head.

When the ambulance arrived, Gerry was barely alive. The bullet had entered his chest but appeared to have missed his heart. He was losing blood by the pints when they took him off to the emergency room. The apartment was soon filled with cops, and I was needed to fill everyone in on the incident. Loo came down as well since it was one of his guys that took the bullet. As soon as he could, Loo wanted to know how I got there and why Louie was also there. I brought him up to speed on exactly what happened—how I ran there from the diner and when I arrived I saw Louie and the others leaving. He saw how distraught I was and didn't push the issue of me and Louie being there together.

47

Later that day when we were writing up the incident, Loo asked me about the timeline. He said, "Dispatch got the call from Gerry at 10:07 a.m. How long did it take you to get to the apartment?"

"It must have taken me five minutes to run the three blocks and seven minutes for the squad car to arrive," I told him. "Why did it take so long for Louie and the other two or three—I'm not sure how many I saw—to get out of there? It was a first-floor apartment, so after the shooting they should have been out of there in seconds, not minutes."

"We'll have to wait on that one," Loo said. "Maybe they were trying to help Gerry. He only took one shot, if they wanted to kill him they had the time to do it. Curious."

*   *   *

Gerry was alive and responding to treatment but still in critical condition when I arrived at the hospital. The doctor said he was in surgery a long time, repairing all the damage the bullet caused to his lungs and chest cavity, but his heart and other organs were all okay, or so they thought. However, it was still touch and go as to whether he would live or not. When I saw him, he had more tubes going in and out of him than any ER patient I had ever seen on a TV crime series. He was not responsive, but I sat with him anyway. I felt responsible for his condition. I sent him off on that wild-goose chase about the dope, and if I hadn't fucked up with Louie, I'd have been with him and this wouldn't have happened. *Shit! I'll kill those cocksuckers when I get them. I'll kill those bastards,* I thought to myself, and then after a few seconds I reconsidered. *Not the right way to be thinking now.*

Loo came in around 10:00 p.m., nearly twelve hours after the incident. "Is he able to talk?" he asked. I shook my head no. "You know, nobody recovered that bag of stuff you had. We looked everywhere—your squad car, the apartment, searched a five block perimeter—nowhere to be found. We asked Louie about it, but he's lawyered up. He's so scared; he knows he's going to prison, so he won't say anything for fear of what they'll do to him on the inside." Loo was just sort of rambling to himself.

"Did he at least tell you who any of the other guys were?" I asked.

"No. Asked for a lawyer right away, so we just booked him. We got a whole team working on this: interviews, lab team, the works. You want in?" I looked at him somewhat in disbelief. He knew how close I was to Gerry, so he should have been keeping me away from this case. "If you say yes, and you find the guys who shot Gerry, can you handle it? I mean, you won't blow up on me will you?"

"I honestly don't know, Loo," I said slowly, realizing the implications of what I had just said. "But I think I can handle myself now. I know where my anger is, and even though I feel I could kill those guys—especially if Gerry doesn't make it—I think I can be professional enough to do my job." I paused to catch his look. "You know I had my gun on Louie when I was in there, and I thought about blowing him away, but I didn't. Actually, I didn't want to shoot him. I just wanted to save Gerry's life not avenge his shooting. Do you know what I'm saying?"

"Okay, then you're part of the team. We're meeting at oh-eight-hundred tomorrow morning. Be there," he said.

*   *   *

Before going in the next morning I checked on Gerry at the hospital; he was still in the ICU and listed as critical. However, he was recovering slowly, and they planned on doing some additional tests to check on his condition. Afterward I went to the precinct to report in for my new assignment on the ad-hoc investigation team working Gerry's case. There were six of us, not counting Loo, at the meeting.

"Okay, listen up," Loo said. "Mitch is on the team now." They all looked at me, and most of them nodded as if to say, "We understand." "Mitch, you'll be working with Patrick—you know each other—and I want you guys to continue on the drug/gang aspect of the case. If you want to interview Louie, then I suggest that both of you do it together." Loo looked at me as if to tell me that I had to be super careful on this one. I fully intended to be.

Driving out in the squad car I filled Patrick in on the stuff I got from Father Pavlos and how we were going to ask Louie if he knew about a gang-related dope scam, and that's where the incident went down—in Louie's pad. Patrick knew about my altercation with Louie, as did everyone else in the precinct, and fully understood the protocol that we would use while interviewing him.

"So just setting up a simple interview with a snitch led to Gerry getting it," Patrick said. "I guess it happens, but Gerry . . ." Patrick was shaking his head. Gerry was liked by everyone. I think he meant that it should have been me, not Gerry, who got the hit.

Ever since my wife left me, maybe even a little before, I'd had trouble controlling my anger—anger at her, my coworkers, everyone. I knew it was my fault she left me, and I knew that in many ways I pushed her into it. I wasn't responsive to her needs or anyone else's. I was only interested in how I felt. This change in attitude was not unusual for someone in my line of work, and I should have sought counseling earlier, but I was too full of myself for that.

"Look, Pat, I'm sorry for the way I've behaved recently, but I can tell you I'm changed now, and Gerry is one of the reasons why. I really want to get these guys, so let's do it—and I mean doing it the right way—for Gerry's sake, okay?"

"Mitch, I don't judge people. I know what you're going through. You know I've done the twelve-step thing with AA, so you don't have to explain anything to me," Patrick said.

I didn't know he was a recovering alcoholic; that made it easier for him to understand my situation. "Thanks for that. You know I didn't need Father Pavlos to point out that my real anger was within me. However, he has helped me focus on the issue and redirect it into doing useful things—like the committee he has me working on. As I told you, that's how the whole thing started."

We were driving over to the crime scene to do some interviews with Louie's neighbors before going back to interview Louie, when I said, "We should probably talk with Father Pavlos first. What do you say?"

"Sounds reasonable to me, the Greek church is not too far out of the way, so let's do it," Patrick answered.

*　　*　　*

Father Pavlos was in his office at the church and was quick to greet us and offer comfort. He had already heard about Gerry, and you could see he was upset by the whole thing.

"Come in, Mitch; yes, do come in," Father Pavlos said, offering us seats at his small conference table instead of a more formal place in front of his desk. "You have no idea how bad I feel about what's happened to your partner Gerry. And to think it happened while you were trying to help us. How are you doing, Mitch? And the other officers—how are they?" he said, looking at Patrick.

I quickly introduced Patrick who explained. "We're a small police department, Father. We all know each other, so it's tough on all of us, but we'll get through it and we'll find out who did this and why it happened." Patrick further related how a team was formed to investigate the shooting. I asked Father Pavlos to tell Patrick the story behind the leaves again.

"He said his name was Alfredo—he was a dark-skinned Hispanic man—and that he found them at work. He seemed so sincere about the package, the Greek cross and all. I knew they weren't cannabis leaves or incense-related herbs, but—"

"Didn't it seem strange to you, Father, that a Hispanic man would be coming into a Greek Orthodox church?" Patrick asked.

"I never really thought of it that way . . . but now that you mention it, I suppose he could have taken them to his own priest," Father Pavlos answered. "Even if he thought the leaves were for an Orthodox service, I don't see why he couldn't have taken them to his priest first and asked about them."

We ended our interview with Father Pavlos learning nothing new about the package of leaves.

"Mitch, do you know of any Hispanic gangs that deal in drugs?" Patrick asked when we were back in the car.

"Yeah, there's a small group of kids in town that identify with the Latin Kings out of Detroit, but they haven't given us any serious trouble. Maybe we should run the name Alfredo through the database and see what we get," I said. I contacted our IT guy by radio and asked him to do the search.

"Alfredo? You gotta be kiddin'. There's probably a couple hundred Alfredos in the gang database. Do you have a last name?" the IT guy asked.

"No, that's all our contact gave us. Come on, you can do it. Just keep it local and try cross-listing it with Louie the Snitch. That should reduce the number significantly," I instructed him.

After a few minutes of waiting the IT guy came back over the radio. "We've got a hit!"

*　　*　　*

Patrick and I returned to the station after our interview with Father Pavlos and got Alfredo's identity from IT. We wanted to fill the lieutenant in on what we had found and get permission to carry out the next step.

"He told us the guy's name was Alfredo Sanchez, formerly associated with the Latin Kings, and listed as an acquaintance of one Louis Smith, a.k.a. Louie the Snitch. That sounds too good to be just a coincidence. What do you think, Loo?"

"Certainly sounds worthwhile to follow up. Go interview this guy before you talk with Louie, and see if it seems reasonable to use him to get to Louie. You got an address?" the lieutenant asked.

"Yeah, and guess what? It's almost around the corner from Louie's apartment where Gerry got it. Patrick and I want to go over there now while it's still a hot lead, Loo, and as you suggest, follow up afterward with Louie."

The lieutenant said he would notify the others on the team in order to have backup alerted and nearby just in case.

It was early afternoon when we drove up to the Sanchez place. It was a small, two-family bungalow on the east side of town in a mixed neighborhood of mostly working-class Hispanic immigrants. It was still raining as it had been for most of the month.

"Let's do this," Patrick said as we got out of the car, trying to look as nonthreatening as we could even though we were both uniformed police officers. Patrick knocked on the door while I stood slightly to one side. No answer.

We tried the door and it was unlocked. "This is too much like a B movie," I said as we walked in. The place was neat, clean, and apparently well cared for. "Hello, is anybody home?" I shouted. We drew our pieces and held them at ready—again just in case. Still, no answer. As we walked through the apartment, from the kitchen we could see into the backyard. There was a man out there attending some trees or bushes. He was a fair-skinned Hispanic man, as far as we could tell.

We opened the back door and as gently as possible, with our weapons down, I asked, "Excuse me, sir, but are you Alfredo Sanchez?"

Shocked at hearing my question and then seeing who we were, he answered very nervously. "Sí, yes . . . I'm Sanchez. Why are you here?"

"We need to ask you a few questions, Mr. Sanchez. Would you mind coming in and talking with us?" I asked in as friendly a voice as I could muster.

Sanchez followed us inside, took off his wet raincoat, and asked, "What you want to know? How did you get in?" He was definitely nervous and distrustful. He also seemed irritated that we simply walked into his house.

52

He kept looking around as if he was concerned we might see something. He repeated, "What you want me for?"

"We understand that you're an associate of Mr. Louis Smith; is that right?" I asked to get things started.

"I don't know no Louis Smith. Why you asking?"

"Maybe you know him better by his street name, Louie the Snitch," I continued.

Sanchez paused a bit before asking, "Why'd you think I know him?"

I noticed Patrick looking around the small flat. He was eyeing something in the bedroom and started to head over there.

"Hey, whatcha doin'? You got some kind of a search warrant?" Alfredo asked Patrick as he headed him off from going into the bedroom.

"I was wondering what was in those plastic bags I saw in there. Mind if I take a look?" Patrick answered.

"Yeah, I mind. You got no business here. You still haven't told me why you come here. You broke into my house, and now you're trying to plant some shit on me. What's this about anyway?" Alfredo asked.

"Where were you yesterday morning around ten o'clock? Were you with Mr. Louis Smith? Were you in his apartment?" I tried to distract him so Patrick could continue with his mission.

"I wasn't with Louie yesterday. I know nothing about what went down there. Who sent you to me?"

"So you know what happened there; do you know who did the shooting?" I threw out.

"Not me, man, I didn't shoot nobody. I got no gun. Who told you about me? Why you think I shot the cop? I was just an innocent person in the wrong place, that's all, man, that's all," he said, noticeably agitated and half scared to death.

"Then who did shoot the cop?" I asked.

Patrick had been in the bedroom and walked out with some bags that looked like marijuana. They were the bigger bags, about a half pound, maybe five hundred dollars' worth of dope in each one, and each bag had a large "LK" for Latin Kings marked on it. Patrick also had a larger, three-quarter-filled bag of something with a funny-looking "T" on it—the bag that Father Pavlos gave me.

"That's not what you think. That's just stuff from plants in the backyard. That ain't dope or anything. It's just used like herb medicine, that's all it is, that's all. Hey, man, test it. You'll see, it ain't nothing; I'm telling you, it ain't nothing."

"Then what's in here?" I asked, pushing Father Pavlos's bag in his face. "And where did you get this?"

"I want a lawyer," Sanchez said as he sat down on a couch, burying his face in his hands and crying.

*   *   *

Back at the precinct we had Father Pavlos come down to identify Alfredo Sanchez as the man who he claimed gave him the herbs.

"I don't see him in the lineup. The man who came to me with the incense was older than most of those men and had a darker complexion than any of the men in there. No, I'm sure none of them are the Alfredo I talked with."

"You're absolutely sure of that, Father Pavlos?" Loo asked the priest.

"Absolutely. I'm very good at remembering faces, and I don't recognize any face in that room."

We thanked the priest for coming down and told him how helpful he was in breaking the case, even if the man who brought him the incense was not in custody today.

"We really don't need the father's identification of Alfredo—we got the right guy," I said to Patrick after the lineup. "He confessed to being there and dropped a dime on the others in the apartment. That's all the Criminal Investigation Unit needs. They'll pick the others up and find out who the shooter was. Those guys will do anything to save their own asses. We got 'em now. Look, it's late, and I want to see Gerry. You want to come?"

"Not tonight, Mitch. I got to get home, but you give him my best and tell him what we've done. He'll be happy to hear it."

At the hospital, Gerry was still in the ICU. He was conscious—groggy but conscious. The doctor told me that they have to do some more tests on him the next day, something called a TEE test to examine his heart. They thought that it could have been damaged in the shooting or the surgery, and they were concerned about blood clots forming in the heart itself.

I went into his room and gently took his hand and said, "Gerry, it's me, Mitch. Can you hear me?"

He opened his eyes, and in a very hoarse and weak voice, he said, "Hey, Mitch, how ya doin'?"

"I'm great," I said. "Just wanted you to know we got the guys who did it." With that I gently put the bag of herbs on Gerry's heavily bandaged chest, just to show him we got Father Pavlos's bag of leaves back too.

But Gerry had had no idea that the leaves were taken during the altercation and that we had recovered them. He looked at the bag with the Greek cross on it and then at me, as if to say, "Why did you bring this here?"

I explained briefly what had happened and how we caught Sanchez. He listened with half-opened eyes, and then he smiled at the story. He reached into the bag and sprinkled some of the leaves on his chest, and then he fell asleep with a smile on his face. I left there feeling good that he was alive and the doctors were on their way to making him well. He was still listed in critical condition, but the doctor was definitely optimistic.

The next morning Gerry had the TEE exam, and it showed that his heart was normal—no noticeable abnormalities or evidence of clots. They did notice something in his heart that they thought was an old wound or injury to the valve, but his records showed no previous heart issues. He was also feeling a lot better and seemed to be recovering normally now from the surgery, so they moved him out of ICU and into the surgery recovery unit at the University of Michigan Hospital. They also did a follow-up EKG to look for any tell-tale signs of an old injury—it didn't show any.

*　　*　　*

The following Monday at the precinct we were able to piece together what happened the day of the shooting. Louie had talked over the weekend and so did Sanchez. The two other guys were picked up, both gangbangers and one of them the shooter.

"It seems that Father Pavlos was right," Loo said to me and Patrick. "Sanchez was selling some leaves, however they proved to be leaves from a false aralia plant. He grows them in his garage and backyard and mixes the leaves up with cheap tobacco. He puts the LK on the bags to make people think that they were part of the Latin King's stash—a very risky thing for him to do."

"So why were those guys there, Loo? What brought them to Louie's in the first place?" I asked. I hadn't done the interviews over the weekend. Loo and some other detectives were doing all the interviewing at that point.

"When Gerry set up the meeting with Louie, he told him that he was interested in finding some guys who might be selling some weed as dope and wanted to show Louie the mark to see if he knew anything about it. It seems Louie knew that Sanchez did that—sell stuff with the LK marking—and so he told Sanchez about it and told him to come over right away. Sanchez knew, or just assumed, it must be some other dude's stuff they got. So hoping to get himself in good with the Latin Kings again, he brought two of them along. He had them all hyped up about folks selling bad shit and calling it Latin King's goodies."

"What an idiot!" I said. "That could have backfired on him so easily."

"Yes, but unfortunately as soon as Gerry walked in with the bag, one of the young Kings with an itchy finger shot him accidentally before he could say or do anything. Panic ensued, Sanchez grabbed the bag just in case it was his, and they all took off after deciding that that was the only thing they could do. They claimed they tried to help Gerry but thought he was dead, even though they heard him yell, 'Officer down,' into his radio. Poor Louie knew he would be pulled in because it was his apartment, but he felt he could talk his way out of it since he had no part in the shooting. Anyway, that seems to be the way it all went down."

"I guess it's up to the courts now, but they shot a cop and in Michigan—even if it was an accident, that's one major felony. I hope he gets the book thrown at him," I said.

"How are you feeling about it, Mitch? Could you deal with this guy in court if you had to, without blowing up?" Loo asked me.

"Yeah, Loo, I could handle it. I don't feel that kind of anger anymore. I don't know, maybe it's the classes with Father Pavlos—going through all those ten steps and learning to be more patient and reasonable—but once Gerry and I started to work on this case, I started to feel good about myself." I told him that I felt I could be a professional again without it getting to me. I didn't know—maybe it was Father Pavlos, or the volunteer committee, or whatever, but all of a sudden I felt good inside, like those demons of anger I used to wrestle with were all gone now.

"Sounds good to me, Mitch. I'm glad I had you go to that anger management class. You're a good cop and we need you here. Now let's hope that Gerry will be back with us real soon and the two of you can continue doing what you guys do best. It looks like you're going to need to be working with the Latin Kings again. Are you ready for that?" Loo asked me.

"Yeah, I'm ready. I think I'd like to begin with the two we got here, starting with the one that shot Gerry. Don't worry. I'm not gonna hurt him," I said with a broad smile on my face. "I just want to get background on him so that I can help the other members of the gang, maybe make sure they don't end up the same way he did. How old did you say he was?"

"He's just a kid—only twenty years old," Loo answered.

"Another young life ruined for absolutely no reason at all. I just hope I can prevent it from happening to someone else."

*   *   *

Gerry survived the gunshot wound and went on to become a detective in the Criminal Investigation Unit. I went on to become a detective too, and I also continued with my work in the Youth Bureau with the gang squad. Gerry told me that the doctors never could explain why the TEE test showed some previous heart damage, yet no subsequent tests or exams confirmed any kind of heart abnormality. It might just have been a fluke because of the gunshot wound that he took to the chest, but they said they'd probably never know. In any case he was healed just fine. But, you know, in some strange way I couldn't help but think how Gerry looked when he put some of those leaves on his chest—like his complexion all of a sudden became rosier. It might have been my imagination, but maybe Father Pavlos's leaves had some strange effect on us, even though that supernatural shit was all nonsense.

As for me, my anger has been well managed since the incident with Gerry, and I was able to forgive myself for all the grief I caused my friends, family, and in particular, myself. It may only be temporary, and the demons may return, but I'll take what I can get—hey, life goes on.

Chapter 5

Father Pavlos

I was sitting in my office, thinking about Gerry and quietly praying that he'd recover soon. I also was thinking about Mitch and how it seemed that he had changed. I sensed he was not as angry as he had been, and I couldn't figure out why. I'd like to believe it was because of my anger management classes, but that might be a bit presumptuous of me.

Suddenly it hit me. *Oh, my God,* I thought. *Oh my God, they got the wrong man! His name wasn't Alfredo. What was it? Ernesto?* It was Wednesday, the day after the arrest, when I suddenly realized that I had given the police a wrong name. I had to call Mitch immediately and tell him about my revelation.

"Hello, Mitch? This is Father Pavlos. I have to tell you I think we've made a serious mistake," I said to Mitch on the phone. Mitch had told me last night about the arrest of the men involved in Gerry's shooting. "The man who came to me with the leaves—his name was not Alfredo. I think it was Ernesto. I'm sorry; I'm good at faces but not so good at names. I'm just not sure what his name was—"

Mitch interrupted me. "Maybe it was just fate that made you say the name Alfredo, Father, because it was that name that led to the arrest of Sanchez and the others. Don't worry; we got the right guys. I'm gonna return the leaves to you today, because they weren't involved in any criminal activity that I know of."

Later that afternoon Mitch came by and dropped off the bag of leaves at my office. He said in some way he was glad to be relieved of them. He thought that maybe they would be of better use to someone else, someone who might need comforting from their touch. I thought that was a most curious way of putting it. As an herbalist, and someone who has used herbs to treat animals, I found it interesting that he would say something that implied that the leaves might actually be therapeutic. It was then that I had a strange feeling, almost like an epiphany, that these leaves would play an

58

important part in my life. Although I was not exactly sure what he meant by comforting, and even though I felt that the leaves were in some way important to my priesthood, I realized that it was time to get them back to their original owner—they'd caused enough trouble for Mitch and Gerry.

I was also feeling a little strange about my coming up with the right name for the criminal involved in Gerry's shooting. It just seemed that it was too much of a coincidence that I should pick *his* name, even though I knew I didn't remember names very well. I had felt so certain about the name Alfredo, like I knew someone named Alfredo was involved. But how could that have been?

*   *   *

I recalled that the man who brought the leaves to me—*Was his name Ernesto?*—worked at the airport as a janitor, or so he had said. Taking a chance, I called Detroit Metro that afternoon and introduced myself on the phone to one of the assistant airport managers.

"I know this is going to sound strange, but I'm Father Pavlos—I'm a priest at Saint Demetrios Church in Ypsilanti."

"How can I help you, Father?" the man replied.

"I'm trying to locate one of your janitorial staff. I think his name is Ernesto, but I could be wrong. He's a dark-skinned Hispanic man, a little on the short side, maybe five foot six, nicely built, and he might be in his early thirties. It's very important that I locate him. Do you think you could help me?" I pleaded.

The manager took my name, address, and phone number and said he'd get back to me or someone would get back to me later. He couldn't promise me that he'd find my Ernesto, but he said that with my good description he'd give it a try. I thanked him and waited. That was all I could do.

About seven that evening, just before I was to leave my office, my phone rang.

"Hello, is this Father Pavlos?" the voice asked.

"Yes, yes, it's me, Father Pavlos. Can I help you?" I asked anxiously, not knowing who was on the line, but I thought I recognized the voice as the janitor who brought me the incense leaves.

"Father Pavlos, my name is Fernando Garcia and someone thought that you might be looking for me. I'm working the afternoon shift today, and so I'm calling you from the airport. Were you looking for me?"

Fernando! Yes, that's his name, Fernando, damn it! I thought, irreverently. "Yes, Fernando, I'm sorry to bother you at work, but that bag of incense leaves you left with me, would you mind taking it back? It's not our incense, so maybe someone else needs it. Could you possibly return it to the storage room where you found it or find out who owns it? I have it here and would appreciate it if you took it back. Can you do that for me?" I said, almost pleading with him.

There was a pause on the line. Then Fernando said, "I think I can do that. I can come to your church tomorrow late in the morning, say eleven? Will that be all right?"

"That would be fine. I hope you'll be able to stay for a while. I have a story that might interest you."

"And I have one for you too, Father. I'll see you tomorrow then. Good-bye."

*   *   *

As soon as he came into my office, I recognized him. "Fernando, so good to see you again," I said as I extended my hand to him. "Here, sit down. How have you been?" This was a silly question since I had seen him less than two weeks ago. As he sat down at the table, I excitedly filled him in on the shooting and how my poor memory for names actually helped solve the case. He sat there quietly, fascinated by the whole account.

"Excuse me, Father, but did anyone who came in contact with the leaves have any serious illness?" Fernando asked.

"Why, no . . . at least I don't think so. Of course, Gerry, the officer that was shot, was in very serious condition. But he's coming around just fine now. I don't know if he had any direct contact with the leaves. Why do you ask?"

Fernando then related his story about his daughter Maria Elena and her miraculous recovery over MD. He was certain that it was the smelling of the leaves burning that cured her.

"How very interesting indeed," I said. "Have you told your priest? What did your doctors say? Were they so surprised as to call it a miracle?" I asked. My heart was beating very hard now. *Was I in possession of some divine product that could cure the sick?* I thought.

"No, no, I didn't tell my priest, and no, the doctor did not say it was a miracle. But I can tell you it was. I know it was a miracle," Fernando said.

I looked into Fernando's eyes, and I could see the passion in the man. How strongly he felt that a miracle happened in his family, to his daughter.

"Well, if what you say is true, then you can see how important it is that we get them back to their rightful owner. You said you found them at work—was there any information that would lead you to know who owned them?" I asked.

"No, Father, the only thing I really know about them is that one of the customs agents had them in his possession for a few days."

"I suppose you don't know who that agent was, do you?"

"No, I don't. There was a name on the confiscation ticket—Sarbanes, I think—but that doesn't mean much. He might have been the duty officer at the time they were taken."

"Well, that's a start," I said. "Will returning them to the storage room get you in any trouble?"

"I don't know. Of course you're not supposed to take confiscated food or plants out of the secure facility. They are taken every couple of weeks to be incinerated, but everyone does it. I suppose if we made a big deal out of it, I could be in trouble," Fernando explained. "But if the incense can help someone else, I'll take that risk, Father. However, if I remember right, the bag was out for a while before I had them, and that guy—Sarbanes—he might be in more trouble than me. After all, I'm just a janitor, but he's a US customs agent."

"You're right, of course. We wouldn't want to get anyone in trouble unnecessarily," I said. "I'll tell you what, if you like, let me follow through in a discreet manner on finding the agent. I think I can do that, and let's see what he says. Unless, of course, you want the leaves back yourself to dispose of them as you see fit. As far as I'm concerned, they're still yours."

"No, no, Father . . . please, you keep them and get them back to their owner. As I told you, they probably were taken from a passenger—I thought one returning from Greece—and should be returned to him. I'll feel much better knowing you're taking care of it," Fernando said.

"Then that's how we'll handle it. I'll try to find out who they actually belong to with my contact at the airport. I think that I could do it in a way that keeps everyone's privacy intact and yet could still resolve the issue."

"Thanks, Father. And if I may ask a favor, please say a prayer for my daughter, Maria Elena, in the hope that she no longer needs—or more importantly, that she'll never need the incense again," Fernando requested.

"That I will do, my son . . . *that* I will do."

I thought it strange that Fernando was concerned that the leaves' cure might not be permanent. But on second thought, I supposed I could understand his hesitancy on accepting such a miraculous cure in such a short period of time.

I was thinking of contacting the assistant manager that found Fernando to thank him, and then just ask a simple follow-up question about Sarbanes. *I better write that name down before I forget it,* I thought. It was then that I actually started my T file to keep tabs on all the people that had come in contact with the tea leaves. I also wanted to know what the leaves supposedly did for them, but more important at this time, I just wanted to keep the names straight of all those who were in any way involved.

*   *   *

I delayed calling the airport right away, still pondering what I would say to the assistant manager in order to find out who this Sarbanes was and how I might contact him. *Sarbanes,* I thought—that's a good Greek name, maybe he's one of ours? On Friday morning I called the precinct to ask Mitch how Gerry was doing. "You won't believe this, Father, but they're thinking about letting him out next week. They've never seen anyone with a cracked chest heal this fast," Mitch said.

"Oh, that's just great, Mitch. Please extend my best wishes to Gerry and tell him we're praying for him often," I said, and then I discreetly asked, "By the way, Mitch, did Gerry have any contact with those leaves? Did he, uh, maybe touch them or use them in some other way?" I said, without implying that he might have smoked them.

"Funny you should ask, Father. When I brought him the bag of phony dope to tell him we caught the guys—let's see that was last Thursday—he reached in the bag and sprinkled some on his chest. I remember he had a smile on his face. In fact I thought that somehow those leaves were comforting him." Mitch went on to tell me that's what he meant when he told you about the leaves comforting someone else. He also said that the next day his TEE test showed that he had a heart injury but it was fixed and that his EKG showed no history of heart damage, which they thought was somehow very strange." Mitch then wanted to know why I asked him about Gerry touching the leaves.

"I'm not sure myself, Mitch. The man who brought them in—by the way his name is Fernando. Did I tell you that? Well, he told me he thinks those leaves cured his daughter's muscular dystrophy. Now that's strange. Anyway, we're going to try to get them back to their owner. I've still got them, but I'll get on it early next week."

"Good idea, Father. And thanks for asking about Gerry. I'll tell him you called," Mitch said. "And thanks for praying for him. Let's hope that he is getting well and there's no more to do about that heart ailment."

When I hung up, I thought about our conversation. The bag of leaves was still on my desk, and I stared at it for a while before I made a decision. I decided to wait till next week to find the customs agent. I knew what I was going to do; I was going to put some of the leaves in the censer during Sunday morning mass. The idea alone terrified me. *Will I be doing something that only our Lord should do?* I thought. *And if I do find out it cures some of our parishioners from serious illness, will I still want to give the leaves back to their owner?* Whatever the outcome, I was determined to use them. *Maybe I'll just be doing our Lord's wishes,* I thought, trying to rationalize my testing the hypothesis that the leaves were God's gift to me personally. Maybe I should have thought a little longer before actually doing it.

*   *   *

I found out Monday morning that on Saturday night during our usual over-forty social program, one of the attendees and his date were "socializing" in one of the classrooms. It just happened that there was a small storage room next to that classroom where we stored our incense and other miscellaneous paraphernalia we used during services. None of it was of such great value that we would have to keep the room locked. Why I stored the leaves there and not in a more secure place eluded me to this day. And why the couple happened to look in the store room, I never did find out, but they did look and saw the bag of Fernando's incense. They called the church to find out about the leaves and made an appointment with me to tell me their story.

That evening Mr. Sarbanes and Mrs. Bemis, the couple with the leaves, came in for our meeting. I was in shock when he told me his name was Sarbanes. I hadn't followed through yet on calling the airport to locate him, but it would seem that by some coincidence, or whatever it might have been, he contacted me. *Was this too a sign from our Lord?* I wondered.

"You say that you and Mrs. Bemis happened upon the bag and you were wondering how it came to be there?" I asked.

"You see, Father, it was me who had marked that bag with the tau. That's how I knew it was mine, or I should say, the one I had in my possession about a month ago," Connie Sarbanes told me. "It's a long story, Father, but I think that bag belongs to a couple from Ann Arbor. I was hoping to get it back to them, but—"

"You're a customs agent, aren't you, Mr. Sarbanes? Would you be risking your job to return it to the person who brought it in? Was that person someone coming back into the country from Greece?" I asked.

Connie Sarbanes told me how he had confiscated them from a couple coming back from Indonesia and how the woman had said they were some kind of an infusion. He then told me the whole story about his glaucoma and how it had miraculously gone into remission after he smoked some of the leaves. It was then that I was convinced the leaves were blessed. I told him the stories about Maria Elena and Gerry, not mentioning anyone's name of course, and how they too overcame serious medical conditions after exposure to the incense.

Mrs. Bemis, who I discovered was no longer married to Mr. Bemis, asked about the religious significance of all of this. "Do you think that this is something from heaven, or wherever?" she asked.

"That really is not for me to say, Mrs. Bemis—may I call you Sally?" She nodded yes, and I continued. "The gentleman whose daughter no longer has MD thinks it was a miracle, but I can tell you that it takes a lot more work on the part of the church than most people are aware of to determine if it truly was a miracle. In any case, we should be more concerned with getting them back to their rightful owner than trying to decide if there was some divine intervention into yours and those other people's lives, don't you think?"

However, I felt she was right and that it probably was divine intervention, which convinced me even more to get the leaves back to where they came from. If I indeed was God's choice to use them for healing, then let that happen, but I felt my Lord wanted me to make sure that they now got home safely.

We talked for a long time and came up with a plan on how to return them to the couple who had originally brought them in from Indonesia. I didn't want Connie to get into trouble, even though he said he was willing to risk everything to get them back. I just asked him to see if he could get any information on the couple and then leave it to me to get the leaves back to them. He was delighted to do that. It would probably not put him at risk, and no one needed to know how the leaves got back to them. After all, what he told me was in confidence, and as a priest I could not violate his confidence. As it turned out, I'd been his and Sally's priest since they had been members (though not very active members) of our church from birth. I did not tell Connie about my putting some of the leaves in the censer during the previous day's services. We would just have to wait and see if that had any beneficial or, God forbid, other effects on any of our congregants.

*   *   *

"Father Pavlos? This is Connie Sarbanes," he said over the phone. "I got that information—or at least I think I did—that we were talking about yesterday."

Connie called me around one in the afternoon. He said that their computer person was able to get the information off of the 6059B customs forms that the passengers filled out when they returned from overseas.

"I recalled the date and time of their arrival, and the database that we keep had the other information. The one 6059 that fit all the details—bringing in tea from Indonesia—belonged to a Mr. and Mrs. Joseph Gilbert. Their address was not readable, just the street; it's Overridge Drive in Ann Arbor. Do you think that's enough for you to go on?" he asked me.

"Yes, Connie. Let's see, that's Joseph Gilbert on Overridge Drive, Ann Arbor. That should be enough. If I need more I'll contact you, but in the meantime I think it's best for you and Sally that you don't tell anyone about the whole affair. I'm sure you can understand why I say that. These things sometimes have a tendency to snowball way out of proportion. Let's just keep it among ourselves for now, okay? I will let you know either way as to the disposition of the, uh, tea. Thanks and I want you to know that you're doing a blessed thing and God will bless you for it, my son."

It was easy to find Joseph and Gabriella Gilbert's phone number in the Ann Arbor/Ypsilanti phone directory. I waited till evening to call.

"Hello, is this Mr. Joseph Gilbert?" I asked.

"Who's calling, please?" he replied.

"This is Father Pavlos from Saint Demetrios Church in Ypsilanti—," I started to say when he interrupted me.

"Yes, Father, and thanks for calling but we don't take any phone solicitations. If you—"

"No, no, no, this is not a solicitation; this is about the tea you brought back from Indonesia," I said in exasperation. Every time I called someone who didn't know me—well, almost every time—they thought I wanted some kind of a donation. There was silence on the other end for a moment, and then he spoke.

"How did you know about that?" he asked.

"Then I take it that this is Mr. Joseph Gilbert and you did bring back tea from Indonesia. I would like to return the package of tea to you. Could you come over to my office tomorrow sometime so that I may explain the circumstances surrounding the return?" Once again there was a short pause.

"Yes, we could do that, say one-thirty in the afternoon, if that's all right?" he said sheepishly.

I agreed on the time and told him how to get here and that I looked forward to meeting him. Finally the leaves would be returned to their owners—or at least that's what I thought.

*   *   *

At 1:30 p.m. sharp the Gilberts showed up in my office. "So nice to meet you. Please have a seat over here," I said as I showed them to my small conference table. The bag of tea was on the table, and I could see Mr. Gilbert looking at it as if he had seen a ghost.

"I'm not sure that's my tea," he said. "Mine didn't have any markings on the bag. I must say though, the stuff inside looks like it, but . . ."

Mrs. Gilbert couldn't stop staring at the contents. "Are you sure that these are ours?" Mrs. Gilbert said. "This is all so strange. How, or rather, why do you have these leaves and who said that they're ours?" She was right to the point.

I told them the story of Mitch and Gerry and the stories I had heard from Fernando and Connie, about how all these people with incurable illnesses suddenly got better. I was anxiously waiting to hear their story as well and wondered which of them or maybe even if both of them had had a similar experience. Once again I didn't use any real names, nor did I identify the people involved. But they, of course, knew that it was a customs agent who confiscated the tea. However, that didn't seem to faze them now.

They sat there in awe after listening to me talk for almost an hour, and then I stopped and waited for their answer.

"Holy shit . . . oops, forgive me, Father," Mr. Gilbert said. "I'm sorry, I guess I'm—rather, we're—a bit overwhelmed by those stories of the people who came in contact with the stuff. Weren't any of them normal? Oh, again, forgive me . . . I'm assuming that you are not—"

"No, that's all right, my son. I'm just as amazed as you are, and in fact just as unholy flabbergasted as you were when I first came in contact with the recipients of our Lord's mysterious alchemy. And no, to the best of my knowledge I'm in good health, so you might say I'm the only person who was not ill, nor was anyone in my immediate family ill. But what about you two, are either of you ill?" I pressed.

Joseph told me all about his pancreatic cancer scare and how after he started drinking the tea he went into remission.

"Did that doctor—Setiawan, you said? Did he tell you what they were? The friend of the customs agent who had them analyzed said that she was told that they were mostly green tea leaves. My own knowledge of herbs, which I might add is more than that of an amateur, tells me that they are definitely tropical in origin. Do you think that we could get Dr. Setiawan to tell us how he assembled them?" I wondered out loud. I also became a little concerned that maybe I was going beyond my position to press this issue and should probably speak with my superiors about the whole incident. *I think that I need better guidance on how to proceed,* I thought to myself.

"I honestly don't know what to tell you, Father. I'm not sure what I'll do with them since I believe I no longer need them. I'm tempted to just keep them around, in sort of a 'just in case' mode, but that would be selfish." He went on to tell me that he was actually torn about taking them back and felt that I was a better judge of what should be done with them. He thought we should get them back to Setiawan and tell him the saga of the bag, which he added looked hardly used since they were taken from him more than a month ago. After all, they were Setiawan's concoction, and he certainly deserved to know what they'd done. Joseph also wondered what I thought ought to be done with them.

I, too, was torn. I would have liked knowing what effect they had on my congregation after being put in the censer last Sunday. Yet somehow I also felt that they didn't belong to me to dole out merely as I saw fit. "I think it best you try to return them to the Indonesian doctor and tell him how much good they've done here in the United States. Do you think you can do that?" I said, a little sadly realizing that I would be giving up stewardship of this remarkable, possibly miracle-making substance.

"We'll try, Father. He has a close friend in Ann Arbor, a Dr. Kahn who has treated me, or I should say, diagnosed me. I'll contact him about returning them to Setiawan. I'll let you know what happens, and thanks for all you've done," Joseph said. Then he added, "Although I must admit, I am tempted to keep them myself just in case I should need them again. That cancer scare was quite a life changer for me."

Once more I could see his fear that his cure was short-lived and he needed to be reassured that he was safe now. I told him he was free to do what he felt was right, but he persisted, saying that they should go back to Indonesia.

I'm not sure why he was thanking me, but thank me he did as they left my office with the bag of tea. I was a little melancholy when they left, thinking maybe I should have stayed more involved with the package of leaves by offering to take the leaves to Dr. Kahn, or even getting them to Dr. Setiawan, or who knows what. I guess I was just sorry that I was giving them up, but in fact I was relieved to no longer have the responsibility of disbursing them. Putting them in the censer was probably wasteful and very inefficient, for I knew not who had benefitted. But if I had kept them, I would have been more discreet as to who should receive them. But then again, how would I know how to choose? Maybe it was for the best that I had just let the leaves go back the way they came. If that was wrong or right, I had faith that my Lord would let me know.

* * *

Summer came and was fading fast. It was now August and I was anxious to see if Dr. Setiawan received the herbs. I contacted Joe Gilbert and simply told him I wished to further inform Dr. Setiawan about the leaves' impact here in Michigan. He kindly gave me Dr. Setiawan's phone number, which he still had in his possession, and I called him.

"Yes, this is Wayan Setiawan, and who did you say you are?" he asked.

"My name is Father Pavlos, and I'm a priest at Saint Demetrios, a Greek Orthodox church in Ypsilanti, Michigan. That's just a few miles east of Ann Arbor."

"Yes, I know where Ypsilanti is, Father. I went to medical school at U. of M. How can I help you?" he said with just a slight accent. I was calling him in

Indonesia and I expected his accent would be heavier, but I was pleasantly surprised at how much he sounded like a midwesterner—like me.

"I'm calling about the leaves that Dr. Kahn, your friend and colleague here in Michigan, sent back to you. Are you aware of what I'm talking about?"

Oh, golly, there I go talking so awkwardly. You'd think that after four years at Hellenic College and three more years of divinity school at Holy Cross, I could phrase a question better than that, I thought.

"You mean the herbal leaves I formulated for his patient, don't you? And, yes, I got them back a while ago. What is it you want to know about the leaves?" he asked. I detected some strangeness in his demeanor, a sense of distrust like I suspected him of doing something wrong.

"Did he tell you about all the people whose lives were changed when they came in contact with them? What I'm trying to say is that there were people who had incurable illnesses and other problems that seemed to be cured when they came in contact with the leaves. I'm wondering, uh, is it possible you could tell me what was in that package? I'm an herbalist also, and I was thinking—"

"To tell you the truth, Father, I'm sorry, but I don't think I can help you there," he told me, cutting our conversation short.

I wanted to press him but thought it best to just drop it. I could tell from the tone of his voice that he was distressed at my inquiry, so I just said, "I understand, I understand. I just thought I'd ask anyway. However, if you should change your mind about sharing your, uh, formula, would you mind contacting me?" I asked.

He said he would and took my phone number and address, but I could tell he would never contact me, at least not to send me any leaves or instructions on their preparation.

I felt disappointed after our conversation and wanted to know so much more about the leaves and if any people in Indonesia had been treated with them or other similar herbs. And if they had, how had their lives been impacted. But I had to stop for fear that I would end up sounding like some kind of a religious zealot looking to see if one of God's secrets was, in fact, being made known to me. I had to quell that perception immediately, but in spite of myself, I couldn't help but wonder if I had truly been made privy to the making of a miracle.

It was then that I decided to keep in contact with those whose lives were changed so dramatically by contact with the leaves. I kept thinking about how fragile they seemed, thinking that their impairments would return and that the whole incident with the leaves was just a passing aberration on their lives, no matter how remarkable the outcome had been. I also thought it was God's will that I should stay in touch with them to chronicle whatever purpose our lord had in store for them, and for me. I also prayed that no unforeseen catastrophe would happen to any of them. As to why I seemed to worry about them more than the parishioners in my own church, I wasn't sure. Maybe it was because I felt that our Lord gave me some special responsibility toward them, or maybe my ambition was getting the best of me.

CHAPTER 6

Wayan Setiawan

I'm a doctor from Bali, Indonesia, and my full name is I Gusti Wayan Setiawan. My full name indicates that I was the firstborn child in my family and that we are members of the Wesya caste. However, everyone—except my family, of course—calls me Setiawan. I grew up on a large vanilla bean and clove plantation that my grandfather owned in central Bali, which was passed on to my father, his brothers, and now to my brothers. Our family was relatively well off, and when I was quite young—just thirteen—I was sent to live with an uncle in Hawaii because the public schools were better in the States. I also grew considerably taller there because of the high meat protein diet of the islands. I'm taller than most Balinese natives, but I'm still very much a product of my homeland. I missed my family, particularly my grandmother who schooled me in herbal medicine and the local Hindu religion, which is based heavily on Balinese folklore and other local beliefs. However, in Hawaii I became a Buddhist because that's what my uncle's family practiced, though I never fully understood the difference. As for religion, I was content to accept my grandmother's belief in many spirits and gods who on any given day could impact my life and family for good or evil. But by following proper etiquette and behavior to appease these phantoms, we could live, for the most part, in harmony with the spirits that are in all things.

After I finished high school in 1977, I attended the University of Hawaii in the Manoa area of Honolulu. It was a magnificent region on Oahu, and the vegetation reminded me of my home in Bali, but I still missed my country. I majored in mathematical biology, minored in botany, and did well enough to get accepted to the University of Michigan's Medical School in Ann Arbor. I had glowing recommendations from my professors, and they all thought that going to Ann Arbor would be good for my career. After all, Michigan had an outstanding reputation and a medical degree from there would let me practice anywhere, but I had always intended to return to Bali when I graduated med school in 1985. I returned to Hawaii first to do my residency in family medicine and community health before returning to Bali. It was there that I met Arti, a petite, bronze-skinned, Balinese beauty whom I instantly fell in love with. She was getting her master's degree in public health and planned on working for the government agency that serviced the indigenous populations on Bali.

Arti and I got married in 1990, right after I finished my residency. I picked up an MS along the way in Native Hawaiian Health, which included health-care practices that use many traditional healing methods, like herbs and incantations. Because of the similarity to my own Balinese culture, I knew this was the area of medicine I wanted to practice back home.

When we returned to Bali in 1991, I received an academic appointment on the Faculty of Medicine and Health Sciences at Udayana University. I maintained a modern practice at the clinic on the Bukit Jimbaran Campus in Denpasar, but I also maintained a number of clinical practices all around the island. I lectured in the medical school on a number of subjects, but my specialty, and favorite courses, were in homeopathic medical practices. Arti and I now had two children under the age of five, and they kept Arti too busy to work outside the house. But she hoped that when the kids were older, she'd be able to go back to work and get out into the field, working alongside me in our remote clinics.

*   *   *

I grew to curse that day in early June 1997 that I got those damn leaves back from Ann Arbor, for nothing has stressed me more of late than they have. Bill Kahn kept bugging me about them, but I never in all my wildest imagination thought that some simple, almost generic herbal remedy for nausea would cause me so much consternation. I wish to God that I had never heard that those cursed leaves had cured all those people. For if I hadn't heard of their unusual powers, I would never have tried to use them myself for comforting—or actually healing—any of my patients, and then all the subsequent anxiety and soul-searching would never have been my fate.

I decided to talk it over with Arti—my concern about having used the leaves.

"So why did you use them in the first place?" she asked. "You knew that they were island herbs; what made you think that they could be more than

T

that? You told me you thought that some doctors in the States misdiagnosed their patients. So what changed your mind?"

"You're right. That's exactly how I felt, and at first that's all I intended to do—use them as they were meant to be used. But then it happened. My cancer patient goes into remission, or whatever, but he was totally asymptomatic after only one cup of tea," I explained to Arti. "I just had to see what else they could do, so I kept using them on all kinds of patients, watching them heal literally right before my eyes, and then I realized that at that rate I'd soon run out of them. That's when all the damn trouble started. That's when things got much too complicated for a general practitioner like me, and that's when I realized that I had taken on something beyond my scope of inquiry, something that was best left up to our gods and other spirits to handle."

"Do you think that's why Bill contacted you? That he knew there was something strange—something uniquely Bali at work here—and wanted to know what you thought?" Arti asked.

"I don't know . . . I don't know, but knowing Bill, I would doubt that. He's too much of a scientist to think that something supernatural would be at work. He would more likely think it's psychosomatic before he'd think it was unnatural. Maybe I should be talking with grandmother. She taught me most of what I know about herbs and the spirits that guide their usage. I think I'll take a trip to the plantation this weekend and ask her what I should do. What do you think?" I asked.

Arti agreed that since I was so upset by the leaves' ability, talking with my grandmother would probably be the best way to go about it. My grandmother had no formal education but was considered a healer in our part of the island. She was also one of the wisest persons I knew and someone I could always count on for sound advice—along with much love and affection—whether I was strapped for an answer or just confused. And now I was very confused by one of life's occasional head-knocks that shook my faith in my ability to rationally understand what was going on.

* * *

It was on Saturday, June 14, when I visited my family homestead in the middle of the island. They were always glad when I came for a visit and immediately chastised me for not bringing Arti and the kids, but I wanted

73

to talk with my grandmother and preferred not to have the children there to distract her or me.

"So, Grandmother, what do you think I should do?" I asked her after telling her about all the healing they did and giving her some of the leaves to study.

She carefully, smelled, tasted, and rubbed the leaves beneath her finger tips. I could see she was in deep thought when she answered.

"Wayan, you must do exactly what I tell you." She was speaking in our native Balinese language and continued almost as if in a trance. "Use the leaves no more. You should not choose who is to get life. Take them and burn them thoroughly, be careful to preserve all the ashes, and then wrap the ashes in a banana tree leaf, take them to Sanur, and gently put them in the water so that the ocean carries them away. After that, you are to make an offering of rice, flowers, and incense and leave it at the shrine on Sanur Beach. Don't smell the burning leaves too long or handle them yourself—they are fraught with spirits that even I don't understand."

I had chills when my grandmother told me that—I had never seen her so filled with spiritualism before. Her eyes were misty and her mouth was thin and almost featureless, not even a hint of emotion. My grandmother was always quick to smile and always had very animated facial expressions that I loved to watch when she taught me things or told me stories—but now I hardly recognized her.

*　　*　　*

The next day I did exactly what she told me to do—I did not want to make the gods angry. I well knew that those gods who gave life could just as easily take it away. I also felt that she was right in saying that it was not for me to decide who got them and who didn't. In a sense I was relieved to have been released from that burden. I also knew that I could not tell Bill Kahn what I had done with the leaves. I didn't think he'd understand how I, as a doctor, could destroy life-giving medicine. I also didn't think he'd believe me if I told him I couldn't reproduce the original formulary because my tech goofed up when he originally assembled the package.

Later, on a Sunday in August, Arti noticed me sitting in our garden, daydreaming, and asked, "You still look troubled—is it because of the leaves?"

"I guess so. I've seen some patients lately who are really suffering, and I wish I still had the leaves so I could treat them. I'm always second-guessing myself about destroying them, but I couldn't forget my grandmother's face. When I see her now, she's back to her old self, and I find it hard to believe how she looked a couple of months ago when she examined the leaves," I told Arti. "I was also troubled by that priest who called a few days ago asking me for the formula. I'm not sure what his motives were for wanting the recipe—to study the leaves or use them—but either way, I guess it was for his own personal ambition. He claimed he was an herbalist, but I think that was just a smoke screen. I wasn't thrilled about sharing anything with that guy. Do you think he knew that they were somehow supernatural?"

"I couldn't tell you, honey," she said. "But I personally think it best that you forget about the whole incident as soon as you can. It's not good for you to be beating yourself over the head with 'could of, would of, should of' things. The herbs are gone, so just go back to being the good doctor you are without any ghostly influences hanging over you—influences that we can never understand. Okay?"

That was good advice from Arti, and I tried hard to follow it. But I still got extremely upset when I saw someone young dying of something I could not cure and thought how just recently I had had the power to save them. I no longer tried to reproduce the mixture, because I knew that even if I found it, sooner or later something would happen to make me regret it. Like my grandmother said, it was not for me to decide who lived and who died. But as a doctor I was at times faced with exactly that choice, so what was the right answer? I wasn't sure I'd ever know.

Episode 2

SEPTEMBER 2001

CHAPTER 7

Father Pavlos

Over the past four years my contact with the recipients of the leaves has been sparse, at best—with the exception of Mitch Foley. I had periodically asked Mitch to serve on various committees as a resource person. I liked Mitch; he was young—midthirties, I suspected—energetic, and an excellent police officer. I also felt some responsibility for him to make sure he kept his temper in check, so as not to jeopardize his career or anyone else's life. Mitch was a big man, and I knew someday he would have quite a paunch if he didn't watch his diet. I also knew he was divorced, living alone, and not doing too good of a job taking care of himself. He looked like a caricature of what the cartoonists would draw for a slightly overweight, loveable Irish cop with a red nose and rosy cheeks. In any case, Mitch was always easy to approach on the subject of the leaves, and I think that in some way they might have touched him too. My anger management classes with him would not have been enough to make the changes that I saw in Mitch since our first meeting early in 1997. But I feared that what had just happened could change all that, and I was concerned that Mitch might be having problems coping with the situation. After all, it was today, Tuesday, September 11, 2001, when the world stood in awe while the United States was viciously attacked by terrorists from a foreign country. The entire country was in shock, in probably much the same way as when on December 7, 1941, the Empire of Japan attacked Pearl Harbor.

I immediately thought about the leaves, and I wondered how Mitch and the others exposed to them would take the attack. I was concerned and hoped that they were still living normal lives, unencumbered by personal tragedies. I sorely wanted them kept from harm for fear that if harm did come to them, they would truly believe that the leaves were just an illusion. I feared if that was to happen, then they might get sick again. I know that's not rational, but that's how I felt. I guess my own faith in the leaves' healing powers was also being tested. I recalled the recipients' fragilities over their cures and wondered if the day's attack had made them even more uncertain as to their future able-bodied status. It didn't take me long to find out.

Chapter 8

Mitch Foley

Whenever things got rough, I always tried to find out what my old partner and friend, Gerry Patterson, thought about the situation, especially if I was feeling that my anger issue might be acting up. Gerry was a detective with the Criminal Investigation Unit downtown. He was on his way up the ladder, as well he should be. He was smart, dedicated, and well liked. It wouldn't surprise me if he became the chief or at least a deputy chief one day, so after the attacks on that terrible Tuesday afternoon, I called him.

"It's a madhouse here, Gerry. What's happening downtown? We're all on twenty-four-hour alert here and doing double shifts, but we really don't know what to do. Washington is supposed to give us directives, but they haven't come in yet. Do you know anything?" I asked him, realizing that I must have sounded totally stressed out.

"I just know what you know, Mitch, but we are being briefed by the FBI this evening. I think they want us to be on the alert for any homegrown terrorist cells that might be in the area. I think you guys in the gang squad might be of help there. Do you know any gangs with Middle Eastern connections?"

"Not really," I said. "I know there are a bunch of small groups of Middle Eastern students at both Eastern and Washtenaw, but I've never had any gang-related problems with them. With the way everyone is so jumpy about Arab-looking people now, I expect that we'll be getting lots of calls soon. You know the kind, from all those folks who come out of the woodwork during rough times," I told him, and then recalled an old incident that both of us were involved with in 1990 when an Arab shopkeeper shot an African American teen for supposedly shoplifting. We had our hands full on all the calls that altercation brought in.

"Yeah, I sure do remember that. That was one of our first assignments together, right? We did a good job on calming both camps down then. I hope we can do the same this time around. And I suspect you may be right about all the calls coming in on this one," Gerry said. "Well, okay, keep in touch, and if I have any news for you after we meet with the feds, I'll let you know. You're working with Patrick now, right? He's a good guy, and you guys make a great team. I'm certain no terrorist will get past you two micks," Gerry said with a smile in his voice.

"Yeah, just let 'em try—two Irishmen like me and Patrick can handle them. Well, Pat's really only half Irish," I said to Gerry, while winking at Patrick.

After I hung up the phone, Patrick said, "What was that all about?"

I filled Patrick in on my conversation with Gerry. We were at the precinct just waiting for an assignment. It wasn't our usual shift, but we had been called in because of the emergency situation, and we were sitting around waiting for orders. In reality things were very quiet in Ypsi.

By Tuesday evening almost all local events had been cancelled. Schools had closed early, and both EMU and WCC cancelled all classes. The two schools were holding special sessions for people who wanted to go in and talk about the attacks with some professors and counselors. There was no air traffic, and with us being so close to Willow Run airport, the quiet skies seemed quite strange. We had been briefed by our Loo and told to stand by for anything special that might arise but to also be prepared to interview any suspicious group or individual that might be fingered by someone as a potential threat.

I, like many of my fellow officers, was beyond pissed. I was worried what I might do if I had to deal with any of those radical bastards. I'm a cop and trained to respond to danger by being aggressive and, if need be, confrontational. Although my so-called Irish temperament had been well controlled over these last four years, I was worried that I might be visited by those goddamn anger demons again.

"Juvenile gangs are one thing but terrorists? That's a whole new ballgame. Do you speak any Arabic?" Patrick asked me.

"Are you kiddin' me? I barely speak English," I joked, and then I got serious. "I don't know. If we have to interview anybody, I think they'll speak English, and it won't be much different than when we interview kids. Maybe a little more dangerous so we'll have to be careful, but the protocol should be the same as if we were asked to investigate any other suspicious activity or location. Let's just keep it simple and not read too much into anything, okay?"

We were finally relieved at midnight and told to stay on alert and be ready to come in if called. We were also asked to return early for the morning shift and be prepared to stay through our regular afternoon shift. Patrick and I had drunk so much coffee we weren't sure we would be able to sleep, but we left the precinct station anyway.

"Want to grab a bite?" I asked.

"No thanks, Mitch. I'm going home. Hey, you want to come to my place? Jane made dinner, and she's keeping it warm for me. I'm sure there's enough for two."

"Thanks, Pat, but I'll pass tonight. I'm really not that hungry. I think I'll just try to get some sleep."

In fact I was hungry, but not for food—I was lonesome. I really wanted to be with someone tonight, but there wasn't anybody. I thought that maybe I should go to church and see what might be going on, but realizing the time, I knew it would look much too strange, so I just went home. I tried to watch some late-night TV, but nothing good was on, and the news was the same—over and over, images of the planes hitting the World Trade Center, making me angrier and angrier. I took a hot shower and went to bed, but my sleep was fitful at best.

* * *

Wednesday was a relatively routine day here in the Ypsilanti Police Department, even under these extreme circumstances. Actually it was quieter than normal. So many events were cancelled, and the day was spent by most people reflecting on yesterday's attacks in New York, Washington, DC, and Pennsylvania. Still, many questions needed answering, but the main question—who did it—seemed to be resolved. Osama bin Laden and his al-Qaeda organization were the obvious culprits, but it would appear from what they already knew that Saudi Arabia, Afghanistan, Pakistan, and other countries could also have been the breeding grounds for the terrorists. In any case, at the police station we didn't do anything unusual or try to interview any suspected potential threats, even though a number of calls had been made reporting what some people thought were suspicious activities. None, however, seemed credible enough to warrant sending out a team to investigate. We went home after the day shift but were reassigned to the day shift for the duration.

On Thursday morning a call came from downtown, asking Patrick and me to investigate some EMU student who supposedly had been acting suspicious. Gerry had called and told our Loo to put us on it. I think it was because he sensed it might be unrelated to the attack, and because of our sensitivity to students from working the Youth Bureau, we could handle the situation better than some rookie cops from downtown. He probably wanted to avoid coming on heavy-handed with uniformed officers. The FBI was raiding some suspected cells in the Detroit area, and the TV news was playing it up big time. Gerry probably thought that we didn't need, or want, that kind of publicity here in Ypsi. I also think that he was concerned about me and wanted to make sure that I would control my anger if the real thing did come along. I think he felt like me about our "cures"—if my demons returned, then maybe his heart problem would return. The attack had shaken our sense of normalcy. Maybe all bets were off now, and we wondered if the strange effect the leaves had had many years ago might no longer be working.

"So how do you think we should play this one, Mitch?" Patrick asked me.

"Like we said on Tuesday, let's just treat it as possible suspicious activity and see what happens. You know the procedure—be nice but be prepared."

We were driving over to the address near the EMU campus. The person we were looking for lived on a street that housed many student rental properties. His apartment was on the second floor in an older house that had been divided into three or four student apartments. It was hard to tell how many subunits were inside from all the various mailboxes and doorbells attached to the side posts off the front porch. We found the bell that matched the name of the person we were told to interview and rang it.

The stairwell door was open and a voice yelled down, "Who rang the bell?"

"I did!" I yelled back up the stairs. "I'm Detective Mitch Foley, and I'm here with my partner Detective Patrick Taylor from the Ypsilanti Police Department. Are you Mr. Osman Qalzai?"

It was quiet for a few seconds, and then someone came down the stairs. He was a young man, early twenties at best, dressed in jeans and a white T-shirt, no shoes or socks. He was a nice-looking kid, and he stared at us before saying, "Why do you want to know?" in a definitely hostile tone.

"Are you Mr. Qalzai? I hope I'm pronouncing it correctly," I said.

He looked at the two of us and then said, "Come upstairs if you like. We shouldn't talk out here." His Middle Eastern accent was heavily tinged with a British affect, and he carried himself like a privileged kid—sure of himself and just a little too cocky.

The apartment was typically student—a mess with clothes, books, CDs, empty bottles, and the usual collection of tchotchkes and posters that one would expect to find in a student apartment.

"Sorry for the mess, but the lady who cleans hasn't shown up. I think she's afraid of me . . . or my roommates," he said.

"Should she be?" I asked.

"My *gawd*, not you too. I should think the bloody police would know better. I'm so sick of you provincial little bastards thinking anyone from my country is a murdering terrorist. It's bad enough you call us rag-heads and sand-monkeys, among many other nasty names, without thinking we all want to murder you in the name of Allah!"

"Hold it, young man, we didn't call you any names, nor did we say what we thought about you. We only asked if you were Mr. Qalzai, and you still haven't answered that question. Please keep your anger under control, and let's see if we can get through this interview without anyone's feathers being ruffled any more than they are now," I said in a firm but nonthreatening manner, pleased with myself for keeping my cool.

There was a pause, and you could see that he was a very troubled young man, when he said, "If you've come to talk to me about Ursama, then I think it best we do it at your headquarters."

*　　*　　*

We placed the young man, who I presumed was Osman Qalzai, in an interrogation room, while we put together a plan. I wasn't sure that as the gang squad we should be interviewing him, so my Loo told me to call Gerry and ask him what he thought we should do.

"I don't know, Gerry. I don't think we have a gang issue here, and I'm wondering if you guys should handle this. Why did we get the call on this one anyway?" I asked.

"The information we got was that a group of students were conducting suspicious activities at that address, and his was the only name offered up. The call came in from someone who wished to remain anonymous, and the call was traced to a public phone at Eastern. Anyone could have made it. I thought it best, considering how uptight people are today, to check it out, and I thought that you and Patrick would keep a cool head on this one, so that's why I asked you two to do it. If you think it's too dangerous or out of your job description, let me know and we'll send someone down to bring him back here."

"No way, Gerry, we can do this. Let me start from the gang approach, and if I get in over my head, I call you, okay?" I knew what Gerry meant by cool heads and was pleased that he considered me to be in control enough to handle it. I thought that there were a number of cops out there who were ready to bust heads at the slightest provocation today. I hung up and sat down with Patrick to lay out a plan.

"Why don't you leave me alone with that murdering son of a bitch for ten minutes? I'll find out who this Osama guy is," Patrick said.

"Take it easy, my friend; let's not go there. We were asked to do this only because Gerry thinks we won't loose our cool. I feel like you do, but it's best we play it straight. Can you do that with me—play it by the book without losing your cool? Oh, and by the way, he said Ursama, not Osama; you're watching too much TV," I said with a knowing smile on my face.

"You're the senior guy here, Mitch. I'll take my cues from you, but I just don't like this guy's attitude. He acts like he's something special, like his shit don't stink, but I think there's a problem with him, so I'm gonna watch him very carefully," Patrick said with real anger in his voice. I had never seen Patrick this way, and I'd never known him to harbor a prejudicial bone in his body. Tuesday's events have gotten everyone riled, and now I felt that I might need to watch Patrick more than I wanted to.

But my immediate misgivings about Patrick proved totally unjustified. We went into the interrogation room where the young man was waiting. He was calmly sitting at the small table with a bottle of water when we sat down and joined him.

"As I said earlier, I'm Detective Foley, and this is my partner Detective Taylor. We are part of the Youth Bureau, and we work with young people who might be having problems with school or family. We've been led to believe that you might be a leader of a youth group."

"Bloody hell, man, I know what the fuck a gang squad is. I watch enough of your American TV. I'm not a kid. I'm over twenty-one and the son of a respected leader in Pakistan, so don't put me on, okay? We know what this is all about—it's about Ursama. He's probably the one who told you to interrogate me, right? Well, he's the one you should be interrogating, because he is the local cell leader for LeT."

The young man told us everything about his roommates without us even asking him. It seemed that Ursama and another Pakistani are Qalzai's roommates at the house where we picked him up. They were all from the same region of Pakistan, but the difference was that Qalzai was not a follower of Hafiz Saeed, the leader of LeT, a known terrorist organization already outlawed in England.

"Do you have any idea where Ursama and your other roommate may be?" Patrick asked in a surprisingly cool demeanor.

"No, I haven't seen them since last weekend when they said they were going out for dinner. They never came back, which is not unusual. They've disappeared before for a few days, and then they come home acting as if they were never gone. They don't like me because I'm not a Jihadist. They could be anywhere. There's a lot of Muslims on campus that would protect them even if they themselves are not members of any illegal organization. They're afraid for their families back home, and some may even be sympathetic because of their hate for the Israeli and American governments."

"And why aren't you afraid? They already tried to implicate you for something bad, so what's stopping them from pressuring your family?" Patrick asked. He was really into this and was doing a top-notch job, so I let him handle it.

"My father is a proud and honorable leader. He is not afraid of Saeed and his LeT henchmen, and he would be furious with me if he even thought for a moment that I would cower from their threats against him or me. No, he would be proud that I stood up against them, especially now after the attacks. I would not be one bit surprised if Ursama knew of the attacks before they occurred. You should find him and his small cadre of ignorant fools who do not follow the true Islam and arrest them."

Qalzai spoke those words as someone who had a strong moral sense of what was right. He might be young and a bit arrogant, but I had to admit I was beginning to admire the guy. Patrick and I thanked him for his cooperation and asked him to stay with us a little longer. We needed better descriptions of Ursama and his followers, in addition to any other information he could give us to help find them. Qalzai was more than willing to stay and help.

*   *   *

Friday afternoon Patrick and I were downtown meeting with Gerry and the hastily formed members of the interagency terrorism task force. We were asked to fill them in on our findings from our interview with Qalzai. They had people from the FBI, the Michigan State Police, and some other unnamed federal agencies that I suspected might be CIA. We were in the large conference room, and Gerry was chairing the meeting. After brief introductions, Gerry asked us to report on our interrogation of the young Pakistani, which we did.

"Are you sure this Qalzai guy is not a member of any Muslim or other extremist organization?" one of the feds asked. These guys were primed for blood—they wanted anyone they could take down, no matter how unaffiliated they might be with any known terrorist group. A few years ago I might have helped them do that, but now . . . maybe the leaves *were* still working for me.

"Our investigation of him, though admittedly somewhat limited, shows no known anti-American activities ever noted," I answered. "On the contrary, he's been very much involved with establishing good neighbor ties between Pakistan and the United States."

"That's the way they work. They try to look as good as they can to avoid any suspicion, but when the time comes—," the same Fed was saying when Patrick interrupted him.

"I checked out his story both here and in England where he went to school, and there is no pattern of wrongful behavior anywhere. I also checked with the State Department, and they know his father, who is a faithful US ally, so I think it best we trust this kid and treat him right. We have enough enemies in that part of the world without going out of our way to make more," he said, coolly and professionally without necessarily putting the federal agent down. I was very proud of him.

"We've got good leads on his roommates, and Ursama's terrorist activities," Gerry said. "We found literature in the apartment that definitely links Ursama to LeT, or Lashkar-e-Toiba, as it's actually called. One of our Pashtun-speaking officers was able to translate the materials, and England confirms that the group is outlawed there as a terrorist organization. There were also some handwritten lists of names and other scraps of paper that are proving very helpful in the investigation. His computer is gone, and if it wasn't for Detectives Foley and Taylor's fast action, we wouldn't even have the information I just described for you."

"I think you guys are doing great on this," the FBI guy said, "and if you need any help from us, please let me know. You know how to reach me in Detroit, Gerry, so just do your job and find them. When you do get them, and I know you will, please contact us so we can treat them right and get as much information from them as possible. I know you checked this out yourself, but those kids are here on student visas—they're not US citizens—so you don't have to Mirandize them, you know."

"I understand all that, and I will definitely keep you in the loop when we get them." But Gerry knew the FBI guy was wrong about the Miranda Act. He knew he would Mirandize them if he caught them, so as not to ruin a good case being built against some possible terrorists.

A few more comments and offers of help from the other agencies were expressed. No one tried to shove primacy on us. We all knew where we stood in the pecking order, but it was nice to see cooperation for a change, instead of the sometimes vicious competition we get between local and federal law enforcement agencies. We also knew that the FBI and the other feds were going to stay on top of this one no matter what we did.

After everyone left, Gerry asked Patrick and me to hang around a bit, saying he wanted to talk with us.

"What's up, Gerry?" I asked.

"I just want to thank you guys for not losing your cool on this kid. I've met him, and he's a little hard to take, especially when you first start talking with him. Had some of our guys got him first, there's no telling what might have happened, and we wouldn't have nearly the good information that we have now. So thanks for a job well done."

* * *

Things were a little more normal the next week when airplanes were back in the skies. Our Loo was not as harried as he was the previous week, but we were still on high alert, and the feds were still trying to calm the nation down. We were feeling great pain for all the victims and their families, but we had jobs to do to make certain those kind of attacks wouldn't happen again, and so we did our jobs. I thought that if I did my job and kept my cool, the demons wouldn't return. I knew that was kind of silly, but hey, I had nothing to lose.

On Tuesday morning—a week after the attack—when we got to work Loo called us into his office. "I found out late last night that Gerry and his team rounded up that kid Ursama and most of the members from his LeT organization. Gerry said he notified the FBI, who immediately came and took them into custody as foreign nationals plotting acts of violence against the United States. They had more than enough documentation to make their case. It looks like you two will be receiving commendations for your work. Congrats, guys!"

Patrick and I looked at each other and smiled broadly at what we had just heard. "And to think I wanted to beat that Qalzai kid silly when we first saw him," Patrick said.

"Not a good idea to tell anyone else that," Loo said, and I nodded in agreement.

Later in the day when things were quiet, I got a call from Gerry.

"Hi Mitch, I'm sure you've heard by now that we caught those kids in the LeT cell," Gerry said. "I don't think they had any knowledge of the 9/11 attacks, but I do think they were planning on doing some things just as evil. They were talking up a storm about all their hatred for us and our 'slaves, Israel and England,' and what they were going to do. I was glad the FBI took charge of them. Let them deal with that filth."

"Yeah, I'm glad that I didn't see them. I'm not sure how cool I would have been hearing all that shit," I said.

"The main reason I'm calling is that I'm recommending you and Patrick for citations, 'for your professional and distinguished work under extremely trying conditions.' Don't tell me you don't deserve it—I know you do." Gerry paused for a moment and then said, "And by the way, I couldn't help but think about that TEE test I had five years ago when I heard LeT—and how much the two reminded me of that bag of leaves we got from Father Pavlos. Maybe it was the Greek tau on the bag—another T—that made me wonder what's up with all these 'T's, but something got me thinking."

"You know, that's funny because I thought the same thing when I heard that name. What do you think that's all about?"

"I think it was the connection to Father Pavlos' bag of leaves. I remember it like it was yesterday when you showed me that you had recovered the bag taken by Louie's friend. I put some leaves on my chest and almost immediately I felt a great relief, like something in my body had healed. I couldn't explain that feeling, and I never told you that, but I think that all those 'T's are now somehow connected. Do you think that might be the case, partner?"

"Whatever you say, my friend. Hey, there are far stranger things going on that neither one of us will ever be able to explain—this could be just another one of those things."

We exchanged good-byes and hung up.

I told Patrick about Gerry putting us in for a citation for our work on the LeT case, and he said, "I'm glad you made me keep my head when I was about to bust that kid's face for being such a wiseass. You're the hero here, Mitch. But I'll take the citation anyway," he said, grinning at me.

Holding in one's Irish temperament could be hard at times, but that was just the Irish for you. I had no problem keeping my anger in check, but I had to admit that I still felt like shit over the attacks. I just wanted time to pass quickly so we could move on. However, I knew, as with other historic national tragedies, we'd never fully get over it. I also knew that my anger demons were just under the surface and that it would take some work on my part to keep them from ever fucking me over again. I hoped that the leaves that comforted me and Gerry were still doing their magic.

Chapter 9

Joey Gilbert

It had been almost four years since Glen and I started our company, and we were quite successful, at least in business. Glen kept getting us more contracts, both government and private—usually as subcontractors to large aerospace corporations, like Boeing, who used our electro-optical devices in their aircraft. He frequently drove me crazy with demands for more products and his willingness to take on any project that promised to bring in money, no matter how difficult it might be or how thin it stretched our resources while we tried to fulfill our other contractual obligations. His dour personality didn't help either, and most of our employees were outright afraid of him and simply avoided him. Even I found myself avoiding him whenever I could.

I was in my office on September 11, 2001, talking with a couple of my engineering staff, when it happened.

"Holy shit," I said as we watched the World Trade Center collapse on TV. We were watching the news after someone yelled out that the country was being attacked.

"Who the fuck are those guys? What's going on here?"

"Wait, wait, listen to the announcer," one of my engineers said. "There's more attacks."

"What's all the racket in here, Joe?" Glen came into my office, which was near his in the executive wing of our new building. Our company had grown to around fifty employees, and we had just moved to Research Park Drive in Ann Arbor. We got Glen up to speed about the situation on the East Coast, and as he watched the TV, I could see he was thinking about something—and I don't think it was the horrendous tragedy that was unfolding before us. Glen's presence was not always welcomed by the other employees, and I could see that some felt nervous about being in my office now that he was there. They were afraid he'd start in on them with his usual rant: "Don't you people have anything better to do?" Most of the time he just stayed in his own office or was at the business part of the wing. He was, after all, our CFO and responsible for getting contracts and taking care of money matters. I, on the other hand, headed up engineering and production, which meant developing, designing, fabricating, and producing the products. We had a successful, if not always cordial, partnership.

"Joe, come see me when you get a chance. We need to talk about some new products, okay?" Glen said as he was leaving my office.

I hung around with a few other people for a while, when I realized that I had to say something to our employees. I quickly drafted a brief statement based only on the facts I had gleaned from CNN's coverage of the tragedy. By noon all four plane crashes had been reported on and analyzed. I asked one of our administrative assistants to gather everyone in the large open space in the production area. I went into Glen's office and told him that after I spoke to our employees, I was going to send everyone home for the rest of the day.

"You think that's necessary?" Glen asked.

"Yeah, I do. You should come too; they'll feel better knowing that we're in agreement on this. We can talk about your ideas after the meeting."

We walked over to production, where most, if not all, of the other employees had gathered. They were standing around, quietly talking among themselves. They looked grim and deeply concerned when I started my brief presentation. I gave a quick summary of the events and then said, "I think it best that you all go home and spend the rest of the day with your families. Some of you may want to go to religious services or other local gatherings. I think that your skills, knowledge, and integrity are needed more by others in the community right now than by our company. Come back to work tomorrow and be prepared to help our country do whatever is necessary to prevent these kind of senseless acts of violence from ever happening again."

Nobody said anything. These were good men and women and would be a source of strength for the community at a very low time in our history. Most of them left, but a few senior employees hung around, finishing up some work and making certain that by leaving the building early their equipment would not be at risk of damage if left unattended for the rest of the day.

I walked with Glen over to his office in silence. When we got there, I said, "What's this new product, or is it a product line that you want to talk about?"

"I don't know if you realize what an opportunity just happened for us today," he said. "The government is going to be in desperate need of all kinds of newer and more sophisticated—and I might add expensive—security devices. Our optical scanning products can easily be modified for passenger security applications. We didn't do it before because it cost too much, but now—"

"Wait, you mean to tell me that you just watched what was probably the most serious attack on this country since Pearl Harbor, and all you can think about is getting more contracts? I can't believe you! For Christ's sake Glen, where the hell is your head at?"

"Oh, for shit's sake—grow up, Joey! Yes, it was tragic, and yes, I'm sincerely moved by all the death and destruction, but instead of sitting around wringing my hands, I want to do something that will prevent it from happening again—just as you asked our other employees to do. Is that so hard for you to understand?"

Glen had a point. He was not one to show emotion, and in fact the last time I saw him exhibit any deep human feeling was when he cried with me after I told him about my cancer almost five years ago.

After a brief pause I said, somewhat coolly, "Yeah, I do remember that we researched something about modifying our scanning devices for security purposes, but I'll need a day to get up to speed on the technology again. I want to call Gabriella now, and then I'll hang around here and pull that concept paper out of my files. I'll get back with you tomorrow on it, okay?"

"Good, good. I'm going to make some calls now to some of our project managers in DC, offering condolences, any help we can provide their agencies, and you know, the usual . . . whatever." Glenn was excited. "I'll also casually mention our work on optical scanning and detection equipment for passenger screening, just in case they might be interested, and tell them I'll get back to them in a few days."

Glen was the consummate entrepreneur. He may have been touched by today's events, but only, it seemed, by how much it would benefit his pocket. I felt ashamed to be his partner.

*   *   *

"Tell him to fuck off already. That place is killing you," Gabriella said when I got home that evening. "You're much too decent to be working with such a schmuck." She paused and then said, "What are you going to do? Help Greedy Fingers take advantage of the situation?"

"I checked out our old work on the possibility of developing different passenger screening methods, and I think it could work. Multifrequency lasers are being developed that we can use in our optic's systems for scanning and detecting all kinds of potentially dangerous things. Theoretically, it should work. It will take some development, but I bet in a year we could have an operational system working at the airport. Maybe Glen is an unfeeling asshole at times, but he has an eye for timely products."

"If your point is that you can help us stop those evil bastards, then I'm all for it. But don't let him exploit your clients," Gabriella said.

"I wouldn't let him do that. He'll propose a research and development contract based on my assessment for labor, parts, materials, and other costs," I told her. I went on to explain that the final product would be priced based on fair accounting practices. The government usually did a good job of due diligence on that end. I waited a bit, looking at Gabriella who was apparently interested in what I had to say about the new product. I said, "I feel good about this. I think this is something that we can do to help out now. Who knows? It just might be my payback for not dying. Maybe it's my ego making me think that I can solve a very complex technical problem, but whatever it is, I feel we should try it."

Seeing the concerned look on Gabriella's face, I knew she wanted to hear more. "And, you know what, honey?" I started to say, and then I glanced over at the window, collecting my thoughts before continuing. "We both know that Indonesian tea I drank years ago must have had something to do with my still being around. And the fact that that priest—Father Pavlos—occasionally calls us asking how I am and how our lives are going . . . he must know something that we don't know about those herbs. It scares me a little to think that maybe God chose to save me for some reason that only he and the priest might know. In any case, I'm going to try to do some good with my life now. I don't want to ever get that cancer scare again."

Gabriella let me finish my apology and then said, "Joey, you're a smart engineer with a good heart, and you've already paid back the world many times over for not dying. Do this, but do it for the right reasons. You don't owe anyone anything because you didn't die from cancer." She watched me with a knowing smile on her face, before adding, "Look, if we don't stop those extremist shitheads from destroying our buildings and killing our people, if we just run away and hide, then they've won. So do it; make machines that will prevent them from doing it again and the hell with Glen's attitude."

"Whatever you say, boss," I said with a smile.

"And as for Setiawan and his tea, we know where we can reach him if you should ever need the leaves again, right?" she said.

Even though I had a thin smile on my face, I felt like shit. It seemed everyone in the country was in some kind of a funk. We all felt like crying, and many of us did. TV offered up all the talking heads with their explanations of why it had happened and what we had to do to stop it from happening again. Most regularly scheduled shows were cancelled, as was all air travel, so it was eerily quiet and very sad outside.

*   *   *

It was a beautiful fall day in Ann Arbor, but on the TV we could see that downtown Manhattan was still smoking and on fire. A haze hung over the city, keeping everyone mindful of yesterday's demoralizing attack. I was at work early to meet with my brain trust in the small conference room to discuss the project.

I started the meeting by saying, "I checked out the concept paper we wrote about a year ago, and it's a valid engineering project that both Glen and I think we should be pursuing. What do you guys think?"

The standard skepticism surrounding any new technical venture was expressed.

"I don't see what multifrequency lasers really buy us here. So they pump at more than one frequency, but will travelers still have to remove all their clothes? What are we looking for—drugs, guns, bombs—and what's the underlying theory?" my top MIT electrical engineer asked.

"Terry, can you come up with a theoretical analysis for optical scattering variations over a mixed frequency field?" I asked our resident mathematician/physicist.

"I think I can do that, Joey," he said.

And so it went until everyone was on board for the project. These were my technical people, and they never asked about funding, but I thought I should fill them in anyway due to the unusual circumstances of the project.

"Glen left for DC this morning by train—you know all flights have been grounded. He has appointments with a number of agencies tomorrow and Friday and will try to get seed money for the project, but in the meantime, even if Glen is unsuccessful in getting any money we'll fund it internally because we know it's the least we can do under the circumstances. Are you guys with us on this?"

Everyone nodded in agreement. Some of my team expressed a feeling of determination, now knowing that we were willing to put our money and talent on the line to help our country get over this crisis. Everyone got their assignments, and they were eager to get out and start working. I had never seen them—or myself for that matter—this excited over a new project.

Late in the afternoon I went around to my team members and got briefed on what they were doing. Much of it was still just paper and pencil or white-board stuff and heavy discussions with their staff. They all had other projects to work on as well, and I didn't have to remind them of that, but most were planning on staying late and working on the new project. I was still in a funk, as I'm sure most people were, and couldn't stay away from the TV. But working changed my spirits. *We're doing something about it!* I thought, and that was a good thing.

Later that night Glen called from DC. "What a mess," he said. "Naturally, I can't get to the Pentagon, and I'm not sure if anyone is really interested in hearing me out right now, but I'll call you if I get anything positive out of Foggy-Bottom. What's new on your end?"

I filled him in on the team and how we had organized our work schedule—how everyone was really gung ho to work on the project like it was their patriotic duty, even if they had reasonable doubts about the outcome.

"You know, Glen, my gut feeling is that it should work, and I think we'll be able to have a proof-of-concept model in two or three months. After that, I'll be able to give you a better handle on when we'll have an engineering prototype ready. I think you can safely say that when talking to the FAA."

"I'm not sure the FAA will be the right people. There's all kind of talk about a complete reorganization of the government's security people, but right now it's just that—talk. I'll touch base with you again tomorrow night."

*   *   *

As things slowly got back to some semblance of normality, it became apparent that the federal government was only interested in going to war with Iraq. There were many people in and out of government who disagreed with that decision, but because of the public feeling about the attacks, those who didn't want to go to war with Iraq were not pushing their case very hard.

"I think we'll get some money for an unsolicited proposal from the FAA, but it won't be for big bucks," Glen told me over the phone on Saturday morning. "Maybe a couple hundred thousand, but that's just enough to cover salaries and the initial proof-of-concept costs. We'll have to buy or lease the laser ourselves, using internal funding. I know they cost a bundle, but that will be proof enough to them that we're serious about this effort."

"It's probably going to take some time for the normal proposal process to kick in, so that's better than nothing," I told Glen. "I'll keep the team working overtime to get it done. Thanks for pushing this through."

We finished our conversation and decided to talk again on Monday. I was planning on going in over the weekend to keep the momentum up.

I got home from work Saturday night just before sunset and was having a drink with Gabriella. I filled her in on our progress. The two of us needed to spend some time just talking about the entire situation and how it was impacting us.

"Maybe we should go to Bali again to talk about this. That seems to be our MO when things get rough," she said with a smile. "Anyway, I'm glad you're at least doing something positive about it." Gabriella paused a while and then said, "I wish you guys would get out of weapon systems, even though it's very lucrative. There are more than enough civilian-related products or other government agency work, like your security scanner. You don't need to be developing new weapon technology to make a good living."

"It's a mixed bag for me. Maybe we should be more in military weaponry now; then again, maybe newer, more sophisticated weapons aren't the answer either," I offered.

I started thinking about Gabriella and her Quaker history. She had always been antiwar, even way back during the Vietnam era. She was only seven when the Kent State shootings happened, but it greatly affected her attitude toward Republican administrations. When the war ended, or I should say, when we pulled out of Nam, she was twelve, and from that time on she was dedicated to the peace movement. When she turned nineteen—during her sophomore year at Michigan—she joined the Quaker movement in Ann Arbor at the Religious Society of Friends Church on Hill Street. She had always had great difficulty understanding why I had to be involved in weapons-related research, but she never demanded that I quit.

Gabriella noticed I was in deep thought and asked what was really bothering me.

"Since that bout I had with cancer, I feel different," I said. "Maybe it was because I was facing death, maybe it was my own Methodist upbringing, or maybe it was Setiawan's tea, but I find it hard being angry at people. I don't feel any hatred toward Muslims, or any one particular group of people. Sure, I'm mad as hell at the terrorists who did this, but I suspect that even they might have some rationale for their militant behavior—I would certainly disagree with them, but—"

"Well, I don't think there is any rationale they could offer me that would get me to either sympathize or understand their stupid-ass actions," she said. "They're just a bunch of ignorant savages intent on destroying anyone who isn't beholden to their fuckin' ridiculous beliefs."

"Why don't you tell us how you really feel, Gabby?"

"Okay, enough already. Are you saying that the tea not only cured your cancer, but it made you Mr. Nice Guy too? Well, I don't think so. You were never a bad person; you were the one always sticking up for the bad guys, like Glen—even when everyone else was telling you you're wrong. But, hey, if you think that maybe you did die and were reborn again, and now you're some kind of an angel, well God bless you!" she said with some mild sarcasm.

"No, I'm not saying the tea did more than cure my cancer—if it even did that," I said. "I just feel . . . or believe that maybe the tea was special and I should be thankful for having had it. And I should not be bad-mouthing anybody for any reason. I don't know what I'm saying. I'm just thankful to be here, that's all, just thankful." I started to tear up, and I didn't know why. Maybe I was frightened that the cancer would return, or maybe I was just confused by everything that was going on. I also suspected that I would be hearing from Father Pavlos again real soon, and I looked forward to his call.

Gabriella sensed my discomfort and dropped the subject, knowing the discussion was pretty much over. I put my arm around her while we both sat quietly on the couch. The TV was turned off and there were no sounds of planes in the skies, but the threat of war was looming very real overhead. It was tense, but in some strange sense, peaceful. I had a purpose now—my chance to help respond to the crisis in a nonmilitary fashion, and I intended to do the best I could. I was not going to judge others on what, if anything, they should or should not do. I was just going to do my job and love my wife with all my heart.

Gabriella wasn't so naïve as to think that all weapons-related research should be abandoned; she just didn't want me doing it. I felt that we should be getting out of weaponry for both moral and business reasons, but I knew that our business model would need serious readjustment if our company was to remain viable. Funny, we never said that to each other, but there was no doubt that we were both sensing each other's discomfort, and both of us wanted to simply say, "It's all right, honey, I love you very much." I think Gabriella knew what I was feeling and snuggled close as we watched that very serene late summer sunset from our picture window overlooking the Huron River and the western rolling hills of Ann Arbor.

CHAPTER 10

Wayan Setiawan

It was late at night on September 11, 2001, when we heard about the attacks in the United States. I kept trying to get the American Forces Network station on my short-wave radio. The TV coverage out of Jakarta was extremely superficial, and what little news we did get was heavily controlled by our government. Indonesia, with its enormous Muslim population, was fearful over the response the United States would take because of the attacks. The fear of internal strife was also there because the government knew that some extremist elements in Indonesia might want to create havoc now. So it was not surprising that this early in the tragedy the TV news would be sparse at best.

The Muslim population in Bali was much smaller in comparison to Java. Most of the population were people who just wanted to be identified as Muslims for job security and other social or political benefits, so the thought of unrest here was not as widespread. But because Bali was a Western tourist haven, many people feared that our own homegrown terrorists might try to make a statement by attacking some of the Western-style resorts, so tension was raised along the beach areas and other tourist haunts.

"Why don't you call Bill Kahn and ask him what's going on?" Arti said. "It's just early afternoon in Ann Arbor, and he might know more about the situation."

"Good idea," I said. "I'm sure he's on top of it and can fill me in on all the details." I picked up the phone and called Bill in the United States. It was an interesting, if not a totally enlightening, conversation.

"So, what's happening over there?" Arti asked. "Are they all right? Do they know anyone who might have been killed in the attack? How are they handling it?"

I told Arti about my conversation with Bill and assured her that they were unharmed—at least physically—by the attacks. "He sounded quite depressed and was concerned that the four incidents might just be the start of something even longer term."

"Four attacks? I thought they just hit the World Trade Center," Arti said. "Where were the other attacks?"

I filled her in on the other details and told her about the state of emergency they were under, as well as how all airplanes had been grounded and the general feeling of outrage and distress the Americans were suffering. The lost sense of security that they enjoyed for years seemed to permeate my conversation with Bill. He had cancelled all elective surgery for the week until they had a better handle on the situation. It was not like Bill to react that radically in an emergency, so I knew the situation in the States was bad. I was wondering what I could do to help alleviate the situation, but I soon realized that it was totally out of my control.

The next day I did call my relatives in Hawaii to find out how they were doing and was relieved to hear that they were okay. As non-native Americans, and coming from a Muslim country, they were concerned that they might be rounded up and put in a camp—like the American government did in World War II to the Japanese Americans—even though they themselves were not Muslims. They were concerned that there might be a crackdown on some radical elements in Indonesia by our government, out of fear of reprisals. But I told them that didn't seem likely at this point.

Later in the day while working in one of my clinics, I couldn't help but think about Bill's patient, Joe Gilbert, and the tea leaves I gave him to help his nausea. Those leaves had come into my thoughts many times over the last four-plus years, and I wondered if the current state of insecurity in the States might have affected him. Maybe he had lost faith in the leaves, and maybe his cancer symptoms had recurred. I should have asked Bill when we were talking, but he sounded so down; I didn't want to add to his already over-stressed life. Also, I didn't want to broach the question again of what I had done with the leaves. I still hadn't told him how I had disposed of them, even though he had asked me about them on several occasions. I didn't think that now would be the time to bring that up.

*   *   *

It was on Saturday morning that a colleague of mine came looking for me in my office at the university and asked me, "Seti, are you busy now?"

"No, no, I'm just thinking about the attacks in the States on Tuesday. I've been reading all the English language newspapers this week, and I'm feeling a little overwhelmed. What can I help you with, Pram?" His formal name was Dr. Madé Pramana, where the name Madé meant that he was the second born in his family. Madé, like Wayan, were two of the most common names on the island.

He came in my office and sat down in a chair by the back wall. "Funny, but I was also thinking about the attacks in the States. Have you noticed a general sense of insecurity or fragility among your patients since the attack?" he asked.

"Yes, of course I have. Many people are concerned about it. They know that the attack will have profound impact around the world, especially on Muslim countries like ours," I told him. "But I don't think we need to be concerned about the United States—it's our own kooks that have me worried. I've been treating my anxious patients with some herbal remedies that I think are safer than tranquilizers. You know how hard it is to get some of these islanders to take correct doses of any medicine. They're old school, thinking that if a little bit is good, a whole lot is better. So it's safer to give them herbs. They respect herbs and won't abuse them, but small pills . . . that's a different matter. Would you like my tech to make you up some packages?"

"I wish it were that simple, but yes, please have him make me some packages for my clinic too," my colleague said.

"Why is that troubling you? What did you mean by 'that simple'?" I asked.

"Seti, my friend, you always have a simple herbal solution for complex medical problems. Fortunately you're right most of the time, but I would think that after learning about the more modern medicine practiced around the world today, you would just once defer to your PDR like the rest of us have to," he said, smiling and chuckling about his referring to the Physicians Desk Reference.

When he left my office, I got his point. I did tend to look at our own traditional medicines for treatment before I considered Western, or modern, pharmaceuticals—not the other way around. Again I thought about Joe Gilbert and the others in America, as well as my patients here on the island. *Could they be in need of some remedies for anxiety too?* I wondered.

I was really thinking about trying to reproduce the tea that cured everyone from all those incurable diseases, even though I knew I couldn't and I also knew I shouldn't. I wouldn't ask Bill about the others in Michigan since I didn't want to open up a conversation that I wasn't prepared to handle over the phone or on e-mail.

Damn! I thought. *I wish to hell that I had never had those leaves in my possession.* They had caused me considerable consternation and bother. Remembering the look on my grandmother's face when she told me what I had to do with them and then destroying them when I knew they were still viable haunted me to this day. But since I did have them in my possession, and I did use them, I could only hope that all who received the leaves' healing powers were still well and continued to pursue useful lives. Furthermore, I felt that I should be thankful for the gift of good health they all received. That, at least, would in some way placate my bad feelings about having had control over the leaves for a short time and not doing the best I could have with them. Maybe someday I'd find out about all the lives I'd impacted with them, and hopefully I'd realize that I lived up to my oath and did no harm. That would actually be the best I could wish for.

CHAPTER 11

Connie Sarbanes

I had been watching the monitors at the airport along with thousands of other passengers that day, all of us wondering what the hell was happening. I couldn't believe the chaos and confusion, not only on the part of the staff but also the travelers.

"Is our flight cancelled?" I heard over and over again as people queued up at the service counters.

I also heard, "Well, I don't care if it's not cancelled, I'm getting the hell out of here anyway!" or similar comments from a number of other folks. I kept asking my boss what we should be doing, and he was totally baffled. Nothing like this had ever happened, and there weren't any Standard Operating Procedures to guide us, so we, for all practical purposes, just muddled our way through. When the word finally did come down that we were in stand-down conditions, we at least had some idea how to react. All flights were being grounded, and arrivals would remain on the ground until further notice. We calmed the arriving passengers as best we could, since many were just finding out about the attacks on the East Coast. Soon FBI agents, treasury agents, state police, and others were at the airport. Even a military contingency out of Selfridge Field showed up in full military battle dress—it was quite a show.

I, like many others, was in a state of shock, still not believing what I had just seen on the TV. As the reality sank in, I actually became depressed, hoping that it was all simply a nightmare that would soon be over. I felt so vulnerable and at the same time so helpless. I was relieved when our boss let us all go home—two hours after our shift was over—with orders to be at work tomorrow as usual.

*   *   *

I filled Sally in on what happened at the airport. It was Wednesday evening, and we were still in shock over the previous day's attack on the World Trade Center and the Pentagon.

"You won't believe what's happening down there," I told Sally, and then went on to describe the entire goings-on at the airport.

"We're at war, Connie. What the hell did you expect?" she asked me, noticeably irritated with the situation.

I then explained to her that even without anymore planes coming in or going out, the place was a madhouse. I also said that we, the customs agents, were all sworn Treasury officers, but we were being treated like the rent-a-cops working security lines for the private contractors.

"They're talking about removing those guys and replacing them with us. That's bullshit!" I said.

"Calm down," Sally said. "Nobody's going to put you in a less important position, especially now. I would think that they need all the experienced and highly trained help they can get. What exactly were they saying, and who was saying it?"

It appeared that some assholes out of Washington told my boss that a whole new agency was going to be created to take over all the security. The idea made me sick just thinking about it. New job descriptions, new procedures, new everything—it all made me very upset and confused.

"Did they say you'd have to do the security check-in stuff?"

"No, not exactly—but there was so much confusion and so much in the way of different, and conflicting, information coming from all these guys that my boss told us to just come in and do our jobs until the dust settled." I then said in a gloomy way, "I guess that's a pretty shitty way of saying it." I was thinking about all the dust in New York. I didn't think the dust in New York was ever going to settle.

"So do like he says; just do your job until you get more information," Sally told me. She then commented, "It seems the feds are so sure that the attack actually came from Iraq that they plan on invading those poor bastards—again! I think they're going to want to keep all Iraqis off of airplanes for a while. That shouldn't be too hard; they don't have any air force left after Bush the Daddy invaded them ten years ago. Do you get many people coming in from Iraq?" Sally wanted to know.

I pointed out that probably more people from the Middle East came into Detroit Metro than any other airport in the country. "With all the Arabs in Dearborn, there seems to be one plane after another either coming in directly from the Middle East or through Paris or through London—"

"Okay, okay, I get the picture. So Detroit's an important place right now—is that what you're saying?" Sally said.

"I should hope so. We may not know who did the attack, but we do know that it was from some radical Muslim group or country. But I doubt if it was Iraq," I answered.

I continued filling Sally in on what plans were being made to deal with the situation. I told her that we were going to have some special training tomorrow from some experts, and they were not sure when the planes would fly again, but we would have to be prepared when they did go up. I was calming down just talking with Sally. She was good for me that way. I hadn't told her yet how I felt, how I was worried that maybe this was a precursor of bad things to happen for us and that my glaucoma would return. I knew that was completely irrational, since the one thing had absolutely nothing to do with the other, but I couldn't help it—that's how I felt.

"Have you talked with Maggie yet?" I inquired about Sally's sister who lived in Queens.

"Yeah, we talked earlier. She's okay—I should say unharmed, but she sure is bad-mouthing the Muslims. She's almost irrational, but that's what fear does to you—makes you irrational." She then changed the subject. "Do you want to watch the news?"

I had seen the news all day at the airport, in between meetings, notices, and the general confusion, and wasn't interested in watching it anymore. The airport was mostly empty when I left, except for a bunch of international travelers stuck in the terminal.

I reflected in silence a bit about the stranded passengers and then said, "I feel bad for all those tourists from other countries out there waiting to get home. They couldn't get those poor folks out, so they've got them confined to one section of the Northwest Terminal. They're really scared, and many are broke. I was thinking that we should be doing something for them, but I don't know where to start."

"Maybe tomorrow you can tell someone how you feel about it, and they can get something done for them," Sally suggested.

We sat there quietly for a while. I tried to break the deafening silence by putting some music CDs on, which helped as we read for a while before going to bed.

* * *

"Hello, is this Judith Spiros?" I asked over the phone. "I got your name from the church's social director—she said you chaired the social action committee. Is that right?" I was contacting her early on Thursday morning to ask her if our church could do anything about the stranded overseas travelers. I originally talked with the Red Cross people at the airport, but they said that they were stretched very thin with all their resources heading out to DC and New York—which was, of course, totally understandable. I decided to act locally and thought the best place to get involved would be with our own church organizations.

"I think it's a great idea," Judy Spiros told me. "I'll mobilize our troops and some others on our ecumenical committee to get them involved as well. I'll contact you later on about where we should get the food and things to the travelers, as soon as I'm a little better organized. But that's what social action is all about—being organized to quickly respond. Thanks for calling me . . . is it Connie?"

She sounded really sincere, and I felt good that I was able to do something for other people caught up in this tragedy besides the poor people and their families directly traumatized by the attack. Those folks were getting all the help they could now, as well they should, but others on the fringes needed help as well. Deep down, I also felt that if I did something good for others, then my glaucoma wouldn't come back. That was silly, I know, but again that was how I felt. Sally was right—fear made you irrational.

"What was that all about, Connie?" my boss asked. I filled him in on my plan, and he was surprised and pleased that we were taking care of the problem ourselves. Like so many others, he thought that someone else would handle the issue, but as so often happens in emergencies, there were many unforeseen matters that nobody dealt with. Somebody had to do something, so it might as well be the person who *saw* what was actually happening.

While I waited to hear from Ms. Spiros, I had to attend the training session being conducted by a bomb expert out of Lansing, who apparently knew his business. He was working with us—the first-line supervisors—so that we in turn could train our staff of inspectors. Customs agents have historically been concerned with revenue and tax issues, but now we had to know how to look for weapons and bombs. It was a good session. We finished around 3:00 p.m., and it was shortly after that I got the call from Ms. Spiros.

"Hi, Connie, this is Judy Spiros. We've been able to put together a team from Saint Andrews, Beth Israel, and the Islamic Center in Ann Arbor. We will have a truckload of ready-to-eat food—you know, sandwiches and the like, toiletries, blankets, and other stuff—by 4:30 p.m. Where should we meet you?"

I told her where to come into the airport and that I'd meet her there with our volunteers. By word of mouth, I hurriedly put together a group of workers, made up of airport employees and some folks from the airlines, to gather up the stranded passengers and get them all over to the International Terminal. When the truck arrived, we had it unloaded and the supplies distributed by 6:00 p.m. What a thrill it was to see some of the older people and children get some food and supplies to last them until they would be able to fly home. I watched as Christian, Jewish, and Muslim volunteers worked together, and I thought that this was how the world should work. *Why in God's name are we trying to destroy each other?*

I had called Sally earlier and told her I'd be late because of the aid work we were doing, and she, of course, wanted to know what she could do. I had her contact Judy Spiros to see if she could help out at Saint Demetrios. When I got home around 7:30 p.m., Sally was beaming.

"There was a whole group of us working at the church, including Father Pavlos! We were making up packages, sorting supplies, and everything else. It really felt good, and you were being mentioned as the hero! I was so proud of you. Father Pavlos was saying that leadership was seeing that something needed to be done and then doing it—that was you, seeing something needed to be done." She gave me a big hug and a wet kiss that felt great.

"Yes, seeing that something needed to be done. And to think that just five years ago I thought I wouldn't be seeing anything by this time!"

*   *   *

It was Friday, September 14, and I was back on the job when my boss said, "Word is that flying will resume either today or tomorrow, but it may be weeks before we can get all these folks back home."

We saw some planes from the smaller commuter airlines being brought up to the gates, but no major activity was going on, like flight agents at their desks. My boss informed us that outgoing international flights might resume momentarily, but no incoming flights were anticipated until much later. It was the usual government practice of hurry up and wait. My gut feeling was that we wouldn't see any action until the next day or Sunday. I didn't have to work that weekend, but my boss asked me to be there anyway to help smooth over operations if needed, and I agreed to go in. Lots of people were coming up to me and thanking me for bringing aid to those unfortunate stranded passengers. I, in turn, told them to thank the churches that actually got the stuff here and distributed it.

"When you go to church this weekend, put a little extra in the basket," I told them, and then I smiled.

That evening Sally asked me, "You want to go out for a bite? I think it would help if we start doing normal things, don't you think? People are starting to come back to the doctor's office now, and it feels good not to think about that horrible incident all the time."

"Sure, let's go somewhere. How about Depot Town?" I suggested. I also thought how things would never be normal again. It would be years, if ever, before we got over this attack. *And what if there are other attacks?* I wondered.

We went to a popular indoor-outdoor hamburger place in Depot Town. It was still warm, even for early September, so we decided to eat outside on the restaurant's patio. It was crowded but not as crowded as a normal Friday night. We only waited around ten minutes for our table. The atmosphere was subdued at best. There was no loud laughing or raucous talk, which would be usual for the Friday night crowd.

"Have you talked with the girls yet?" I asked Sally.

"Funny you should ask. I called them on Wednesday to see how they're doing, and just to touch base. Especially with Madison, her being pregnant now—our first grandchild," she said, looking up and smiling at me. "Cindy's doing fine, as I would expect from her. She's always been the tough one. Madison has always been the sensitive child. And you know, both of them asked how you were doing. They were worried about you more than themselves. I think it would be nice if you called them. They'd love to hear from you. I probably should have told you sooner, but with all the commotion . . ."

"I was thinking about calling them. I haven't talked with them in more than a week—like you said, what with all the shit that's been going on." I loved those twins, even if I was only the stepdad, but the grandkids—they'd be mine as if I was their blood-related granddaddy. "But I'll call them tomorrow to tell them not to worry; we got it all under control now."

We ate our dinners in silence for the most part. I was thinking about the girls. *What will Cindy do after graduate school? What will Madison name her kid—or kids? She still doesn't know if she is having twins.*

There was a slight haze in the evening air, and Sally asked, "Do you think the haze is from the fires in New York?"

"I doubt it—our winds mostly come from the west. It's just a late summer mist coming in over the river, but it does go to show you how we can't get the attack out of our heads, doesn't it?"

It was dark when we got home. We tried watching the news and then the *Late Show with David Letterman* but couldn't concentrate on either.

* * *

"Hi, honey, it's me Connie. How ya doin'?" I asked Madison. I had just finished talking with Cindy, trying to reassure her that all was well and we'd be all right.

"Hi, Connie, I'm fine . . . or I should say we're fine," Madison told me. "The baby's growing, and we think it really might be twins—but don't tell Mom yet, okay? Mo is so excited he can't see straight. The doctor said that by next month he'll know for sure from the ultrasound, but right now it's still a little too early to be absolutely certain."

"Oh boy, I can't wait till you tell your mom. I know she'll be thrilled—but not as thrilled as I am," I said with my chest all puffed out like a granddad's should be. "I'm just checking in to find out how you guys are dealing with the attack. Are you all okay?"

"We were worried about you, being at the airport and all. How are you doing? You must be seeing a lot more than we are. Do you know what's going on? Are we really safe? I feel funny about bringing kids into this kind of world. What do you think? Would you feel okay about having kids now?"

I thought before answering her, because I didn't want to appear too glib with my answer. I wanted to give it to her straight yet make her feel as safe as possible, even if my own sense of security was greatly shaken.

"You know, honey, ever since I can remember we've been fighting some group of radical nuts—Vietnam, Cuba, Grenada and Panama, the Gulf War, then there was that deal in Serbia and Yugoslavia, and now they're taking about invading Afghanistan and Iraq. Also, don't forget World War I, World War II, and Korea; and all of those wars were just in this century alone. It seems that war is with us whether we have babies or not. I can't say for sure that we'll be okay, but if history is any indicator, I think we're gonna be all right," I said. "What you gotta remember is that this is a great and powerful country—it's gonna take a lot more than that to take us down. Also, keep in

111

mind that you got lots of family to love and care for you, so I'm telling you straight: you bring those babies into this world without any more fear and anxiety than you would have if the attack had never happened."

I had tears in my eyes after saying all that and was glad Madison couldn't see me. I was still feeling troubled and wondered when my glaucoma, or something even worse, was going to happen to me, but I didn't want the girls to know that.

"Connie, you're the sweetest man I know. I'm glad Mom found you, and I can't wait to make you a grandpa," she said with a tear in her voice.

We talked a little more before I called Sally in to take the phone. In a few seconds I heard the shrill shriek of a woman who was about to become the grandmother of twins. I sat there reading the paper with a big smile on my face that couldn't be wiped off, no matter how bad the national news was.

When Sally finished her long conversation with Madison, she came into the den where I was still reading, or pretending to read.

"What's up?" I asked her.

"Twins!" she yelled.

I acted surprised and jumped up and hugged her and kissed her and then started to babble like a silly fool.

"Why are you acting surprised? She told me that she already told you, you big klutz!" she said as she gently pushed me back down on the couch. "Isn't it great? At least we think it's twins. Twins just like her and Cindy. I hope it's boys this time, don't you?"

"As long as they're healthy, good lookin', and rich, I could care less," I answered like a wise-ass.

"You shithead," she said as she punched my arm. "I'm so excited for her and Mo. He's a nice boy, isn't he?" she said, not really looking for an answer.

We sat on the couch for a long time, occasionally making some nice comment on how good the world was to us, in spite of the current situation on the East Coast. We both truly believed that this too would eventually pass and the world will once again make sense. And we would do all we could to see that our grandkids lived in a better world than the one we inherited.

However, there was little doubt that we were still feeling uncomfortable about the world situation. For the first time in my life I was experiencing doubt as to whether or not this attack could be avenged or prevented from happening again. And I knew Sally was feeling that way too. It would have seemed to a casual observer that we were in good spirits, but we appeared that way only for each other. I think we hoped that by doing so we would feel better ourselves.

When we went into the bedroom that night, I looked at the tau cross hanging over our bed and said, "Just like my mother always said it would bring us good luck, and it did."

"Then tomorrow you can polish it. But tonight let's just dust it off a little," she said with a sexy grin on her face, and then she jumped on top of me in the bed.

CHAPTER 12

Nando Garcia

I was teaching at West Middle School now and thrilled to be here because Maria Elena was also here. However, today all the teachers were made aware of what had happened (many of us saw the events on the TV in the teacher's lounge), and we were advised to stay home with our families tomorrow. Also, since no one knew the full extent of the incident at this time, the school administration felt it would be safer for the kids to be at home rather than at school where they might be more vulnerable to a violent attack. I picked up Maria Elena from her class around noon, while some other teachers and administrators hung around waiting for all the students to be safely on their way home.

Maria Elena was a good student and one of the most active kids in her class. She participated in everything she could, and we let her as long as she kept her grades up. I guess we indulged her because of the years she had spent in treatment for her MD and the special ed classes she had had to take. She definitely wanted to make up for lost time, so sports were her passion; softball, volleyball, and soccer were her sports, and she was good at them. In middle school she wanted to try out for all three, but they told her to pick soccer for now and wait for the other sports when they were in season. She was good enough to make the starting team, which was made up of mostly older students.

In the car on the way home Maria Elena was very upset about her classes being cut short and school not opening the next day.

"Papi, what's going on? Everybody is so upset about some buildings on fire in New York. They said there's no school tomorrow; could someone set our school on fire?" Maria Elena was asking me as I was driving her home. *How do I explain the attacks to a twelve-year-old?* I wondered.

"Honey, some very bad people did a terrible thing in New York City and Washington, DC. They destroyed some very large buildings and hurt many people. A lot of those people who were hurt died. The school is taking tomorrow off so we can decide how to stop it from happening in other places."

"Why? Do they want to hurt us too?"

"No, I don't think they want to hurt us actually. They have some different beliefs about what they think their religious leaders want them to do, so they did a very bad thing, attacking some buildings in order to hurt the people in them," I explained to her. "They think that the people they hurt were trying to destroy their culture. Do you understand what I'm saying?"

I knew she was probably right in thinking that they wanted to hurt us too. And that was bothering me, just as I sensed it was bothering her. I felt that I had to assure her the world would survive and all would be well again.

"Not really—I couldn't hurt someone because they're not from Ypsilanti. Is it because we're Catholic or American? Is that what you mean by culture?"

"I guess, I mean yes, to all those things. Our culture is based, in part, on our Mexican roots, the fact that we are practicing Catholics—Christians—living in a small midwestern American city, and you know . . . things like that."

"Where are these people from? What is their culture, and why do they think we want to destroy their culture?" she asked, repeating my characterization of the terrorist's motives.

"We're not exactly sure yet who they are, but all indications are that they are from some place in the Middle East, like Afghanistan or Iraq—Islamic countries. You know the part of the world I'm talking about, don't you?" I asked.

"Yes, we talked about Muslim countries in our class because their big holiday, Ramadan, will be in November. We plan on having a school party when they have their big dinner—some feast I can't pronounce—when Ramadan ends in December. We'll celebrate it in school along with Christmas, Hanukah, and Kwanzaa. But why do they want to hurt people in New York? There are kids in my class who are Muslim, and they don't want to hurt anyone—or do they, Papi?"

I could see how concerned she was, maybe even thinking that they could cause her to have MD again—or was that my own fear I sensed?

"No, no, honey, they don't want to hurt you," I said, shaking my head. "The people who destroyed the buildings are not the same people as the kids in your class."

"Do you think they'll cancel soccer practice?" she asked.

"Yes, honey, I think all school activities will be cancelled for at least a couple of days. But don't worry; they'll make up for it as soon as everything gets back to normal."

When we got home, Maribel was anxiously waiting for us. She had been watching TV all day and had called me at school just to make sure we were all right and that I would be sure to drive Maria Elena home.

"Can you believe what's going on?" she asked. "Do all the kids know what happened? How are they taking it?"

"Papi explained it to me on the way home," Maria Elena told her. "He said some stupid people from the Middle East burned down buildings and killed a whole bunch of people. Do you know any more about it, Mami?" she asked.

Maribel looked at me as if to say, "What do I tell her?"

"Honey, that's enough for now I think. When we—Mami and me—find out more, we'll tell you. Why don't you have a snack and then go and study till dinnertime?" I said.

With that Maria Elena went to the kitchen for some cookies and milk and took them into her room. She shut her door, and I assumed she started to do her reading. I didn't think she had any homework assignments to do, but she loved to read and hopefully that would keep her busy until we figured out what was going on and how much we needed to tell her.

* * *

The next day, Wednesday, we stayed home and listened to CNN all day. Maria Elena had been very quiet, coming out of her room only for meals and asking very little about what was going on. That wasn't like her, so I told Maribel, "The next time she comes out of her room, let's sit her down and talk to her about the whole thing. Tell her not to worry, even though it's a great tragedy; our country will get through it and stuff like that. What do you think?"

"I think she's a lot more knowledgeable about it than you give her credit for. She's been on the phone for hours, and I think that's what she's been talking about with her friends."

"I hope they're not scaring her . . . you know, with all kinds of misinformation. I'll talk to her when she comes out."

I had no sooner finished saying that when Maria Elena walked into the front room and looked at the TV, and then said to us, "Mami, Papi, I have to ask you something about the plane crashes in New York."

I said, "Sure, honey, what is it you want to know? We were just thinking that maybe we should sit down, as a family, and talk about it. What is it you want to know, sweetheart?"

"I've been on the phone with my teammates, and we decided that we want to do something about the attack to help the people who were hurt. We plan on having a Walk for New York demonstration this Saturday. We're going to ask people to pledge one dollar for every mile we walk. If we all walk ten miles and get a hundred people to pledge, that would be a thousand dollars! That should help, shouldn't it? Will you give me ten dollars if I walk the whole route?"

"Whoa, that's a pretty big undertaking. Who will do all the organizing: set up a route, call the police to get permission, take care of the money, all those things? Who will do that?" I asked.

"I will, Papi," she said. "I've already talked with the police and told them about the time and route for the walk. I've got most of the girls—there are eighteen of us on the team—willing to walk ten miles. We figured that if each of us gets our parents and five other people to pledge, we'll have made over a thousand dollars."

Maria Elena further explained that as good athletes they would be able to walk the route in around three hours, so if they started at nine in the morning, they would be done by noon. They would then spend the afternoon collecting from their pledges and finish collecting on Sunday if they had to. She wanted to know it they could wear their soccer uniforms so people would know they're a team.

"I'll check it out, but I don't see any reason why you can't at least wear your shirts. You have to make sure that people don't think the walk is sponsored by the school, but that shouldn't be a problem," I said as I got caught up in her plan and started to realize how well thought out everything was. "Where will you send this money?" I asked.

"That's what I wanted to ask you, Papi. Where do you think we should send it?"

"Send it to the Red Cross," Maribel said. "That's what everyone seems to be saying. You can designate it for New York, and it will all go there to help their efforts in the relief. I think you're doing a marvelous thing, honey. God will surely bless you and your friends for all your hard work."

"Maria Elena," I said, talking to her like an adult now, "I want at least one other parent to call me on this so we can help out where we may be needed. Will you do that for me?"

"I already have, Papi. My girlfriend's father, Mr. Washington, he'll call you later today to talk about it. He's a teacher too. I knew you would want some help on this, so I took care of it. Like you always used to tell me, 'It's no shame to ask for help when you can't always walk alone.' Remember that, Papi?" she said.

I had the feeling that she wanted to walk for something good so that something bad would not take away her ability to walk again—but maybe that was just my feeling with it.

Maria Elena quickly ran out of the front room to continue with her organizing tasks and left Maribel and me looking a little dumbfounded.

"Can you believe what we just heard?" I asked Maribel.

"You know, to think that less than five years ago she couldn't walk at all, and now to be able to organize a walk-a-thon all on her own—I can't believe that we are so fortunate," Maribel said. "Don't misunderstand me, I'm truly upset by what's happened, but that doesn't make me any less proud of our daughter. That's what I think."

We spent the rest of the day reflecting on the attacks and occasionally answering questions for Maria Elena. She was on the phone most of the time, making final arrangements. I had to talk with the police about monitoring the walk, and I had to talk with a school administrator about their soccer shirts, but nobody wanted to discourage them, so all the details were easily worked out. A number of the parents called and offered to help as well on Saturday, so the whole thing—that is Maria Elena's soccer team walk—would come off without any glitches.

*　　*　　*

"Well, that's it! I just got my last ten dollars from the Schneider's next door. Have you heard from the others yet?" Maria Elena asked me.

It was about 4:00 p.m. on Saturday afternoon. She had just walked into the house with all her tally sheets and an envelope full of bills. Her accounting sheet showed that they had more than $1,200 in pledges. I had already received envelopes with money from most of the other girls, but I hadn't added it up or even looked at it. We planned on taking the money to the local Red Cross office in Ann Arbor on Monday.

On Sunday, when all the money had been collected, we counted up the totals from each girl's envelope and were surprised to see that the first envelope we looked at contained $260 in it. In fact most of the envelopes contained far more than the ten dollars per pledge as expected. The grand total for all the girls was $5,380. It was not a fortune but significantly more than we had anticipated. It seemed that most people donated more than ten dollars, and in some instances donations were in the hundreds of dollars. What an outpouring of giving!

"Did you know that people would be giving so much more than ten dollars?" I asked Maria Elena.

"Not until I went around collecting the money. Most of my pledges gave me at least twenty dollars because they said that was for their family—ten dollars for each person. The other girls told me the same story, and some told me that some of their neighbors who pledged gave tons more than ten dollars. That was okay, wasn't it, Papi?" she asked enthusiastically.

I selfishly thought that the more money they collected, the better her chances of not becoming impaired again. And maybe she was right—maybe she was cured so that she could do some good for the world, and this walk of hers was one way to accomplish that.

"Of course, honey. All the money donated will go to the families, and it's nice to know that people trusted you and your teammates to get the money to New York. What a great job that was. We're so proud of you and your friends, and I'm sure their parents are proud too."

Maribel looked at me with a warm smile of approval.

Maria Elena noticed and said, "I'm glad you like what I did, Mami. I'm just so glad that I can do that—I mean that I can walk—to get help for those people. Maybe if the people who did it—I guess they're calling them terrorists—see what some school girls in this country can do, they'll not hate us and won't try to do it again. Do you think that might happen, Mami?"

"I don't know, Maria Elena, maybe—but I don't think so. But I do think that when they hear that a girl who once had MD organized the walk and participated in it, they'll realize how tough you are. And that may get them to think twice before they try to do it again," Maribel answered.

"Well, if it does happen again, I'll organize hundred-yard dashes to raise money, right, Papi?" Maria Elena said, looking right at me and smiling.

Dash—Mr. T, I thought.

And with that, Maribel picked up Maria Elena, hugging and kissing her with warm tears streaming down her face. As I watched them hug, I thought about our families still in Mexico. When Maria Elena came down with MD, they were devastated, and when they heard she was cured, they were beyond happy. Although I was still worried about the world situation in general and how the attacks would ultimately affect all our lives, I knew how proud both our families would be to see Maria Elena today. I knew she would never disappoint them.

I silently prayed that Maria Elena would always remain healthy, and that she would continue to live a normal and constructive life.

CHAPTER 13

Father Pavlos

It had been a month since the attacks, and I needed to know how my recipients of the leaves—one of the collective terms I used for them—were doing. I had a feeling that the events of last month's attacks might have been a bit hard on them and that their faith in the leaves might have been shaken. It had been some time since I talked with them, so I decided to call them and see how they were coping. I also wanted to see if I could find out more about the leaves' influence on their lives, especially now after the attacks. I pulled out my T file with my notes about the events of almost five years ago to refresh my memory. I called Connie first.

It was a Monday evening. I recalled seeing Sally Sarbanes helping out with the preparation of food and supplies for the stranded travelers. I thought it might be nice to give them a call now that things were slowly getting back to some level of normalcy, and since we worked together on the project, I had another excuse for contacting them.

"Hello, is this Connie Sarbanes? This is Father Pavlos from Saint Demetrios."

"Yes, this is Connie, Father. Nice of you to call. That was quite a job you and the social action committee did getting all that food and stuff out here for those poor stranded passengers."

I went on to thank Connie for all his efforts and ended by saying, "You know, Connie, it's times like these that test our humanity, and you and your staff passed brilliantly."

"Well, thank you, Father, but as you said, it was important for me too."

Obviously feeling a little uncomfortable with all this praise, Connie changed the subject.

"And how have you been, Father? I see in the church bulletin that you seem to be taking on more duties. Is Father Timotheos retiring?"

I continued with the small talk about Father Timotheos's retirement before getting—or I should say trying to get—on track about any concerns over the leaves' efficacy that he might now harbor. I awkwardly said, "Time goes by quickly, and it seems that there is so much more to do." *That was some kind of a non sequitur,* I thought as I tried to compose the important question in my mind. "Are you coming to church more regularly now that you're married?" I asked, not sure why I would put the poor man on the spot like that. *I'm really messing this up,* I thought.

"We try to get there as often as we can, but I'm sure it's not often enough."

"Connie, another reason why I'm calling is to ask you about the incense, or herbal tea, you had in your possession five years ago. Has your medical condition changed any?"

Connie must have been surprised by the question and answered somewhat tentatively. "No, Father, it hasn't—why are you asking? Has something been brought to your attention about the leaves that made you ask that question?" I could sense immediately that I had upset him, maybe even leading him to believe that the leaves' effects were transitory, when I was hoping to find out just the opposite.

"No, no, I was just curious. The fact that you feel your eyesight was saved by the herbs . . . I was wondering if you thought that what you did for those stranded travelers might have been . . . like something you had to do?" I wasn't putting this right, and as a priest I should have been doing better, so I tried to reword it. "What I'm asking is do you think that it might have been divine providence that saved your sight, just so you could be able to help others?"

Connie waited a moment before answering. I'm certain that he thought it was some kind of a trick question.

"I don't think I can answer that one, Father. In all honesty, you know I'm not the most religious man, but I am a believer, so it would be very hard for me to know. I guess I believe that God is responsible for everything, so in some sense it probably was divine providence that I should still be able to see. Does that make sense, Father?"

"Yes, yes, of course it does, and it was an unfair question at best. It is after all the Holy Spirit that moves us all to do good deeds whether we can see or not," I answered.

Connie was thoughtful. "If you ask me whether I feel blessed by not having glaucoma anymore, and that being cured in some way makes me want to pay back the favor, or I should say blessing, then the answer is definitely yes. But I must admit that the events of last month have troubled me, and now I feel a little insecure about my . . . cure."

"Are you saying that you feel the leaves' effects might only be good for a finite time?" I asked.

"No . . . not that as much as I feel I have to keep deserving the gift of sight. That if I forget what a gift God has given me, I may lose it. Does that make any sense, Father?" Connie asked me.

"I don't know, my son. But I do know that faith has helped cure many people over the centuries, so all I can say is that you should keep your faith in our Lord, and I hope that He continues to bless you and Sally so that the two of you will continue to live a full and healthy life of Christian charity."

"Well, thank you, Father. We are truly blessed—Sally's daughter will be having twins in the near future, and we are both very excited at the prospect of being grandparents," Connie told me.

"Congratulations to both of you and, of course, the future parents of the twins. How grand that is!"

And with that last exchange we politely ended the conversation.

I felt upset with myself for the way I had handled it. I was looking for something that I should have known I couldn't possibly get from Connie Sarbanes. I wanted confirmation that I had possessed some leaves with the power of healing that our Lord gives to only a few of his flock in any given century. All I did was make Connie uncertain about his gift and now probably less likely to want to come to church—and I was no closer to finding the answer than before.

I would have to flesh out and then prepare a better reason to call the other people than the one I offered Connie. My biggest problem coming out of college was in public speaking, which was not good if one wanted to be a priest. But I had learned that by proper preparation I could deliver a good sermon without stumbling over my words and talking in long, convoluted sentences. I was determined to be better prepared for my next calls. I didn't ever need to make anyone else feel that uncomfortable again.

*   *   *

Scripture tells me that He made the blind to see and the lame to walk. He healed the sick and cast out demons of anger and hate, among many other miracles, and always for a purpose and compassion, or so I am to

123

believe. So why did He use herbs this time? And why did He choose these people? I had to admit I was puzzled by the whole experience and felt compelled to find an answer, if there was one. I had studied my T file, but the answer still eluded me. I was still not even sure what questions I needed to ask or, aside from Holy Scripture, how to research it if I did know the questions. I also decided that this study of mine should not involve other clergy, at least not at this point.

So who do I call next? I wondered. It was Tuesday evening and I decided to call Mitch. I knew him best, and I thought I could ask him almost up-front if he felt that his anger was still under control, without making him uncomfortable. I had sketched out what I had wanted to say before calling.

"Hello, Mitch, Father Pavlos here. How are you?"

"Father Pavlos, always good to hear your voice. I'm fine and how are you?"

"Good, thanks. I read in the paper that you are being cited for helping to catch those potential terrorists. That must have been very rewarding—and probably dangerous as well."

"I don't know about dangerous, but it was an interesting case, and fortunately it resulted in good arrests. So to what do I owe the privilege of your voice, Father?"

I had thought this one out a little more carefully when I said, "Mitch, after the events of last month I thought it might be a good idea for me to follow through on those herbs we came in contact with five years ago. I'm trying to determine if the effects were long lasting. I'm also interested in seeing if their powers are still active, even though the leaves are no longer available. What's your take on them?" I paused, realizing that I had put a lot of information into one question, so I asked, "Do you even remember what I'm referring to, Mitch?"

There was a short pause, and then Mitch told me about his conversation with Gerry and how the terrorist group, LeT, had reminded both of them of the leaves and the impact they had had on Gerry's health in the hospital.

"It's amazing, Father, but both of us were aware of the leaves' significance almost as soon as we heard the terrorist organization's acronym. Gerry never actually told me before about how he felt when he put the leaves on his chest. So you can image how moved I was when he told me."

"Do you feel the leaves' healing power still exists, or is it wearing off?" I asked.

"That I can't tell you. All I can say is that I've been a changed man since taking your anger management class and coming in contact with that stuff.

But you know the events of last month have still got me wondering why that happened to us, and they have scared me into thinking that nothing may be forever. You ask if I'm still healing—I don't know, you tell me."

"I think you are, my son, I think you are. Thanks for your time, Mitch. I appreciate the feedback. Oh, and by the way, would you mind coming here sometime this month and telling the story of your arresting those people to our ecumenical committee?" I threw that in at the last minute. I liked when Mitch came to visit—his presence always cheered me up.

When we ended the conversation, I felt much better about asking the tough questions. I made notes in my folder about what Mitch told me, but I didn't try to analyze them. Analysis would come when I had talked to all four of my subjects. I was worried that if I started the analysis now, it would color my other two interviews, and I wanted to avoid bias at all cost.

*   *   *

It was now early Wednesday evening, and I wanted to call Fernando before our church council meeting at nine. "Hello, is this Fernando Garcia?" I asked.

"Yes, it is, and who's calling, please?" Fernando answered in a pleasant manner. "Fernando, this is Father Pavlos. Do you remember me?"

"Of course I do, Father, and how may I help you?"

I then posed the question to him that I had posed to Mitch about the herbs' long-lasting effects. He immediately filled me in about Maria Elena's walk-a-thon for the victims of 9/11, her activities in school, and all the other wonderful things that she had accomplished since her cure.

"Father, there is absolutely no doubt in our minds that God has intervened on her behalf and continues to make his presence known by her actions. I just wish we could do for everyone who's suffering what that incense did for Maria Elena." He hesitated a little before saying, "But I should also tell you that she seems a bit more fragile now. The attacks have greatly influenced her attitude about trusting people in other parts of the world. I hope she'll get over it as time passes, but . . ."

"Yes, yes, I know what you mean. There seems to be a general sense of loss for the stability we've known for so many years now, and it is not surprising it affects the young even more than older individuals," I told him. "I'm sure her anxiety will pass, and this issue over 9/11 will be dealt with for the betterment of all. I know you're active in her education and religious training, and I have faith you'll work it out with her."

We talked a while longer, and I was surprised, and pleased, to find out that Fernando taught at West Middle School, Maria Elena's school, and was no longer a janitor. And then I wondered about that, because being a janitor—an occupation more associated with the common people—was something that struck me as more in keeping with Jesus's actions for healing. *Stop it!* I thought. *No analysis until I'm through with all the interviews.*

I couldn't keep my mind on the council meeting that night. My thoughts kept drifting to the herbs, 9/11, and the fervent hope that I had been witnessing a miracle—or a series of them.

I was still daydreaming when the council president asked, "Do you agree with that statement, Father Pavlos?"

"Oh, yes, yes I do, uh . . . however would the secretary be so kind as to read it one more time for me just so I'm certain that I can fully endorse that proposal?" I said.

After the meeting our president stayed around and asked me if the events of last month were still bothering me and if that's why I seemed so preoccupied. I had given a very moving sermon (or so I'd been told) on the Sunday after the attack, and he asked me to write it up for wider publication.

"Yes, that and some other things have been on my mind lately, but I assure you the church's business is important to me, and I promise not to be so wistful at our next meeting." We shook hands, and I promised to write up the sermon as he requested while we both were leaving the council room.

*   *   *

"Mr. Gilbert?" I was on the phone again on Thursday, "This is Father Pavlos from Saint Demetrios, and no, I'm not asking for a contribution," I said jokingly. I wondered if he remembered our telephone conversation of five years ago, or if he would think I was some kind of a screwball.

"Father Pavlos," he said laughing into the phone, "and even if you were—asking for a contribution that is—I would take your call. How are you?"

I filled Joseph in on why I was calling, and he, too, had a great story that he wanted to tell me. Though he just outlined his idea about the security device he was working on—I'm not sure I would have understood it anyway—he said he felt his second life, as he called it, was a blessing and shouldn't be wasted on unimportant things. He also mentioned his discomfort working on weapon's research now and hoped to do something about that soon.

"So there's no doubt in your mind that Dr. Setiawan's tea is still active?" I asked.

"If you mean by active that I'm still cancer free, then yes, it's still working."

I decided not to push him any further about the tea's effect on his whole person. I thought he had given me enough of an answer without my having to get too personal. He hadn't heard from Dr. Kahn or Dr. Setiawan after the tea was returned. However, he felt certain that the leaves would be put to good use if it was in any way still possible. I wondered about that—wondered if the leaves needed something, or someone, more to make them work, someone like a priest or another true believer.

*   *   *

I now had all my data and I pored over my notes on the interviews, trying to draw some conclusions. My first conclusion was that all the recipients of the healing herbs remained cured. My second conclusion was that they all had become, or were still, caring and righteous people. But my third conclusion was that it was not clear that all the recipients were necessarily from the common people—people who might deserve more compassion from our Lord than others suffering from the same afflictions.

I also noted, more as an aside than as a conclusion, that all, like most Americans, felt a great loss of security after the attacks. But I think for those who received the healing leaves, it also made them wonder if the leaves' effect could possibly wear off and their conditions would return again. I detected that sense most of all in Connie Sarbanes when he asked with deep anxiety in his voice about my question concerning the leaves' effectiveness. He was truly concerned that the leaves' power might be fading and that he might go blind after all. However, with Connie that could have been because of the way I phrased my question. In any case, what I still didn't know was why these people had been chosen, and just as importantly, why I was given possession—one might even say stewardship—of the leaves. I would ponder that question and many more about the leaves for the rest of my life.

Episode 3

June 2005

CHAPTER 14

Father Pavlos

It had been some time since I followed up on the chosen few—that is, the people who were healed by those mystical herbs. Things had quieted down since the 9/11 attacks of four years ago, but the war in Iraq was still dragging on in spite of our president's proclamation. I knew that they had all felt very strongly about the attacks of 9/11 and immediately became involved, trying to make things a little easier for those hurt by the events. I thought their reasons were altruistic, but I also sensed that they felt that they had to pay back somebody, or someone, for having been blessed by receiving a better quality of life, or as in Joe Gilbert's case, life itself.

I wondered how they felt about their gift now, eight years since they were first exposed to the leaves. It would seem that the entire country's mood had changed since the war, and I sensed that most people were conflicted by their own change of heart over the war's outcome. At first many of us supported the incursion into Iraq, but now most of us doubted that it was the right thing to do—especially since no weapons of mass destruction were ever found, and they were probably never there to begin with.

I wondered how that sense of lost purpose might have impacted on the leaves' recipients—did they too feel conflicted over our government's policies? And if so, did it make them unsure of their cure's sustainability? My guess was that as the national bad mood continued, they too were affected. I also guessed that they might feel that anything they'd done for the war effort in the past had little or no impact on making the world a better place to live in. I recalled them telling me that they all felt the need for their lives to have a special meaning, since there must have been some reason as to why they were chosen to receive their special gifts.

I knew that I had had conflicts over my faith, as we all have, but I resolved my conflicts through prayer and, in some cases, even divine guidance. I wondered how they handled their personal conflicts and what, if anything, guided them. I knew that I would soon have to find out the answers to all those questions by contacting them once again.

I continued to pray that all of them were still well and trying to do good, and that none had suffered a cataclysmic fate—like having their infliction returned. Not only would that be devastating for them, it would also raise serious doubts in my mind about the leaves' purpose in the first place. And of no less importance, but still a question for me to get answered, was what my role in this grand saga meant.

I had to admit that I too had reason to be concerned over the leaves' status—my ambition. I would be forty-six in a couple of months and had recently read about the bishops who were appointed in other areas of the country. I noted that most of them were in their mid to late forties or early fifties at best—in other words, around my age. I began to realize that my promotion to bishop was getting less likely as time passed. I had not published many things—only a couple of sermons—and my personality was not considered charismatic enough to garner any large regional attention. There was little chance that as a priest in Ypsilanti, Michigan, I would be able to get any national notoriety unless I was associated with something extraordinary, like herbal leaves that cured the sick. It was also that realization that prompted me to get actively involved with the leaf recipients again in the hope that I would be noticed as someone who possessed, or was blessed with, the Lord's gift of healing. *Stop being so damn ambitious*, I thought to myself.

CHAPTER 15

Connie Sarbanes

It was the first of June and the TSA had been around for almost four years now, but it was far from perfect, at least in my eyes. I just couldn't understand the reasoning behind some of their new operating procedures and it bothered me that I was in the position of having to support them. My gift of sight, that I believe I got back by smoking those mysterious leaves eight years ago, depended on my doing what I saw was right, not what my bosses told me was right. Well, at least that was what I believed. I was worried that if I continued just blindly doing what I was told, then I might lose my sight for good the next time.

I had been reading the newspaper and came across the article about a six-year-old kid who was randomly selected for a complete screening before he was able to board his plane. There was a picture of him with his little arms outstretched and the TSA screener running the wand over his tiny body.

"It's just so much bull. You wouldn't believe what kind of shit the new screeners have to take now," I said to Sally. "I know the TSA is still learning the ropes, but the current situation has everyone crawling the walls. I mean, how much more embarrassment can you cause a kid like that—having to open his belt and stand there while everyone watches, thinking he's a terrorist."

"Honey, wasn't it you who said that the airport is too easy going and that anyone could get on a plane with just about anything they wanted?" Sally asked me.

"That was a long time ago. Look, the terrorists know that it's going to be very hard to get on a plane with a weapon or an explosive today, so they aren't going to try that trick again. And in any case, all the goddamn terrorists have been Middle Eastern Muslims—none have been six-year-old white kids or grandmothers in wheelchairs, so why are they screening them?" I asked, more or less rhetorically.

"Yeah, but that plane they blew up over Lockerbie around twenty years ago was caused by a bomb that a nice-lookin' Irish girl brought on board. I can remember that so well. The twins were only ten and about to go on their first flight out East. I was terrified and didn't want them to go."

"That wasn't al-Qaeda, that was one of Quaddafi's nutty followers from Libya, and that was a one-time shot. They caught the guy, and he's rotting in jail in London or somewhere. How can you compare that incident with the 9/11 murderers?" I asked.

"Because it doesn't matter where or who they are, anyone with a grudge against us could use some six-year-old or some one's grandmother to bring some kind of bomb on board. And I would guess that those poor souls wouldn't even know they had a bomb, just like that Irish kid, who probably thought it was only a radio. If I'm traveling, I want safety, which, by the way, reminds me—what time are we leaving Friday?" Sally said, changing the subject.

"Huh? Oh, yeah . . . we're leaving on the evening flight—six-oh-five. Should be a fun weekend—I like your sister. And I guarantee you'll be safe traveling with me. But that still doesn't mean I can stop them from patting you down and searching you if you're randomly selected. I know who I would search—I see them every day coming and going from the airport, on their way to Dearborn or some other Arab ghetto in the Detroit area. Probably planning the next 9/11—"

"Hold it there, my friend—that's not like you; that's not my Connie. We have a number of friends whose families come from the Middle East, and you never said anything like that before. What's eating you now, all of a sudden?" Sally asked.

"I'm just mumbling out loud. But I see these people, and they're not like our friends. If I was a screener, it would be them that I would look at carefully. I can see it in their eyes—shifty and—"

"If I didn't know any better, I'd think I'm talking with a red-neck from Ypsi-tucky."

Sally was right; I wasn't acting like I normally did. I had never said hateful things like that before, and I felt ashamed. I was so fed up with all the new directives we were getting, the constantly changing responses we were supposed to undertake based on the security advisory color codes. Nobody actually knew what they meant or how we should respond when

T

they changed. But they did say very specifically that no profiling would be done. *Well, if we didn't profile, how the hell are we gonna catch anyone? I* thought. *Certainly not by frisking old folks and kids. My God, even a blind man could see that,* I murmured, still worried about losing my own sight.

"What did you say?" Sally asked.

I didn't answer.

*   *   *

The flight on Friday into LaGuardia was uneventful. We took a cab to Forest Hills in Queens, where Sally's sister, Maggie, lived. Maggie was a young widow—if you could still call fifty-three young. She had one married son working in Manhattan in what they called the rag trade—clothing. The sisters were very close, and we tried to see Maggie at least a couple of times a year.

"So how was the flight?" Maggie asked. Even though she was raised Greek Orthodox and was now a practicing Catholic, I always associated her New York accent with someone who was Jewish. I guess my midwestern bias showed through in that way.

We were in her apartment and quickly unpacked our things for our two-night visit. "How you been, Maggie?" I asked.

"Fine, Connie, I'm just fine, especially now that you and Sal are here. So what do you want to do this weekend—museums, eat out, what's your pleasure?"

"We came to visit with you; entertainment can wait. But I would love something to eat now," Sally said. "We ate little on the plane, and we left Detroit right from work. Do you have anything in the house?"

"Boy, have I got a treat for you—pastrami from that delicatessen on Queens that you liked last time you were here. How would you like a sandwich on some good kosher rye bread?"

"Did you get pickles? I love New York kosher dills," Sally said.

And so the small talk continued through our late dinner, catching up on family business, Maggie's son, the twins, and other relatives still in the Ypsilanti area. I was just window dressing, but I didn't mind. I didn't have a big family, so in some sense this was my family now, and it was interesting just listening and seeing the sisters have so much fun talking and reminiscing.

After a couple of hours and just before it was time to get some sleep, Maggie asked me, "So, Connie, what's happening at the airports? With all

135

the *michigas* I'm reading in the papers, what with level orange and level yellow—what's that crap all about anyways?"

I explained to her briefly what the color codes were, but I didn't get into the constantly changing orders as to what we and the public were supposed to do under the various colored threat levels.

"If you ask me, and I know nobody did, I would just stop all Arabs from getting on airplanes—it's that simple," Maggie offered.

"Not you too," Sally said. "Why would you discriminate against a whole race of people because a few of them are crazy nuts?"

"Look, my Israeli friends have it right when they tell me that even though not all Muslims are terrorists, all our terrorists have been Muslims. Do the math. You call it discrimination, I call it protecting our own asses; and there's nothing wrong with that, is there, Connie?" Maggie said, looking at me to back her up.

"I agree with you a little, but you know and I know that in this country we can't do that, and I'm grateful for that. It's easy to see that pulling aside all Middle Eastern passengers and doubly screening them might be one approach to security, but it would completely destroy our society—first the Muslims, then the Maronite Catholics, then who? Where would it stop?" I said. "I'm afraid that passenger screening has to be blind to color, religion, ethnicity, the works. We'll do fine doing just what we're doing—trust me." I caught Sally smiling at me out of the corner of my eye. I also thought about what I had just said about screening having to be blind. *Was that the leaves talking for me?* I wondered.

"Coming from someone who almost went blind, that's powerful stuff you're saying," Maggie said in true New York fashion. "Okay, I'll trust you, but only because you married my sister."

*   *   *

"How about we take in the matinee at the Midway and see the new *Star Wars* picture?" Maggie said Saturday morning while having breakfast. "What's it called?"

"*Revenge of the Sith,*" I said, "and how did you know we wanted to see that movie?"

"Because I heard that you're a fan of that stupid character, what's-his-name, and he's in it," she answered.

"If you mean, Jar Jar Binks, I'm no fan of his. Are you sure he's in this one?"

We went to the 2:00 p.m. show in 3D, and after almost three hours in the movie house, we walked out into gray skies and drizzle. "Let's walk down to the deli. It's only a couple of blocks, and we can have an early dinner there," Maggie said.

It was early for dinner and late for lunch in New York, but there were people there at five in the afternoon anyway. We decided that since it was raining we would take our time and enjoy our meal while debriefing the film.

Sally and I talked about the various elements of the film, raising all kinds of questions about its meaning and purpose, when Maggie chimed in.

"Both of you are making Lucas far smarter than I think he is. He's a movie man not a Nobel Peace Laureate. It was just a movie, that's all, just a movie to make lots of money for the people who made it. I think anybody with any kind of an axe to grind can make it out to be something that supports their way of thinking. With so much shit going on in the movie all the time, what with whites and blacks and every imaginable color of aliens, who come in all sizes and shapes, with wars and prejudices and mistrust, and a whole *megillah* of issues, it's easy to pick a cause and say, 'See, that's what I believe'!" Maggie said.

"Are you sure you're not Jewish?" I asked Maggie jokingly.

"Look, in New York you're either Jewish or you wanna be Jewish, but just to put you at ease, tomorrow morning we're going to a Greek Orthodox service at a great old Greek church here on the island. I think you'll like that."

*   *   *

Sunday morning it was still dreary when we walked into the glorious Saint Constantine and Helen Greek Orthodox Church in Flushing. Maggie reminded us that we were all members of Saint Demetrios in Ypsilanti when we were kids and thought it would be nice to once again participate in a traditional Greek service. When a young priest was swinging the censer on the altar, the sweet smell wafted over to us and I closed my eyes, thinking about what Father Pavlos told me. He said that the father of the little girl who was cured of MD felt it was the incense that had cured her. I felt I needed curing now from my mixed feelings of hate for our Islamic enemies and hate for having feelings of prejudice—two very powerful forces. I also had to smile when I thought about how Sally and I went looking for a pillow to prop up our love-making position in that little storeroom (before going into an empty classroom) that Saturday night and found my bag of leaves with the tau on it.

The priest started his sermon by saying, "And are there doubters here? Those of you like Thomas the Apostle who had to see Christ's wounds before he could believe; are there still those among you who have to see the face of God before you'll accept his existence? Then what are the blind to do? Are they without faith? For 'blessed are they that have not seen, and yet have believed.'"

After quoting the gospel, the priest went on to point out the power of blind faith and the need for faith in order for us to truly accept God in all his glory. *Was my finding the leaves in that storeroom a sign from God? Was it some way of seeing his face?* I thought. But I was never a doubting Thomas—I had always had faith.

I started to think about if I had gone blind but somehow kept my job. How would I teach my agents and the screeners what to look for when searching for terrorists? Impossible—I had to see in order to search and screen by definition. Nor could I be blind to what was going on around me and not see who was doing what to whom. I was truly conflicted.

*   *   *

"Why the silence and dark mood?" Sally asked me as we were driving in the cab to the airport later Sunday afternoon.

"I was just thinking, that's all. I hope the weather clears before we leave. I hate flying out in a rain storm," I said.

"The clouds are starting to break up—it'll be all right," Sally said. "I always feel a little sad after visiting with Maggie. The weekend went by so quickly. It seems we hardly had time to visit, but I could see you had had enough and it was time to go home."

"No, that's not true. I hadn't had enough. I love visiting with Maggie. It's just that I'm still troubled about our conversations about profiling people who get on airplanes, that's all. I'll get over it," I mused.

"I was real proud when you explained to Maggie about why we can't do that—profile based on race. That was the Connie I married."

"Actually, what I was thinking at that time, and what the priest said this morning about seeing . . . what I was thinking was what if I was blind? How would I profile if I couldn't see their faces? What criteria would we use besides a noticeable ethnicity? I find it all very confusing."

"I'm not sure I follow you. Not seeing someone doesn't mean that you still couldn't be discriminating against a person who's not white. I think you're comparing apples to oranges."

"And why not, they're both fruit? No, it's deeper than that." I looked out the window of the cab and then said, "Tomorrow at work I'm going to make a concerted effort when I watch my agents and the passenger screeners working to see if they appear to be harsher on Middle Easterners. And if I think they are, I'm going to talk with them about doing their job without any bias toward a person's background. I don't know if that's right or wrong, but I'm going to practice being blind again."

*   *   *

When we were going through security, Sally was randomly singled out for a more thorough screening. She was enraged. "That was one of the most embarrassing things I've ever gone through. It was like they were looking at me naked and all the other passengers were staring, thinking I'm some kind of a terrorist. And you didn't do anything. Couldn't you have told them who you are? Why did you let them do that to me?"

"Honey, it would have made no difference. I could have been the one selected, and I would have gone through the same thing. It's quite an ordeal and not as easy as they would have you believe. The nonsense about 'if you have nothing to hide than you shouldn't care' is just that—nonsense. You feel violated. And to think that there are some people who would want all Muslim travelers to go through that. How blind could they be?"

"You know, sometimes you can be such an asshole—but you're my asshole, and I love you. But right now you're the smartest guy in the room," Sally said with a smile on her face.

The clouds were just breaking up and the evening sun was coming out. It was going to be a smooth flight home. I still felt confused as to why I should not be 100 percent behind our government on this color coding and scaring the shit out of everyone, yet by the same token, I also wondered why our government seemed so pigheaded about the whole war thing in general. All I knew was that it was no longer easy to know who was right on this and who was being the jackass—me or the guys in DC. But what I was most concerned about was not doing what was right and the gift of being able to see being taken from me—taken by whoever gave it to me through the leaves. *Was that too selfish of me?* I thought. I hoped not.

I was also thinking that in about six short years I would be eligible for retirement and wondered what I would do when I did retire. I would still be relatively young—in my fifties—and I thought it would be nice to go back to school and get a college degree, or at least a certification in some helping profession that could lead to a more satisfying work environment for me. I wanted a job where I knew what was right and what was wrong, where conflict over my work would not get in the way of doing good for people. I still remembered how nice it felt helping those stranded passengers four years ago. I would love a job that would make me feel like that all the time. Maybe I'd look into other professions and see if there was something new for me out there that would get me to a better place emotionally about my work than where I was right now.

The sky was blue and gold above the clouds, and the sun was beginning to set in the west—what a marvelous sight to see.

CHAPTER 16

Joey Gilbert

Bush was reelected last year—again, by a narrow margin—in spite of his "mission accomplished" gaffe. Today in 2005 I, along with many moderate Republicans, was getting more disillusioned by the current administration. Even more importantly, my gift of life that the leaves had given me seemed to be wasted. I hadn't done enough—at least that was how I felt—to pay back for my new life. Maybe I was worried that whoever or whatever gave me the gift would now want it back—like it was on loan and could be taken back at any time. In any case, like the rest of the country, I was in a noticeable funk.

We were watching the evening news when Gabriella started in again on the relevance of the war.

"This war sucks—we should never have gone in there, and we should get out now!" Gabriella said.

I tried to respond thoughtfully because with Gabriella's antiwar sentiments, I knew where this was going, but I went there anyway. "I don't know, I thought it was the right thing to do at the time, but who knows now. With Bush's approval rating going down the toilet, you'd think they would do something more to convince us he was right, but . . ."

"How could they convince us he's right? His whole premise was based on bullshit, and now that we know there were no weapons of mass destruction, why the fuck are we still there?" Gabriella said while making big blow-up movements with her arms. She was livid.

It was Wednesday, the first of June, and I had just gotten home from work. We were trying to relax over a drink when we saw on the news that eighty more Americans had been killed in Iraq during May. It set Gabriella off.

"And God only knows how many of those poor Iraqi bastards got killed last month; I'm sure it was more than eighty. I get so fucking mad every time I see that shit. When are we going to learn? Violence begets violence!

141

Enough! Enough, Mr. President—stop the carnage!" she was yelling at the TV but not to any one in particular. Gabriella, like many people, was totally unconvinced that we should have gone into Iraq two years ago. She was very much in favor of hanging Osama bin Laden but never knew why we chose to invade Iraq.

"Joe, you're in the arms business, tell me why we should be there. Give me one good fucking reason why we're there."

I got this from her all the time—lots of foul language and blaming me for being in weapons research. She knew I'd agree with her for the most part about Iraq, but she couldn't understand why I would be doing weapons research and development if I felt that way about our invasion and the subsequent destruction of a country—a country that was for all practical purposes completely out of the 9/11 loop.

"I could tell you, honey, but then I'd have to kill you," I said, trying to lighten up the conversation.

"I'm not in the mood for that now. Seriously—I promise I won't yell at you—with your military contacts, you must have some idea why we're fighting this war. What is it?"

I tried to figure out in my mind how much I could tell her without violating security and not endangering her.

"Honey, the people I work with out of the government labs really don't talk about the politics of the war. Our only interest is to prevent as many American casualties as we possibly can . . ."

"Well, it seems to me that one way to do that is to get the fuck out of there!" she screamed. I didn't respond, just waited. "Sorry, I know I said I wouldn't yell at you. Go on."

"Our company makes optical tracking and aiming devices—I should say, parts for the devices—that are used on robots that can go into combat, do the shooting, and keep our soldiers and airmen out of harm's way. I think that's a good thing. If I can prevent just one of our guys from getting killed, then I'm okay with it." Since my cancer cure, I had been concerned—you might even say obsessed—with trying to cause no harm to anyone.

"But if we didn't have those devices, would the government still put these guys in the field, knowing they were going to get killed? Maybe if you stopped making them—"

"Stop it! If I stopped, someone else would pick it up. This way I know I'm doing what I can for our guys in the field, and that's who I care about.

We have this same conversation all the time. I'm frustrated about it, and so are you, but we shouldn't take it out on each other, clear?"

I got up to make myself another drink, and Gabriella quieted down. She was still staring at the TV, and I could tell that this conversation was not over.

* * *

It was raining on Thursday when I went to work. I had an early morning meeting with Glen to discuss our product line, and my argument with Gabriella was sitting heavily on my mind when I walked into Glen's office.

"Did you see the latest casualty figures?" Glen asked as I sat down. "We got to do more; we should nuke those bastards back to the Stone Age where they belong. All the crap coming from those Islamic fundamentalist shitheads about God knowing who's his own as the justification for the indiscriminate killing of women and children just drives me up the wall. Why are we pussy-footing around with them?"

"I think one of the reasons is that we're fighting in Iraq and bin Laden is probably in Afghanistan or Pakistan, or some other fuckin' 'stan,' and we should be concentrating on him. We're spread too thin over there and fighting people who aren't our enemies. We're letting our real enemies—like the Saudis—off scot free," I retorted.

"What are you talking about? The Saudis are old and loyal friends of our country. The Bush's and the royal family are as tight as brothers. How can you say we should be fighting them?" Glen asked.

"Then why did most of the 9/11 attackers come from there? And why are the Wahabbi clerics in Saudi Arabia still screaming for our heads, and their government, including their goddamn royal family, has said nothing?"

"That's not fair. You know they can't say anything against the Islamic clerics. But they didn't support the attack or were in any way involved with the attackers. Be fair, Joe," Glen offered.

"Glen, you're a finance guy—who do you think is funding those terrorists? Well, I'll tell you—it's the fuckin' Saudis!" I screamed.

"You just said we're already spread too thin, and now you want to start a war with the Saudis. I'm sure glad you're not making these decisions. Bush has an expert team in Wolfowitz and Rumsfeld. They make these decisions and I trust them. And you should too. Anyway, we're not meeting to talk politics; our job is to help them win the war, so let's get on with it," Glen said dismissively.

"Let's take a break. I need a time out here before I can seriously talk about our product line, okay?"

Glen agreed and I offered to stay late to talk with him. My argument with Gabriella last night had gotten to me, and I'd been thinking about this all night. *How could I support saving our soldiers lives by making it easier to take other people's lives?* I wondered. But after that little political dialogue with Glen, I thought it best that I wait until both he and I had cooled down before presenting him with my idea. I never should have lost my cool like that. Glen and I were both Republicans, and we'd had our little disagreements in the past over politics, but this war was driving us apart. I had to do something to stop this battle before it ruined our partnership and the company.

*   *   *

"Glen, what's our military versus civilian product line split?" I asked that evening. We were in my office now, and everyone had gone home but the cleaning crew. We could hear their buffers at work down the corridor along the executive office wing. It was still raining, and although still light out, the dark clouds gave the appearance of late evening.

"Still the same—sixty-forty, 60 percent civilian products and 40 percent government. You interested in changing the mix? Want to go more military?" he asked.

"Actually, I'm thinking we'd be better off going 100 percent civilian, or rather zero percent classified weapons. First of all it's more sustainable, and secondly our government weapons' stuff has peaked. They also squeeze the shit out of us since we're only subs. The primes get all the money and the long-term benefits, while we get the aggravation and scraps. I think it's time for us to focus on an all nonmilitary line."

"And what happened to our patriotic duty? You once told me that the least you can do is see to it that our fighting forces are as safe as practicable. What's your take on that now, and why has it changed?" Glen asked but not in a hostile manner.

"I've been thinking a lot about it lately. I know—and you agreed—that it was to protect our men in the field that got us so heavily involved in weaponry. Also, our airport security line was quashed because it was too expensive and a little impractical, so we felt that we needed the more lucrative military contracts to meet our fiscal needs." I paused, and then said, "In any case, I no longer feel that our weaponry efforts are that vital, nor lucrative, and that our efforts could be better spent on other projects."

"So what do you want us to do now?" Glen asked with a little touch of sarcasm in his voice.

"Glen, remember when I was diagnosed with terminal cancer and you came over to my house? And then, for some reason that no one has really been able to explain to me, I went into complete remission." I stared out the window for a while, getting my thoughts in place. "I honestly believe that I was given a second chance at life. And with that chance I pledged never to take a life—for any reason. Life is much too precious. And now I find myself in the awkward position of helping someone else take lives. No matter how justifiable I feel it is to kill enemy combatants, I just can't support that anymore."

"Joe, my brother, I can completely understand that. You don't have to explain anything to me. If you want us out of the military, that's okay with me. We'll finish up our contractual obligations by October, and then that's it. I won't ask for any more proposals from you for weaponry." Glen caught my watery eyes and continued. "Joey, we've been friends and partners for a long time. I can see how this is affecting you, and I'm behind you all the way. In fact, I was thinking almost the same thing. What with civilian aircraft, the auto industry, and all kinds of manufacturing and construction programs going on, our LED digital services should be targeting those markets anyway. I think there's easily enough money—maybe more—to fill the gap left by dropping weapons research. I'll put together a new business plan in a day or two that doesn't include any classified or weapons-related programs. Is that all right with you?"

Glen was smiling broadly, and I somehow got the feeling he had wanted to go that way before we had our conversation on defense programs. Only now he was doing it for me—not the company or him. I wasn't sure why, but I felt uncomfortable exposing my feelings to him. And for some reason I couldn't explain, I still didn't completely trust the guy.

* * *

"You say he bought it up without an argument? Something's going on there with Glen. He never gave up a chance to make money no matter how he came by it," Gabriella said.

We were having a late supper and I told her what had happened at work.

"No matter, sweetie, I'm so proud of you. If enough small business people did as you do, then maybe those assholes that are running the war would get the message and we'd get out of there," she said.

"I doubt it, honey. Our company not doing any more classified R and D is going to have very little—if any—effect on Bush's war policy. In fact, they'll have absolutely no idea as to why we're not bidding on any more proposals. Also, we'll still be doing other government work, just no weapons or other classified military stuff."

"That's plenty! I love you very much for that. For taking a stand—"

"Okay, Gabby, I'm still a Bush supporter, and I still believe he's getting a lot of undeserved grief from the left on this. Remember, they invaded us on 9/11 not the other way around."

"Iraq invaded us? I don't think so."

"Here we go again," I said. "Let's just leave it at that. I'm out of the weapons business, and I'm keeping my pledge not to assist in the taking of a life—anyone's life. That's all I can do; I can do no more. Now can we finish dinner in peace, or do you still want to yell at me?"

We went to bed early that night and watched the late news in bed. Iraq was still in the headlines, of course. They were summarizing the earlier trials around Abu Ghraib prison and the demotion of a senior military officer over the debacle.

"They should put electrodes to his balls—"

"Will you stop it! First of all the colonel is a *she*, and the poor bastard probably had absolutely no idea what was going on. Enough already with your bad-ass attitude. These are not bad people," I said.

"I know, they're good people doing bad things. Well, it's time these good people started behaving like good people."

"You're incorrigible," I said and rolled over on my side and tried to sleep.

* * *

Sleep did not come easily. As I lay there, I recalled my father's stories about his experiences in Korea. He was an enlisted man who served in the marines, and on occasion I could get him to tell me a story or two about his battle scars. He didn't like to talk about it, but he usually ended his stories

T

by telling me, "Joey, you see there are a lot of evil people in the world who want to take what you and I have. And they'll do anything to get it. We have to be prepared to stop them and willing to do whatever it takes."

I believed him and miss him terribly. He died when I was just fifteen years old. That little speech of his still haunts me, and by my giving up on developing better and more sophisticated weapons, I somehow feel very conflicted. I felt I was letting him down by not doing more weapon development work.

I just hoped that my pledge of not wanting to take a life had not caused me to lose sight of what was truly right and important. I also prayed that because I'd taken a stand against killing people, maybe my cancer wouldn't return. And maybe, just maybe, I shouldn't have sent all the tea leaves back to Indonesia. Only time would tell—but then again, maybe it wouldn't.

Chapter 17

Nando Garcia

It was Friday night, actually Saturday morning, and Maribel and I were up late waiting for Maria Elena to come home. Since there was no school tomorrow, we were a little more liberal about her staying out late on Friday and Saturday. However, it was later than she should have been out, and I was worried. I was always a little tense when it came to Maria Elena's health—worried that if we did something wrong or if we were not deserving parents, her MD would return. I knew that was all nonsense, but I worried all the same.

"She drives like a maniac. If she doesn't stop driving like that, I'm going to take away all her driving privileges," I was telling Maribel. "Ever since she turned sixteen, she's been acting nuts—driving crazy, partying, staying out late. I don't know how she keeps her grades up, but if that changes too—"

"Yes, and then what will you do, Nando? You're all talk when it comes to her. She can do no wrong in your eyes. You complain to me, but do you say anything to her? Say something to her. She ignores me, but at least you can get through to her sometimes, so do it!"

Maribel was right. I was much too easy on Maria Elena, but so was Maribel, so it was not all my fault. I decided that as soon as she came home I would talk to her. School was almost over for the year, and I wanted to know what she had planned for her summer. I also wanted to know why she wore a red-and-white bandana around her neck every day. I'd been around long enough to know about gang colors, and this looked like the real deal. If I was right, then we had some real problems.

When Maria Elena walked in, I looked at my watch—12:22 a.m., twenty-two minutes past her curfew and past her legally allowed driving time. I didn't say anything but waited until she went into her room and then followed her in.

"Did you have a good time tonight, honey?" I asked in as much of a nonjudgmental tone as I could muster.

"Just hanging out with some friends, nothing very exciting," she said as she started to get ready for bed.

"You know it's after curfew, and if you had been stopped while driving, they would hold up your regular driver's license. You have to take your driving responsibilities more seriously—stop speeding and driving recklessly and driving after curfew. If you continue to behave this way, you won't be able to take your mother's car anymore. Is that clear?" I said in a gentle but firm way.

"Yes, Papi, I promise to be a good little girl, and I'll drive more carefully and I wont drive after hours, okay?" Maria Elena said with a lot of sarcasm in her voice. I didn't want to get into a fight with her so late, so I thought it better to change the subject.

"What is this kerchief you wear all the time now?" I asked, holding it up. "Is it some kind of a club thing? I see that some of your friends also wear them; are they in the club too?" I gently asked, trying to feign benign interest.

"It's just a kerchief, that's all, and I like the colors. I look good in red and white, and so do some of my friends. We just like them, that's all. Why are you so interested in what I wear now? Is everything I do a problem with you? Maybe you'd like me better if I was stuck at home in a wheelchair with no friends for you to worry about. Is that what you want?"

And so the confrontation started. She was always ready for a fight and challenged everything I said lately by getting hostile and accusing me of wanting to control her life. I put the kerchief down on her dresser and walked out of her room with a disgusted look on my face.

*   *   *

"She's angry, isn't she?" Maribel said.

"When isn't she angry?" I answered.

"Nando, we have to do something about her behavior before she gets into some serious trouble. I think we should write out rules for her and give her penalties if she doesn't follow them."

"I tried that, remember? We cut her allowance, restricted her car use, grounded her, and all she did was go back to her bad behavior at the first chance she got."

"This time make it even harder, like no car at all or no allowance or staying in the house for a whole weekend—things that will really cramp her social life. That should do it?" Maribel offered.

I didn't answer her. I just nodded as if I approved and then went into our room to get ready for bed. I could hear Maria Elena's radio playing softly. It was nice music, not the shit that most kids listened to today, and all I could think of was how thoughtful and gentle she was as a child. But I also remembered how helpless she was with MD, and yet she never lost her temper or complained about not being able to walk. Maybe she was right about my wanting to have more control over her actions, but not if it meant she would have a recurrence of MD. There were times that I wished I had kept the leaves when Father Pavlos asked if I wanted to. But that would have been even more selfish, and who knew if they would work again. I fell asleep, troubled over my thoughts and determined to keep Maria Elena safe and healthy.

* * *

It was Monday morning and I was at my desk in West Middle School. I decided to call the police officer who was permanently assigned to Ypsilanti High School. I wanted to know if there were any gang activities involving red kerchiefs.

"Hello, is this officer Cheryl Delahaney?" I asked. After she acknowledged that it was her, I said, "My name is Fernando Garcia and I teach over at West. I'm just curious, but is there any gang activity going on at the high school—gangs that wear red-and-white kerchiefs around their necks?"

Officer Delahaney answered quickly. "I know what you're referring to because I do see some very active students wearing these things. However, as of now I don't see any organized gang activities."

"What do you mean by active students—active in a good sense or a bad sense?" I asked.

"In their case, neither. I mean I see them all over the school actively talking in groups, hanging out together, going to class together. They're all sophomores and juniors—at least that's what they look like to me—and they just seem to be having a good time. They haven't been in any trouble, but they seem to be looking for trouble. You know what I mean?" She paused and then said, "Anyway, I know a detective in the Youth Bureau who's a gang specialist. I'll call him and ask if he's aware of any activity going on

T

involving gangs wearing red kerchiefs. Oh, by the way, you said your name is Garcia—are you Maria Elena's father?"

"Yes, I am, and I was concerned that maybe she might be hanging out with the wrong crowd. Now that she can drive, it seems that there's no end to the worry a parent can have for his teenage daughter."

"I understand completely, Mr. Garcia. If it's any consolation, I promise to keep an eye on her and her friends. I've known her since she started here, and she's always been a top-notch kid. I'm not sure why she gave up sports—she was so good at soccer—but it's not unusual for them to take a break from organized sports as they get older. I'll let you know if I hear anything, but in the meantime, I wouldn't get overly concerned. Sixteen and seventeen are tough years for kids—almost adults but still kids looking to define themselves. But, hey . . . you're a teacher—you know that, right?" Cheryl said.

"Yes, I do, but it seems it's always a little harder when it's your own kid that you have to deal with." I thanked Officer Delahaney and hung up. I was somewhat relieved that Maria Elena wasn't involved with a known crowd of bad apples, but I was still concerned. I was determined to talk it out with her this evening, no matter how angry and uncooperative she might get.

*   *   *

"Hi, honey, what are you reading?" I asked as I walked into Maria Elena's room that evening. Her door was open so there was no need to knock. It always seemed to me to be a little too formal for a parent to have to knock.

"Just a book about Vietnam. Why did we fight that war, Papi? It seems that we're making the same mistake all over again in Iraq. And didn't we make the same mistake in Korea too? Didn't Bush say something like the war was over a couple of years ago?"

"Yes, his infamous "mission accomplished" speech. What a fiasco that was."

"Then why are we still fighting if it's over? You know some of the kids I know are going to be old enough to be drafted soon. I can't bear to think that they could get killed fighting in a stupid war. Haven't these guys learned anything about fighting in a foreign country, on someone else's land—you can't win!" she said with such maturity it almost frightened me. I decided that I would try to talk to her like she was an adult, because at sixteen she was.

"I'm not an expert on war or foreign policy, but as a naturalized citizen I find it hard to disagree with my government. After all, they've done so much for us. I would like to believe that they know what they're doing, even if at times it makes absolutely no sense to me."

"Then you agree—the war is senseless!" she proclaimed.

"No, I didn't say that. I said that at times our policy is hard to understand from a rational point of view. But I have to give them the benefit of the doubt. I have to assume that they know things you or I will never know." I waited a bit, and seeing how troubled she looked, I asked, "Has the war been bothering you, is that why you don't participate in sports anymore?"

Ignoring my question Maria Elena said, "Papi, if I was a boy and you knew I might be drafted in two years, how would you feel?"

"The war will be over in two years. It can't go on much longer."

"No . . . but if it did, how would you feel about me being drafted?"

I hesitated before answering. Looking into her deep dark eyes I saw for the first time that my child was no longer a baby. "I would not be happy and neither would your mother, but if it was to happen, I would pray for your safety and for God to give our leaders the wisdom to end the conflict as soon as they could."

"Pray for my safety? Is that all you could do? I don't think so. If it was me and it was my son who might be asked to be killed in a meaningless war, I would send him off to Canada or even Mexico before I would let him go." Maria Elena looked away from me after saying that. I was totally taken aback by her logic. "Look," she continued, "my friends and I have formed a pact that we won't fight in the war if we're called, and we all wear our kerchiefs as a sign that we disagree with Bush. I gave up soccer, like my friends have given up some of their activities, to protest the fact that kids like us are being killed in Iraq and other places for no reason at all. Maybe if all the kids do that, they'll stop taking us."

"Honey, they aren't drafting anyone for the military."

"*Yet!*" she said with emphasis. "But I bet by the time I graduate they will be. And they'll probably draft girls too, because everyone else will be too pissed off at them and won't want to join up."

I couldn't argue with her feelings, because I could see she was totally convinced in the righteousness of her mission. All I could do was to try and channel her activities away from self-destruction to something positive. *But how can I do that?* I wondered. I tried to appease her.

"The war has gotten us all upset, just as 9/11 upset us a few years ago, and most people feel we have to avenge the innocent people who were killed in the attack. I understand how you can feel that it may be time to do something else, but . . ." I looked at her again. I could see she was hoping that I could explain it all to her, make sense of all the bloodshed, but I couldn't. I simply said, "Peaceful protest is a very American way of letting your government know you disapprove of their policy. I respect you and your friends for expressing yourself that way. I would hope that you would continue to peacefully demonstrate how you feel in a nondestructive way to you and to others. That's all I can say, other than your mother and I love you very much and we'll always love you."

"I know you will, Papi. But at times it's hard. We kids sometimes feel that we should be living for today, because who knows what's going to happen tomorrow."

"But tomorrow will come just as surely as the sun will rise, and you'll have to live in tomorrow just like you live in today. There will be a future, and you and your friends will be a big part of it. So take care that you stay healthy and get a good education so you'll be able to make a better future for all those you care about."

I felt that was enough preaching for one night, so I kissed Maria Elena and left her to her thoughts.

When I went back into the front room, Maribel asked, "Did you tell her what penalties she'll get if she doesn't change her ways?"

"Let's go to bed now. I'll tell you all about it in there," I said. It was getting past ten, and we all had to be up early tomorrow for work or school, or just to live another day.

*   *   *

It was on Wednesday that I got a call from Officer Delahaney reporting to me about her conversation with the Youth Bureau detective. "He told me that he's not aware of any gang problems associated with kerchiefs being worn around the neck—at least not locally. But he said that wearing colors usually is the first sign of kids organizing for something—recognition, criminal activity. You know the drill, Mr. Garcia," she said.

I filled her in on my conversation with Maria Elena on Monday night and asked if she would watch out for her. Maria Elena was emotionally

153

involved with her new cause, and I hoped it would not lead to her or her friends getting into trouble.

"You know, Mr. Garcia—"

"Please, call me Nando."

"Okay. You know, Nando, there's a civics teacher here in school that I think would be a good resource for these kids. He could direct them as to how they may present their case to the rest of the school. In fact, if I'm not mistaken he teaches sophomore civics, and I think Maria Elena and some of her kerchiefed friends are in his class," Officer Delahaney informed me. "I'll talk to him, if you don't mind, and see if he'll get involved. Maybe he can have them do a march for peace or something like that. I'll let you know what happens, okay?"

* * *

The next day when I came home I found Maria Elena with two of her friends busily involved in some kind of organizing activity. There was no doubt that they were excited about what they were planning. I peeked into her room, and I politely asked what was going on.

"Hi, Papi, meet my friends. That's my dad," she said, introducing us. "We're forming an official school club on international civics and Mr. Gorstein, our civics teacher, is sponsoring us. Do you know him?"

"No, I don't, honey, but I'm delighted that you're doing something like this. Not much time left in the school year, but it's a good start for next fall, right?" I said. "Have you planned any activities yet?"

"No, someone wanted us to do a march for peace, but we feel that's so yesterday. We're more concerned about educating people as to what it means to be a good international citizen. There are kids in a number of countries who have already formed international civics groups, and we want to team up with some of them, so we'll be at it all summer long. Who knows—if enough kids get involved maybe we can achieve a real 'mission accomplished,' right, guys?"

I left her room feeling so much better about her proposed summer activities than I had felt a couple of days before. It was bad enough that I felt so ambivalent about our government policies, but kids should feel more certain and secure in the knowledge that their government was doing right by them. I walked into the kitchen where Maribel was preparing snacks for the kids—I should say young adults.

"What do you think of our daughter and her Pancho Villa bandoliers? With their red kerchiefs they look like quite the revolutionaries, don't you think?" I said with a broad grin on my face.

"Stop teasing, Nando, they'll hear you. Here, take this tray in. I'll bring drinks," Maribel ordered.

I hoped that Maria Elena's new activity was the end of her dangerous behavior and the beginning of a more constructive approach for her social discontent. But my main concern was that Maria Elena and her club would give them some satisfaction that the world was actually listening to them and that their efforts were not all in vain. When kids lose faith in their government, it's not hard to extend that to losing trust in other institutions, like religion. If it truly was God that had sent the incense, then maybe he would take back the cure, like in the book of Job, just to test our faith. I prayed that wouldn't happen to Maria Elena. Only time would tell if the war would end, and our daughter could believe in a bright future for herself, her friends, and the students from around the world she'd be meeting with. For me, well I could only pray.

Chapter 18

Mitch Foley

It was Monday afternoon in early June and the weather was dank. My partner Patrick and I were doing our routine cruising. We had plans to go over to police headquarters later in the afternoon. Gerry was being promoted to captain; he would be heading up the entire western division. He was on his way to becoming chief someday, and he deserved it. He'd be a captain for maybe a year or two before moving back to downtown with all the other brass. I was pleased to hear that he had passed his physical and they had found no problems with his heart or other organs. I guessed that meant that Father Pavlos's leaves were still working on him—I wondered if they were still working on me too.

I got a call on my new cell phone and took it in the car.

After I hung up, Patrick asked, "What was that all about?"

"I just got a call from Officer Delahaney at the high school, wondering if there were any gangs out there wearing red-and-white bandanas or neckerchiefs. Have you heard of anything like that?" I asked him.

"There was that gang out of Detroit, Mitch, that wore red kerchiefs with white flowers on it," Patrick answered. "They wore them on their heads like do-rags. I don't think that would go over well at the high school here. And that Detroit gang did not include high school kids—they were older and dealt in drugs, if I remember right."

"Well, you know these kids, always willing to copy something that they think will buy them even more street cred. Makes them look tough."

We drove over to the school to see if we could find any unusual activities like clusters of kids hanging out.

"Look, there goes one of those bandana wearers. Should we stop him and ask what's with the scarf?" Patrick asked.

"What for? We have no beef with them, do we? Why don't we wait until we have a better idea of what it's all about before we stop anybody, okay?" I said. "It will be nice seeing Gerry get his promotion this afternoon. Not too many people will be there, but we will. I already told Loo we'd be going, and he says it's okay. We might be running a little over shift; is that all right with you, Pat?"

"Not a problem, Jane knows I can be late anytime, so she's all right. I'll give her a call when I can anyway, just so she won't worry," Patrick said as we pulled into City Hall and parked in the police area.

The promotion ceremony was brief since it was only Gerry getting his captain's bars and two other officers being promoted to lieutenant. The chief and the mayor did all the talking and handed out their bars and certificates, and that was it. Most of the people there were family members of the two lieutenants, so I was glad that we were there for Gerry. When the ceremony ended, Gerry asked us to hang around and talk with him a bit in his old office. He had already packed everything up and would be in his new office tomorrow, but for now he was still in the detective's area of the Criminal Investigation Unit.

"Thanks, guys, glad you came today. It was a nice service—simple but nice, don't you think?" he asked us.

We nodded in agreement and wished him the best. We offered him our complete support and told him he could call on us anytime for anything. It was just standard stuff that you say when your friend moves up the ladder and you're pleased for their accomplishments. He then told us about why he wanted to see us—that he was glad we were working in the Youth Bureau and would be relying on us to keep him up to speed as to what might be going on in the streets. I think he just wanted us to hang around so he could thank us for coming to the ceremony, but his comment about the bureau led me to ask him about Officer Delahaney's call earlier in the afternoon.

"By the way, Gerry, have you heard anything about a red-bandana gang in the area? Cheryl Delahaney—you know her—at the high school called me about it today. I was wondering if there were any bulletins on this or anything from the State."

"I haven't heard anything, Mitch. Do you know what they're into?"

"No, and Cheryl didn't know either. Just a hunch at this time, but you know, better safe now than in deep shit later, right?" I said.

"If anything does turn up, Mitch, I'll let you know, but keep your eyes open on this one. I am getting notices about more than usual unrest in high schools around the country. They say it has to do with the war, but I'm not exactly sure why that's creating unrest. It's not as if we have a draft going on right now, so it's not the same as Nam. These things go in cycles, so I'm not greatly concerned. Hey, thanks again for coming, and as I said, keep me up to speed on this high school gang thing, okay?"

"Will do, Gerry, will do, and again, congrats, well earned."

"Yes, congratulations again, Gerry," Patrick chimed in.

We left the station and still had some time left on our shift, so we called dispatch to say that we were back in service and continued to cruise for another twenty minutes before returning to the station.

*   *   *

It was Wednesday afternoon when we stopped by the high school again. As Patrick and I walked into her office, I told Cheryl, "We were in the area so we thought we would stop by to see if there was anything new on the neckerchief gang."

"I just finished talking to one of the kids' dad's. He was the one who called me on Monday to ask about a possible gang connection—he's a teacher at West," Cheryl answered, smiling as we sat down to talk.

I hadn't worked with Cheryl very often, even though both of us were with the Youth Bureau, but she was known here at Ypsi High as a good officer who was well liked by the students and teachers. I was thinking I should probably work with her more often, as we sat down in her small office.

"So what did he tell you?" I asked. Cheryl filled me in on her conversation with the teacher, and I was a little surprised that his sixteen-year-old daughter—someone so young—could be that concerned about a war so far away.

I'd known Cheryl a long time. She was a friendly person and had been with the school for many years. She was also a nice-looking woman, with just enough meat on her bones to let you know she was all women but far from chunky. I liked that type of woman, and I couldn't help staring at her. She was younger than me, maybe in her late thirties, and had been with the force for around fifteen years.

Cheryl and I were both Ypsi kids who married right out of high school. I was told by one of the other officers at the precinct that she was going through a rough divorce, and having been through one myself, I wanted to tell her that I understood and that I was there for her. But I didn't know her that well—*yet*. Cops, in general, found it hard to stay married, and suicide was almost endemic among police officers. My spouse never really got it, and I suspected Cheryl's husband didn't either. But we get it, and maybe that's one reason why cops should only marry other cops. I had never really thought about Cheryl in a sexual way before, but for some reason today she turned me on.

"I'm going to put those kids' civics teacher in touch with them. He's a good guy, and I think that will help end any gang possibilities. What do you think, Mitch?" Cheryl asked.

"Any way an adult can get involved to channel their energy toward something positive can't hurt. I think you're doing it right, Cheryl. You agree, Pat?" Patrick had been quiet, and I thought it was time to bring him into the conversation.

"Why are these students so angry? Do any of them know someone who's been killed in Iraq?" Patrick asked.

"I can't answer that one, but it does seem that the older students seem angrier than normal, and I guess the war has something to do with it. I think they're afraid that the draft will start, and they honestly don't know why they should go," Cheryl explained. "By the same token, there are many other students who plan to enlist right after they graduate, but I think it's a totally macho thing and has no relation to our foreign policy. I don't think the kids really know what's going on over there."

"Does anyone?" I asked. Patrick gave me a strange look when I said that, but that was Patrick, always defending Bush policy.

"Either way, this is the time of year that students go *zooey*—just before summer vacation. So it's not unusual for some kids to act up now for no apparent reason at all. We shouldn't read too much into their behavior—they're not that complicated," Cheryl said.

We chatted a little longer, telling Cheryl to call us if anything did turn up, and we promised to keep her in the loop as well. Back in the squad car I asked Patrick what the look he gave in Cheryl's office was all about.

"What did you mean when you told her you don't know what's going on? Didn't we help catch some terrorists a few years back? That's what's going on!" Patrick was angry.

"Yeah, we did, but they weren't Iraqis. Look, I'm no genius and politics isn't my best sport. I grew up in an Irish factory worker's family, so I was born a Democrat. But I'm also a police officer and I follow orders. If the president says, 'Shit,' I ask how high and how deep, just like you. But you know, Pat, just between the two of us, if I was a kid today I would probably join up. You know why? Have you seen all those ads on TV? They promise them the fuckin' moon for enlisting. But do they say why we're there? Hell no! Why? Because they don't fuckin' know either."

"What do you mean, they don't know? You don't read the paper or watch the news? Iraq was planning to attack us with WMDs, and they supported al-Qaeda in their attack on us. Why the fuck do you think we're in there? To get more land? Who wants a fuckin' desert?"

Patrick was passionate, so I thought it best to avoid any more arguments. We both had our beliefs, and we'd never know who was right. I also knew that his so-called reasons for war with Iraq were a little outdated. But worse than that, I was getting angry as we argued. It was something I had avoided or controlled for a long time, and I wasn't about to blow it now. I wondered if maybe my contact with the leaves more than eight years ago was wearing off. I knew that Father Pavlos had had them at one time, and I wondered if he still had any left. Maybe I needed another dose or two. *But Gerry isn't getting sick again, so why should I be getting my old demons back?* I thought to myself.

"Maybe you're right, but at least admit that you can understand how some kids might feel about it—the war that is," I said to Patrick.

"Unless they personally know someone who was killed in battle, I can't see why they just don't support our country on this one. It's the right thing to do." Patrick continued. "And even if they do know someone who was killed, then they should honor that person by not saying he died for nothin'."

We were silent for a while, just talking when we had to as we drove back to the precinct to log out for the day. Once again Patrick invited me home for supper with him and his family—he did that a lot—but as usual I declined. I thought about Cheryl Delahaney and how nice it would have been having supper with her. *Maybe sometime in the future that will happen.*

*　　*　　*

"Loo wants to see you, Mitch," the desk sergeant said as I walked in Thursday morning.

"What's up, Sarge?" I asked.

"You'll have to ask him, but he seems irritated about something. You guys been doing something naughty on watch?" he teased.

"Patrick in yet?" I asked.

"Haven't seen him."

I went upstairs to the detective's area and walked into Loo's office. "You wanna see me, Loo?"

"Yeah, Mitch, come in. You have to go downtown to Internal Affairs and talk to someone there about a dead guy. It seems that Louis Smith—you know, Louie the Snitch—OD'd recently and they want to talk with you. You okay with that?" he asked.

"Why would IA want to talk with me? I haven't seen Louie in years. In fact I'm surprised he lived this long—I thought he was dead already. What's the skinny on this, Loo?" I asked, feeling the anger rise in my chest over being called in by IA to talk about Louie. *They only want to catch bad cops, so why do they want to see me?* I wondered.

"I'm not sure, Mitch. Look, just go there and see what the hell they want. I'll have Pat work here in the station this morning, and you can team up again this afternoon. He'll brief you on anything new that would concern the two of you. If you're really concerned you should call Gerry and see if he has a take on this."

I walked out of Loo's office and immediately went to my desk to call Gerry.

"Gerry, Mitch—what's the deal with IA wanting to talk to me about Louie? You know anything about this?" I asked, without letting Gerry say anything.

"Yes, I heard yesterday that they found him dead in his apartment. His landlord called when she smelled something bad coming out of his room. He'd been dead for a while. At first glance they thought it was an OD because of the stuff they found there—you know, needles and other drug paraphernalia—but on a closer look they saw that he was badly beaten. They won't know for sure what killed him until the ME tells them later today, but in the meantime they've started an investigation. I didn't know that they contacted you, but don't get excited. Just go in and see what they want. I'll be here if you should need me, okay?" Gerry said like a true friend.

Patrick had come in by then and asked what was up, and I filled him in.

"Why IA and not the Criminal Investigation Unit or narcotics?" Patrick asked me.

"I'm wondering the same thing. It could only mean they think I did something wrong. I'm feeling a little pissed because it's been more than eight years since my run-in with that scumbag, and I haven't seen him in more than five years or more. Why should IA want to talk to me?"

"Well, don't get pissed, and whatever you do, don't lose your cool. That's all you need to do with those guys and it could mean your entire career turns to shit. Just go there and see what it's all about. Oh, you may want to take your log with you just in case. Do you want me to call our union rep?" Patrick asked.

"Wise words, my friend. No, don't call him yet. I'll get back to you if I need that call, okay?" I was getting angrier by the minute and realized that everything was coming back—how pissed off I was at my wife and taking it out on Louie. *Why are the leaves letting me down? Do I no longer deserve to be sane?* I wondered.

*   *   *

When I walked into the IA office downtown, I felt a little less comfortable knowing that Gerry was not in the building. He was my main man, and I knew I could call on him if I had to. I was trying my best not to get angrier—controlling myself as well as I could. I tried to remember all the anger management lessons I had had with Father Pavlos—taking deep breaths, thinking good thoughts. I knew the drill well.

"I understand that you wanted to see me. I'm Mitch Foley, Detective Kevin Foley," I said in a controlled voice.

"Yes, we know who you are, Mitch. Come on in. Have a seat." The other officers in the room introduced themselves and said that they were investigating the suspicious death of Louis Smith, a known police informant and habitual narcotic user. He had died approximately one week ago as a result of an overdose of heroin, or he was beaten to death. They said that they'd find out the cause of death later that day, but in the meantime they were pursuing a number of avenues and asked if I'd be willing to help them.

"I'll always cooperate on a criminal investigation, but I'm not sure why IA would be involved. Do you suspect that some cop did it?" I came right out with it to avoid any more bullshit about cooperating. My blood was beginning to boil. The two investigators looked like a couple of pansy-assed college kids, and all I could think about was that if one of them got smart, I'd take him down.

"The reason IA is in on this one is that, yes, we think a cop might have been involved, and we were hoping you can help us there because we think you know who that cop is," the talkative one said.

I was about to stand up and face off with the asshole when the other one joined in.

"About five years ago—it was after you and Louie had worked together—a narcotic's officer by the name of Adela Patricia Russell came on the scene and took over control of Louie. Do you remember her?" he asked me.

I was confused at first—why were they asking me about her when they thought I killed Louie? Then it hit me that maybe it wasn't about me.

"Uh, yeah, yeah . . . I vaguely remember her. We had a meeting . . . I guess it was five years ago. She wanted to know all about Louie. Said she'd be handling him for narcotics and took him out of the gang squad's control. He was getting older and more involved with the real dope dealers, not just the young gang members. By the way, you know that I beat Louie up about eight years ago, don't you?" *Get it out now,* I thought. *It's now or never, and I have to find out.*

"Yes, of course we know, but that was long ago and we know you haven't had any contact with him in years. Why, did you think we were looking at you for this one?"

"You never know . . . you never know. Anyway, what's with this Russell woman, and how can I help you?" I said, a lot more relaxed now.

They explained that it would appear Officer Russell had teamed up with Louie on selling dope, and she had disappeared a week or so ago. They were drawing up a profile on her based on interviews with any officers that she might have spent some time with. The fact that she and I had met to talk about Louie was why I was on the contact list.

"Do you recall—I know it's been some time—anything in her demeanor at that time that would lead you to believe she might go bad?" he asked me.

"Ouch, that's tough—how does someone know that a cop will go bad? She was young and relatively new to the department. If I remember right, she was one of the first women officers to go to narcotics, and I thought that was strange. But who wouldn't at that time? There weren't a lot of women—if any—dealing drugs. Or if they were, it was their pimp who got picked up for trafficking, not them. Why they would put a woman in narcotics then I never understood," I told them.

"But nothing outright different about her, like wanting to know his sources, contacts, customers, and all that?"

"Of course she did—that's why we were meeting. She wanted to know all about Louie's business. I didn't think her questions were wrong. They were the same as any other officer getting the assignment would have asked." It was then that I realized why I was so nervous about IA: if they got a beef against you, they were going to make out a case against you no matter what.

163

We continued along this line for a while until it was clear that I knew little or nothing about Officer Russell and couldn't help them anymore in their investigation. They thanked me for my cooperation and asked that I keep the interview confidential until they finished their investigation. Being the good cop, I said that anytime they wanted to talk with me, I'd be available.

When I left headquarters, my anger had significantly decreased, but I was a little scared thinking how close I had come to getting in that one investigator's face and destroying my career. I wondered if this whole war issue was making me angry; if my confusion over our country's policy was ramping up my emotions and turning my feelings of frustration into anger. I knew that could happen, and it worried me. But I did keep my cool, so maybe the leaves were still working on me after all.

*   *   *

I called Gerry later and filled him in without giving up the Russell name, since I had promised confidentiality. I think he knew what was going on, but couldn't give it up either.

"From what you just told me, maybe you should see Father Pavlos for a refresher course on anger management. Do you really think you'd have popped that investigator?" Gerry asked.

"No, I don't think I actually would have done him any harm. But those demons of anger are there, and I have to remember that they're always there and it's up to me to control them, right?"

"I guess so. But you know, maybe somehow those phony dope leaves you played with all those years ago . . . maybe they're still helping you with your, uh, problem. What do you think?" Gerry asked.

"Hey, who's to know? In any case I'm gonna call Father Pavlos and ask about a refresher course like you suggest. I feel it can't hurt, and I like talking with him; he calms me down. Take care, my friend, and let me know what happens in Louie's case. You know, in some sense I'm gonna miss the asshole. He was always a reminder to me to keep my cool, and like so many other people now in this fucked-up world, I need a reminder to stay cool."

I ended our conversation feeling a little better about myself and knowing that I'd be seeing Father Pavlos to help with my issues. It was good to know that there were people in this world who were there for you no matter what, and Father Pavlos, like my pal Gerry, was one of those people for me.

CHAPTER 19

Father Pavlos

I was sitting in my office thinking about my recent conversation with Mitch. He had called to tell me that he needed a refresher course in anger management, but I sensed it went deeper, especially when he told me that he had come close to getting physical again with someone. I asked him to come in to talk about it with me this evening for two reasons; first, I don't think attending another class would help him in his case, and second, I was curious about the lasting ability of the herbs' curative powers.

I also felt it was time that I faced the issue of my role in the whole leaf affair. I knew it was my overactive ambition that gave me this feeling that I was somehow special, but I needed to know once and for all if my role was actually divinely inspired in some way or I was just an observer passing through all the others' lives.

I heard the knock and said, "Come in, Mitch," knowing it would be him.

"Hey, Father, how are you doing?" he asked as he walked in and sat down on the sofa. "Nice new office—glad to see you're moving up," he said with a smile.

"Hello, Mitch. Always a pleasure meeting with you. So, tell me, how have you been?"

Mitch repeated his story about getting angry with the other police officers and was wondering about needing what he called a refresher course. He also added, "And guess what? They just found that Russel woman in Mexico working with one of the drug cartels, so they really weren't looking at me," to more or less confirm that his anger was irrational. "I was getting very angry and maybe even a little paranoid. But you know, Father, looking back at it now, I don't think I would have hurt that guy, even though the feeling was so powerful. I guess I've been getting angrier lately what with Iraq and all. Maybe I should join the army," Mitch said in lighthearted way.

"No, that's not the answer, Mitch," I said, chuckling at his suggestion. "You know that there really isn't anything more I can teach you about controlling your anger that you don't already know. I think you're doing fine since you really haven't hurt anyone in anger in more than eight years. Is there something else you haven't told me?" I asked.

Mitch looked over to at my bookshelf, gathering his thoughts before answering me. "As a matter of fact, there is, Father. You know, I seem to notice that a lot of people are angry today, especially the kids; they seem to be going nuts with anger and distrust of our government. I was wondering why that is. Gerry thinks it's a war thing, like Vietnam years ago, but I don't know. What do you think, Father?" he asked me.

"I wish I did know, Mitch, but I'm sure that whatever it is—societal or otherwise—it will work itself out." I went on to tell him that I thought it was in large part the world situation, the unknown or unpredictability of world outcomes. I felt that it was the young who sensed it the most since they had the most to lose—their future. I then told him that I sensed a loss of faith in many of the young people I came in contact with, and that was what really concerned me.

I said, "They should know that our Lord's love for them is without bounds, and they need to trust his wisdom—just as you do, Mitch—in knowing that He is responsible for you being able to control your anger. Don't you believe that, Mitch?"

"It sounds reasonable to me, Father, but I would hope that at least in my case—you know, with the leaves and all—I'd be more sure of myself and my beliefs, but I'm not. That's why I think I'm getting angry. Maybe I've put too much trust in those leaves, and maybe they aren't the cure-all we thought they were. And if that's true, then maybe I should be scared—or I should say, concerned," Mitch confessed.

"You think the leaves effects are wearing off? Has Gerry been ill recently?" I asked, anxious but staying calm so as not to upset Mitch.

"No, Gerry's great. He was just promoted to captain and had to pass a tough physical, so I know he's okay. No, it's just me that I'm worried about."

I continued to counsel him, saying, "Mitch, your anger seems to be well under control. You shouldn't worry about having a breakdown. As for the leaves losing their efficacy, I have no idea if that will happen, but be assured that your faith in God will guide you to do what is right."

Mitch seemed relieved with those words and thanked me for meeting with him. We promised to stay in touch as he left my office. It was then that

I realized that my role was indeed important. Helping Mitch to keep his faith and put his trust in God more than the leaves was indeed my role, and that was not at all a bad thing. I now knew it was time to call the others to see how they were coping.

* * *

It was a Thursday in June, and I had my T file out with all the previous data I had collected on the recipients of the herbs. I wanted to brief myself before calling. I didn't want to make mistakes on their names, so I carefully read all the information when I called Connie.

"Hello, Connie Sarbanes, this is Father Pavlos calling. How are you?" I said.

"Father, good hearing from you again, and how are you?" he asked. I detected some guilt in his voice because I had not seen him in church in some time, but I was determined not to make him feel guilty.

"Fine, just fine, Connie. Connie, the reason I'm calling is to see if your health . . . that is, your past eye problems . . . are you still free of the disease?"

"I'm fine, Father. In fact Sally and I just got back from visiting her sister in New York, and my eyes are just fine, thanks."

Connie told me about the trip and then filled me in about his concerns about racial profiling at the airport. But upon hearing a sermon at a sister church in Queens on how Doubting Thomas had to see Christ's wounds before he believed, he realized that he would have to be "color blind" and still have faith that he could do his job without putting others in danger. However, his feelings of uncertainty about having to do what was right and what was safe were still with him.

His message was a bit convoluted, but I got the gist of what it was he was trying to tell me. In fact, as I had suspected earlier, all the others had similar stories about feeling conflicted by the impact that the war was having on their lives and how it was straining their justification as to why they had been selected to be cured. They felt that maybe they should have stayed ill or even died, as in Joe Gilbert's case, rather than have to decide what was the right response for them to the war in Iraq. Joe, in particular, was very much torn about giving up weapons research at a time when our country needed it most. Even Nando's daughter felt conflicted about being able to walk now and not wanting to do anything special with her new mobility while the country was at war.

I made careful notes on all the conversations and tried to make sense out of what I had heard from these chosen few. I wrote in my file notes:

> My conclusion is that in some sense I know now, or at least rationalize, why they were chosen. They have all gone on to show concern for all people on earth, regardless of their own personal conflicts for their own well-being and the safety of their loved ones. Could that be why our Lord felt compassion for them? And will his compassion continue, or might some tragic ending still befall one of them? But if it does, will it be because of their exposure to the leaves or in spite of it? I can only hope that one day my Lord will inform me about these matters, but for now I have to wait for Him to make these mysteries known to me, if He so chooses.

As for the personal conflict they felt, I could empathize with them in part. I had also undergone a contradictory experience of faith, but it was during my college years. In my sophomore year I met and fell in love with Vicky Lasko, a lovely young woman of Greek heritage, studying social work at Hellenic. We dated for almost two full years, and I think we were very much in love. We remained celibate, deciding to wait until we were married, which was very difficult at that time. I also felt driven by the fact that if I did remain celibate and did not marry before I was ordained, then I would be eligible for a bishopric at some future time as a celibate, unmarried priest. I guess you might say I was already thinking way ahead about my priestly ambitions.

As it turned out, Vicky and I parted in our senior year. We were still very much in love, but my vacillation about getting married convinced Vicky that I was not someone she could depend on, so we parted amicably but with much sadness on both our parts. I was tremendously conflicted about that decision for some time. And I must admit that to this day I still have carnal thoughts about her—and other woman. How I handle these feelings is known only to me and my confessor. In any case, when I entered the graduate program at Holy Cross, I knew I had done the right thing by deferring marriage.

In my graduate program I became interested—in fact, you might even say obsessed with—priests who were healers. In particular, the life of Saint Savvas, who was beatified and known as a miracle worker, fascinated me. I thought that I could be like that, or rather live the life of an ascetic. If I was chosen as one of our Lord's miracle workers, then that would be more than I could hope for. Through all of this I realized that conflict is expected in life, and sometimes having to deal with conflict can lead to decisions that are far more important to the world around us than they are to us directly.

I read and reread my conclusions many times, which made me recall what I was once told at a Jewish Passover Seder to which I was invited by a member of our ecumenical group. While reading the Passover story from Exodus—as it is the Jewish tradition to do at the Seder—they got to the part about the Red Sea parting and the children of Israel crossing over on dry land. The story related how the Egyptian soldiers followed after them, and once the Israelites were on the other side, the sea closed up and drowned the soldiers. On seeing the soldiers drowning, a cheer supposedly went up from the Israelites, and in their telling of the story, God was heard to say with deep sadness, "Why do you cheer? My children are dying."

My survivors of the leaves, as I liked to call them, would never cheer if any of God's children lay dying. They would try to help or at least solemnly understand, even if it was their enemy who lay dying. I was taught to love my enemy, so maybe, just maybe, that was why they were chosen—because they would not cheer their enemy's death.

I decided then not to bother these good people for a while—to let them live their lives as they saw fit. If anything catastrophic happened to any of them, I would try to counsel them, like I did with Mitch, but only if I was wanted. Otherwise, it was time to let life take its course. I also felt that at some future date someone would contact me again about the leaves, and maybe, if that happened, I'd be in a better position to discuss the whole affair. I had enough to do in my church and with my parishioners to keep me busy and not be sidetracked about things I could neither understand nor hope to deal with in my short time here on earth. I put my T file away and tried to think about my current responsibilities with the church.

But try as I might, my thoughts kept returning to the leaves.

Episode 4

APRIL 2010

CHAPTER 20

Joey Gilbert

Gilbert and Masden Digital Optics, Inc. was supposedly doing well financially on that April Fools day in 2010, or so I thought as I tried to put the pieces of the puzzle together. My partner, Glen Masden, and I were both wealthy beyond our wildest expectations, but something was wrong. I wasn't quite sure exactly what it was, but something was definitely wrong. I was pacing back and forth in my office, showing my lawyer, Brent Collins, bank statements, company accounts, and other personal financial records.

"I can't see any issues here that would concern me other than the fact that the vast majority of your wealth is tied up in company stock, Joe," my lawyer told me. "Look, tomorrow is Good Friday and Sunday is Easter and today's April Fool's Day—are all these holidays making you uptight?" he asked.

I know he was just trying to lighten things up, but I persisted. "Brent, stop patronizing me. It's not just the financial items that are making me nervous, it's the attitude of . . . friends and family. You know what I mean? I told you before that Gabby has grown indifferent toward me, and now I find I can't get Glen to look me in the eye. I'm not paranoid—something is going on here. Either it has to do with money or sex or something, but something is definitely going on."

"Do you want me to recommend a private investigator?" Brent asked.

"I don't know. What do you think?"

"If you're as concerned as you say you are, then that's the best way to do it. Have an unbiased third party who's trained in these things take a look for you. That's what I'd do.

"Do you think you can get someone to start right away? My paranoia is getting to me physically." I said the word paranoia while twirling my finger in front of my ear.

"Okay, okay, I get your message, Joey. I'll let you know when the guy I use for these things has anything to report. It probably won't be until the middle of next week, or maybe even later. Can you keep a lid on it till then?"

I assured Brent I could handle it for now.

The gnawing feeling in my stomach would not go away, but my doctor told me that it was nothing but nerves. Still, the discomfort was there and it was preventing me from doing my best engineering. I was easily distracted, and my crew looked like they wanted, or needed, better leadership from me. I was also nervous about my cancer returning. I'd never been comfortable as to why I deserved to be singled out for the cure thirteen years ago. If I had only saved some of the tea leaves, like I had originally wanted to, then maybe I wouldn't be so anxious.

Glen hadn't said a thing, but I knew he had noticed the change in my work habits and the restlessness of the people in my department. He saw my guys loafing around, acting like they had nothing to do, and yet he said nothing to me. I knew something was wrong. Worst of all, Gabriella and I hadn't had sex in months, maybe even a year, yet she hadn't said a word about that. In the past she would have made some cutesy comment in an effort to get us to make love again. *Are we getting too old for sex?* I wondered. I'd be fifty this year, in fact in about a week or so. But Gabriella was only forty-seven, and that was still young for a woman to be disinterested in sex. *Something's going on.*

* * *

"What do you say we go to Bali for a quickie vacation?" I asked Gabriella that evening during dinner. Lately we hadn't talked much during meals.

At first she looked surprised that I had said something, and then she answered as casually as I had asked, "When do you want to go?"

I was floored at first by how quickly she reacted. There was no hesitation and she was apparently willing to go away with me, unless she thought that because it was April Fool's Day, I was kidding.

"How about, uh, for my birthday? We would have to leave next Friday or Saturday. Would that work for you?"

"Next Friday? That'll work. Why not? Let's do it," she said.

"Okay then. I'll have Dottie make the arrangements. You want to stay at Poppies again? That would be fun, you think? Or would you prefer a little more elegance now, say some fancy resort on Nusa Dua?"

"I don't care . . . a little more luxury might be nice this time. It's been thirteen years and who knows what Poppies might be like now. Let's go for luxury."

The next morning at work I told our office manager to make all the arrangements. "A second honeymoon, Joe?" Dottie asked.

"You might say that. Actually, we went there thirteen years ago for a second honeymoon, so this is maybe a third one?"

"What account do you want me to charge this to? Glen is getting all fussy again about keeping accounts right. You'd think we were paupers the way he's been getting on everyone."

"Charge it all to my personal account. I don't intend to do one bit of business on this trip. It's strictly for pleasure . . . or therapy. And what's this about Glen getting on everyone?"

"Oh, you know how he gets sometimes—acts like we're going broke and gives the guys in accounting all kinds of fits about spending. It's the same ole' shit." Dottie was in her late fifties and had heard and seen it all. She was not easily rattled, but this time she looked concerned about Glen's behavior.

"I'm glad he handles the money and not me. I'd have spent it all on fast cars and wild women. Speaking of which, my wild wife wants this to be a luxury trip, so spare no expense. We're going first class all the way, including a top-of-the-line resort on Nusa Dua. That's what I call therapy," I told Dottie, not wanting to bore her about my personal problems. "That should convince you we're not going broke."

I figured I'd probably have to cancel the trip anyway when I got the private detective's report. I was so sure that we were through that I had played it out in my mind already. I pictured the silent fight, the banging of suitcases, me leaving our nice house, and going I didn't know where (probably a hospice so I could die of cancer in peace). I could see the relief of it being over, the pain of it being over, and being alone. Maybe I'd retire, move to Bali, and spend the rest of my life as a bum on Kuta Beach. The gnawing in my stomach started again. *I'm certain my pancreatic cancer has returned? I need a pill,* I thought.

*   *   *

The Easter weekend was uneventful, and it wasn't until the day before we were to leave that I heard from Brent.

175

"I understand that you and Gabriella are going to Bali tomorrow. Good for you! Don't you have to pack?" Brent asked as he handed me the detective's report.

"Depends on what's in this report," I said as I opened the envelope marked "Confidential and Personal." "Do you know what's in it?"

"Not really. I would prefer you read it first and then if you want to talk about it, well . . . I'm here."

I skimmed through the various paragraphs that succinctly noted what the detective had seen, how he had followed her, the places she had gone, and all the other minutia that he needed to report on in order to justify his fat paycheck. Finally, on the last page was his summary.

> SUMMARY: Mrs. Gilbert was not seen with any other men or women in any intimate or any overtly friendly or compromising setting. I did notice an inordinate amount of cell phone activity, and on investigating her records, I found that a large number of calls were made to 734-663-8990. I have been unable to locate the owner of that number and did not try to call it. Aside from a variety of shopping trips, and as I mentioned, cell phone activity, I am unable to corroborate any clandestine or nefarious activities on Mrs. Gilbert's part.

"God, what an officious schmuck that guy must be," I said as I read through some of the details on Gabriella's activities. "He used the term nefarious like I thought she was some kind of secret agent. All I wanted to know was who, if anyone, she was fucking! It certainly isn't me, so it has to be someone," I said with some disdain to Brent.

"Maybe you're jumping to conclusions. Maybe it's really nothing. I think it's wise you're going to Bali, some place nice this time of year. Get away from all the dreary rainy days we're having, and just settle your issues with Gabriella. You two are such a perfect couple—don't let it end without at least talking it out, okay?" Brent told me. He was a good friend and sincere in his concern for our marriage.

"What the fuck is this number she keeps calling? I bet it's the guy she's having her affair with. I wonder if there's some way I could find out. You'd have thought that the PI could get that information or just call them."

My paranoia was becoming too much for Brent. He wished me safe travel and left after explaining why the private eye would not call an unknown telephone number received during a client-initiated investigation.

When I got home, Gabriella was packing even though it was just late morning and we weren't leaving until tomorrow.

"What's the rush? We don't need that much in the way of clothes for Bali. I thought I'd pack tonight," I said.

"Suit yourself. I just like to have things done so there's no last minute panic."

"When have you ever panicked over a trip?" I asked.

Our conversations were like that lately—short and snippy. Gabriella just ignored me and kept on packing. I thought about our last trip to Bali and wondered if I should try to contact Dr. Setiawan again. Maybe he had some herbs for my stomach. I was recalling that when we got the leaves back from Father Pavlos, I didn't make any more tea, nor did I save any for the "just in case" situation I had mentioned. We took them to Dr. Kahn, and he said he'd get them back to Setiawan. From the few conversations I'd had with Father Pavlos over the years, I was certain he did.

"Are you thinking what I'm thinking?" Gabriella asked me.

"What—about the trip?"

"No, about Dr. Setiawan. Are you going to try to contact him again?"

"Why would I do that? And what made you ask?"

"Nothing, nothing . . . you're in such a shitty mood lately. I can't ask you anything. What the fuck is eating you anyway?"

"Nothing's eating me! I just wondered what made you think about Setiawan after all these years. You got something wrong with you that you need some herbal tea for?" I said sarcastically.

And so it went. Then the silence, always the silence, nothing resolved.

* * *

We checked in at the Intercontinental Bali Resort around eight in the evening on Saturday. It was a long flight with a short layover at Narita Airport in Japan and then an all-day flight to Bali. The weather on the island was great as always: soft tropical breezes, temperatures still in the low 80s, and the smell of tropical flowers everywhere. It didn't have the intimacy of Poppies Cottages, but it did have luxury.

"How do you like this room?" I said, looking around the room with its dark teak wood floors and exotic-looking tropical furniture. Gabriella went over to the balcony and stood outside, staring at the beach and the black ocean beyond. "Let's unpack later. How about a drink?" I suggested "There are a couple of bars here. I'm sure we could find one that has good scotch. What do you say?"

"Sounds good to me," she said. "Even after traveling first class, I still need a drink on the ground just to relax." She had a smile on her face, something I hadn't seen in a while. It was nice.

There was a lot of activity going on in the various restaurants and bars—music was playing in some places, dancing in others. We found the sunset bar that was open to the beach; it was furnished with comfortable chairs and small tables. There was only a handful of other people there, all talking quietly and into their own conversations.

"What can I get you, please?" the waiter asked, putting a bowl of mixed bar nuts in front of us. I saw his name tag—it said Madé.

"Lagavulin neat, if you have it, and a Stoly Martini for the lady, Madé," I said, and I couldn't help but smile when I said his name.

"Olives with that, mum?" he asked.

"Yes, please—do you have any stuffed with anchovies?" Gabriella asked. Madé nodded in the affirmative and went off to place our order.

We were quietly commenting on the nice surroundings and watching the evening activities in the pools and on the beach when our drinks arrived.

"Thanks, Madé," I said.

After the waiter left, Gabriella said, "Would you believe that we have a waiter with the same name as the waiter we had at Poppies—coincidence? I think not." She raised her eyebrows in a conspiratorial way and sipped her martini. "Hmm, that's good."

I sipped my first taste of the good Islay scotch and tried to relax. But it was hard to relax with the 1,500 pound gorilla looking at us over our shoulders; we knew he was there but were afraid to acknowledge him.

"You relaxed now?" Gabriella asked me.

Here it comes, I thought. *Either the confession or the accusation, or both. Which will come first?*

"Feeling fine. Why do you ask? Got something to tell me?" I asked.

"As a matter of fact, I do. You've been so busy these last few months, so short-tempered that I couldn't talk to you about anything. I was thrilled when you asked me to go on this trip with you. What's it been, two years, three years, since we've gone away together?" She took another sip of her drink and looked at me to judge my mood.

I just sipped my smoky scotch, steeling my emotions for when the gorilla would pounce on me.

"There's something I've been wanting to talk to you about, but I couldn't before, so I'm going to do it now while we're both in a better place and you can't run out when I tell you."

My God, she's dragging it out, I thought. I was wondering if she was going to tell me his name or that she was leaving me or something else. *Just get on with it.*

"I've been in contact—in fact quite a bit lately—with a lawyer—," she started to say.

"What the fuck do you need a lawyer for? We have a number of family lawyers? Why do you need a fucking lawyer?" I asked, getting very testy.

"Okay, just relax; it's not what you think—"

"How do you know what I think? You've been so out of my life lately? How could you possibly know what the fuck I think?"

All of a sudden Gabriella blurted out in an emotionally wrought voice, "I want a child! I want a kid! I want someone or something to make my life more meaningful, now that we can afford it. We couldn't have our own—I know we never really wanted any—but now I need something more, something more than just us, our friends, and your business. Something for myself—I want to care for someone who needs me." She was sobbing softly when she said, "Don't get angry. This is not about you for once; it's about me for a change. Can you understand that?" she asked, and she started to sob even more, quietly but noticeably. Madé noticed our situation and stayed discreetly in the background, giving us as much privacy as possible.

I couldn't believe what I had just heard. All of a sudden the gorilla was gone—poof! I was at a loss for words. I wanted to laugh, I wanted to hug her, I wanted to dance. *God, I love this woman more than life itself,* I thought.

"Why didn't you tell me about this?" I asked.

"I couldn't!" she sobbed. "Every time I tried to talk to you, something else more important seemed to take you away. It just got so bad . . . it was just easier not to talk at all."

"God, I'm sorry . . . I'm so sorry. Had I known . . . had I realized I would . . . I would have . . . I don't know. Glen's driving me crazy at work, and now he's just . . . I don't know." I stopped talking, realizing I was doing

179

it again, making it all about me. "But let's keep this about you, okay? You're right, enough about me. So what's this baby all about? Who's this lawyer, and what's he going to do?"

I was so relieved, so filled with love, so excited for her to tell me all about her secret desire and how she was handling it. I called Madé over to order more drinks. He noticed our change in attitude and behavior and was delighted to serve us. He was truly a native Balinese.

"I want to support an orphanage overseas. Not the entire place—we can't afford that—but at least to some major extent. I want a place I can go to a few times during the year to see what they've done with *our* money, and to work there for a few weeks, to get to know the girls and to help them with . . . oh, just so many things. I want to be the mother or the special aunt they never had. I can't tell you how happy this makes me feel. I've been on the phone with Rosetta—she's my lawyer—every day, in fact many times a day. I have such a good feeling when I'm talking with her."

And so it went for hours talking about Gabriella's project—which countries she was looking at, the ages of the children, what organizations were involved, how much she was planning on giving, and all the other details both large and small. She had been at this for almost a year now and was about to finalize it all. She was so pleased to share it with me finally. There was so much she wanted my opinion on. I said yes to everything and more. I was also relieved to know that the 663 telephone number was actually her lawyer for the project.

"Can I go with you sometimes on your stays? That might be fun. How old did you say these girls were?" I asked.

We closed the bar well after midnight. We were the only two left and Madé stayed with us all the time. We felt very relaxed and more than just a little high on the booze, having eaten only bar nuts all night. When we got back to our suite, we ordered grilled cheese sandwiches and apple pie from the room service menu and then ate our very late supper while we continued to talk and plan *our* new venture. When we finally went to bed, we made love and hugged and kissed and giggled as if it had been years since we last enjoyed each other's bodies—and maybe it had been.

* * *

For the next couple of days it was just like it was thirteen years ago, only we spent most of our time at the resort on the beach or in one of the pools instead of going around the island. We ate, drank, and made love like we were in our thirties again, and we simply enjoyed the amenities of a five-star resort. On Tuesday I tried to contact Dr. Setiawan just to touch base and tell him I was in remission—in case he hadn't heard. His old phone number had changed, but I was still able to get through to him.

"Hello, Dr. Setiawan? It's me, Joseph Gilbert, Dr. Kahn's patient. We met thirteen years ago. You probably don't remember me—"

"Yes, yes, I do remember you, Joe. How are you doing? I understand that you've been in remission . . . what is it now, thirteen years? I'm delighted to hear that. I hope all is still going well for you. What can I do for you?"

"Actually, nothing now—I just thought it would be nice for me to thank you personally for the tea leaves you formulated for me. I believe they had something to do with my getting well and just wanted you to know that."

"Well, I'm glad they made you feel better, but herbs alone can't cure serious illnesses like the one you had. I bet your doctors had more to do with your recovery than my herbs. In any event, thanks for calling. If you see Bill Kahn tell him hello for me, and best of luck to you."

"I was a little surprised at how curt he was, like he didn't want to talk about the leaves," I told Gabriella after my conversation. "I guess he wasn't fully aware of the other recipients and how they too were cured, or you would have thought he would have wanted to talk more. Oh well, at least I had the opportunity to finally thank him after all these years."

"Maybe there are other reasons he didn't want to talk about them. Maybe he was aware of their potency, but he too couldn't explain it just like your doctors couldn't. I would think that might bother a doctor—curing someone but not knowing how they did it," Gabriella said. She always had a better intuition about these types of touchy-feely things than I did. I was a little too rational or scientific, where she was far more spiritual. The fact that I was feeling 100 percent better now and the certainty that my cancer had not returned made me drop the whole issue, and we went on to enjoy the rest of our day.

* * *

On Wednesday, however, I had to see what was happening at our company. I had turned my cell phone off and avoided plugging my laptop into the resort's Internet access port, because I just wanted to relax and not think about the office. The pain in my stomach was gone, and just the thought of going online to check my e-mail made me queasy. Gabriella was still in bed and didn't want any breakfast, so I quietly connected my computer and opened my company's site to access my messages.

When I opened my e-mail page, there were around seventy-five new messages that didn't get filtered out and another fifty or so from before that I hadn't dealt with. "Contact me ASAP use phone not e-mail VERY IMPORTANT" was the subject in the first message that caught my attention. It was from Dottie. Dottie was like my Major Domo; she was our chief of staff when neither I nor Glen were around and had our absolute trust. Although her official title was senior office administrator, we were a small company, and with her experience and knowledge of business operations, she was much, much more. She was not one for hyperbole, so if she said it was very important, then it was.

It was around 10:30 a.m. in Bali, so it was around 9:30 p.m. Tuesday back in Ann Arbor. I called Dottie at her house.

"What's so very important?" I asked Dottie.

"Joe, glad you called. Hated to bother you because I know how much you and Gabriella wanted this time together, but I got to tell you what's going on. Glen hasn't been in all this week, and nobody knows where he's gone. You know that's not like Glen—he's such a control freak. Anyway, the guys in finance are going nuts. I tried to charge your trip to your account, but they say it's frozen! They say that all the accounts are frozen! Nobody knows what's going on. I'm scared on this one, Joe, and you know that's not like me. I think you have to find Glen or come home or both!"

Chills ran down my spine when she told me she was scared. I had never bothered with the financials—that was Glen's bailiwick. My recent hunches about Glen and the company's finances now seemed to be significantly more than just a hunch. Dottie understood the financials better than I did, so if anything dealing with money came up that Glen didn't take care of, Dottie did.

"I'll be there as soon as I can. I'll have the concierge get us home—hopefully today or no later than tomorrow. Hold things together, Dot. Gabriella and I will be coming back as soon as it's physically possible," I said with a false sense of confidence.

I filled Gabriella in on my conversation with Dottie.

"Oh, honey, do you really think it's that serious?" Gabriella asked. She was definitely concerned, not just for us but for all the others at the place. She knew them all well. Glen was not married and seldom socialized in the sense of having Christmas parties or other company events, so Gabriella did it all. We packed quickly and were checking out when the manager approached me.

"Sorry to bother you, Mr. Gilbert. I know you have some kind of emergency to attend to back in the States, but your bill was not paid for by your company. Would you mind settling up with us now? Your personal credit card will be fine if that's all right with you," he said in his perfect Australian accent.

It was the same at the airport when I went to turn in our old tickets for new ones. I had to pay either in cash or use my personal charge card. The old bill had not been paid by the company.

Gabriella asked, "What can be going on? You said the company was in good financial straits and that there was lot's of cash around, so what could be happening?"

"I honestly have no idea, honey. I can't for the life of me imagine what's going on. But what I am envisioning is not very pretty."

* * *

It wasn't until Wednesday night Ann Arbor time that we were able to get back. I called Dottie immediately to let her know I was home and would be in first thing in the morning. Glen still hadn't shown, and things had gone from bad to panic.

"Call the department heads tonight and tell them we have an emergency meeting at eight tomorrow morning. I'll call Brent to make sure he's there too. Tell finance that they need to bring everything they've got to the meeting."

Gabriella and I did not get much sleep that night. Jet lag and anxiety gave us both restless nights. Gabriella wanted to know if she should be there in the meeting tomorrow morning.

"No, honey, I think it best we keep it with just the employees for now. I'll call you as soon as I can and let you know what's happening. Thanks anyway . . . I love you very much."

At eight the next morning everyone was in my office: Dottie, Brent, accounting, IT, and personnel.

"Gordo, what's going on?" I asked Gordon Baumgarten, our VP for finance and the head of the accounting department.

"It's serious, Joe. All the accounts are frozen, not just the company's internal accounts, but the bank accounts that fund those are closed too. I can't write checks, pay bills, make financial commitments—"

"Who says they're frozen? You have authority over all those accounts. Can't you unfreeze them?" I asked.

"Not really, Joe. You see Glen has the final say on all funding elements, and only he can get things out of the bank accounts. Yeah, from a company accounting perspective I have the authority, but the money is actually in the bank, and those accounts are all under Glen. You don't even have that authority, Joe. But worst yet, according to the bank—actually an old friend of mine at the bank told me this under strict confidence—all our money was wired out over the weekend to an out-of-country bank. He could not legally tell me the name of the bank or the country it's located in."

"Well, how much is all?" I asked.

"Oh, I'd say maybe ten million in checking, CDs, and savings. At least that's what I have on the books. I don't know—there may be more in accounts I never even had access to. Don't you know how much the company has, Joe?" He was not being sarcastic, he was just deeply concerned.

"What about the stock account?" Brent asked. "Is that held separately? How much in the way of stock is held by the company?"

"You know that's funny, uh . . . no, I mean strange too. The transfer company that holds our stock account was not returning my calls. Last I checked it was still being traded OTC, but way down, under two dollars a share. Just last week when I checked it was more than thirty dollars a share. I have no idea what's going on there either," Gordon said.

Everybody started talking at once. There was a sense of panic; we all had significant portions of our savings in company stock, and we were just beginning to realize what was happening—Glen had stolen all the company cash and was gone. He probably somehow unloaded all his stock as well through a foreign exchange office that did weekend trading, which drove the price way down. We both had about five hundred thousand shares, and with him dumping that much at one time—well, that would scare anybody.

"I'm calling the police and the feds, and I'll have them start an investigation immediately," Brent said. "I should tell you that if he's in some other country—which I strongly suspect to be true—we may never see him or our money again."

"That's way too much for us to believe, Brent," I said, totally devastated. "And what about us now? What about the company? What the fuck are we supposed to do?" I was completely heartbroken by the thought that the company might go under.

Brent didn't know the answer to that one. We started to make plans on how we could survive the crisis and still be a viable company. The first thing we did was to notify all the employees about the situation and Glen's alleged larceny and desertion. The company had around ninety people employed; fifty of them were engineers or scientists. We still had around four large major contracts, and we knew funds would be coming in if we continued to work on them. The real question was whether we could get enough money to tide us over until receivables flowed back in. It was up those of us in the room to find out if we could reorganize the company and make that happen.

*   *   *

It would take a long while for us to get things turned around. Because of the economic situation, we couldn't get enough private loans to keep us afloat. In addition, once the government agencies that were funding some of our work were informed about our senior man stealing corporate funds, the auditors were all over us like flies on shit. I wondered what might have happened if we were still doing classified research. They'd have shut us down in a heartbeat and probably gone after Glen no matter where in the world he was. My guess was that was why Glen agreed years ago to give up classified research; he was planning even that long ago to pull this stunt off._

In order to save the company and the employees' jobs, we agreed to be bought out by the corporate vultures who loved to prey on situations like ours. By late August the old company was dissolved and a new company was formed as a subsidiary of the giant global enterprise, Schlossberger, Ltd., a joint English-German group with their US headquarters in California. They took over the debts we had accumulated over the time we were trying to stay afloat and kept me on as the head of engineering and production. They were able to get the auditors off our backs, and they actually brought in some new contracts, but things were definitely not the same—they never are when you've been your own boss and are now, once again, just another employee. But the others in our small company were grateful to have kept their jobs; good-paying jobs like theirs were very scarce.

* * *

"So, what's the verdict, honey?" Gabriella asked me. "Just how broke are we?"

"You know of course that we can kiss the millions in stock we had good-bye. All our savings were essentially in the old company's stock. We still have around 185,000 left in various checking and savings accounts, and my salary is not all that bad. We also have a few shares of stock in the new company—nothing like we had before though. But we can't afford this house anymore, so we should start looking to downsize. Also, I'm afraid your orphanage plans will have to go on hold for now."

"What a shitty housing market to have to sell our home in. What's it worth? You think we can get one and a half million for it? We paid more than two million and still owe more than a million. Ouch!" she said.

"On the bright side, we should be able to get something nice—maybe a condo—that we can afford for around three or four hundred thousand," I said.

All this talk about finances, downsizing, starting over at fifty—you'd have thought it would depress me, but it didn't. My stomach wasn't in knots anymore, and the relief that the company was no longer my responsibility was in some sense invigorating. I did feel terrible about Gabriella having to put her dream on hold and asked her about it.

"Of course I've been in contact with Rosetta. I've had to tell her what's happened financially, so our big plan is on hold," Gabriella said. "I guess that's a nice way of saying I have to scale down too. In any case she's been great. I'm still staying involved with the orphanage but on a volunteer basis and as a fund-raiser. Hopefully, I will get there one day, but in the meantime I'm in constant communication over the Internet and Skype with many of the girls. Actually, I'm much more personally involved with the girls, and I think that's even better than what I had planned. The great benefactress was not really me."

We sat there looking lovingly at each other for a while—basking in the aura of knowing that we'd gone through an earth-shattering event and survived. I think it was then that the thought hit both of us simultaneously—what if I had died of cancer thirteen years ago? We faced that challenge then, just as we faced the challenge of losing the vast majority of our material wealth now, and we got through it. Of course we had the tea leaves thirteen years ago, and now we only had faith that they were still working.

186

Smiling at me, Gabriella said, "You know this all could have been significantly worse—we may have never reached this point at all. We should be very thankful that we still have each other, a good job, a future . . . a life!"

I had to agree; no matter how bad things seemed, they could always be worse. Setiawan's tea might have cured the cancer, but it must have been something else that cured me and made me what I was now. I actually liked myself, and I was still very much in love with Gabriella, and that wasn't all that bad.

CHAPTER 21

Wayan Setiawan

Even though it had been thirteen years since I ordered that tea for Joe Gilbert, I had never gotten over the whole incident. I was planning on being back in Ann Arbor in a couple of months for our twenty-fifth medical school reunion, and I would be staying with Bill and Lenore Kahn. I knew he'd want to know about the leaves—whether I used them, what I finally did with them, and all the other details about their remarkable properties. I was talking with Arti that Tuesday evening, after I got the call from Joe Gilbert. She knew all about the leaves and what I did with them after talking with my grandmother, so she knew how I felt about them.

"His call today really bothered you, didn't it?" she said.

"I'm not sure 'bother' is the term, but it did upset me. It brought back all those memories of what the leaves could do, and my grandmother's admonishment about all the spirits they contained," I told Arti. "I'm sure Bill will want to know about them, and I'm certain he'll ask. I hope he's forgotten about the whole incident by now, but if he hasn't I'm still trying to figure out how much I'll tell him."

"Tell him everything!" she said. "He's a good friend and he should understand what that medicine put you through. Tell it to him straight out—don't even wait for him to ask, just get it off your chest the first opportunity you get. That way it won't be a burden on your friendship." She caught the troubled look in my eyes and continued. "I wish I could be there with you, but the kids will be starting a new school year, and it's such a long distance for such a short stay. It's just not worth it."

"That's okay, Arti. I know you would have come with me if you could, but I'll be all right," I said. "I think I'll wait till he asks about them and then I'll tell him, but I don't think I'll tell him what my grandmother said or how she told me to get rid of them. He's a Western doctor trained in hard science, and it will be difficult for him to understand our culture and our way of life."

"If you're comfortable with that, then that's what you should do," she said. "But he might be more understanding than you give him credit for. He knows that there are many things in this world that science alone cannot explain, and the leaves are certainly one of them.

*   *   *

The next day I was sitting in my office during my regularly scheduled office hours and thinking about Joe Gilbert and the leaves. I was feeling bad that I was so brusque with him and thinking maybe I should have talked to him more about his situation—how he felt now, what his take on the leaves were, did he believe that his cure was supernatural in any sense. Not that I could have shed any light on his case, but the question would have been more for my own edification.

I kept thinking back to my grandmother. She had never said that the phantoms in my leaves were good or bad, or just benign as they sometimes are. But I knew that she never liked getting close to or talking about the spirits that inhabit all things. She had great respect for them, and I would say it almost bordered on fear. On the other hand, I have always had an interest in them for medical purposes, but I haven't met anyone as knowledgeable as my grandmother, rest her soul. I had older aunts and uncles who I thought possessed her knowledge, but it turned out they didn't. So all I'm left with is what she taught me years ago and what she told me to do at times when I was confronted with the mystical aspects of healing.

I was interrupted in my thoughts by a graduate student.

"Dr. Setiawan, do you have a minute?"

"Yes, of course, come in," I told the student. She was in the homeopathic medicine and pharmacy department, working on her PhD in pharmacology. "You've caught me at a good time, since I was just thinking about herbs and herbal cures. What can I do for you?"

"I'm at an impasse in my research for my dissertation," she said. "I can't seem to find a good research method for evaluating the efficacy of traditional herbal medicines. The majority of my data is anecdotal, and I know that phenomenology alone will not cut it. Can you show me how I can evaluate nonstandard medicines that have never been through any clinical trials?"

I gave her a mini-lecture on surveying clinicians and then using some multivariate statistical methods on her survey results. It was not easy and still based in part on anecdotal data, but at least it was scientifically more rigorous than softer methods. I knew that herbs were either something unique in their own right or a manifestation of some special chemical combinations. I gave my student some good statistical references to use, told her to pick a few methods that seemed to make sense to her, and then come back and I'd help her put together her research agenda. She was pleased to be pointed in the right direction and thanked me. She left clearly excited to be moving forward on her thesis work.

*   *   *

Working with my grad student brought back my training on research methods. For the next few weeks I spent much of my free time wondering if I could come up with a way to scientifically analyze my own leaves for the nausea remedy I gave Joe Gilbert. I took out all my charts on the patients I gave the tea to thirteen years ago, to see if there were any patterns that I could discern from their treatments. I also wanted to see if there was enough data there to be able to do some good scientific analysis.

There were around two dozen cases that I had treated before I incinerated the leaves. I still remembered some of them quite well and was surprised to see that in almost all cases, once I treated them I never saw them again, with the single exception of the first person I treated since I was able to follow up on him. Most of the others were treated in their villages or in my primitive clinics located at major country crossroads, so it didn't surprise me that I didn't see them again. I suspected many of them died, since I only treated patients that I thought had a slim chance of surviving. I knew they would never consent to come into a modern hospital. I just tried to relieve their pain and make their last days as comfortable as possible.

There were a few patients who came back over the years—but not as patients. They came in with other family members who were sick and seeking treatment specifically from me. I didn't make any notes in their records when they came in to have someone else treated, but I remembered that they were always praising me for saving their lives. They didn't mention the tea, just the fact that I had treated them, and that they thought I was the one that had the power to heal—at least that was what they told me. Some even told me about major devastating events that occurred in their lives that ended up being good for them and their families. They also thought that was due to my treating them.

I didn't think that was unusual at the time, since Balinese people were very spiritual and it wasn't surprising that they thought that a doctor would have mystical powers of healing. I got similar responses from patients that didn't receive the tea. But as I recalled, the ones that I saw that did get the tea seemed different. They had an aura, a glow, that my grandmother claimed to see in some people. She told me that those people had been blessed by the gods. She said that I, as a doctor and as her grandson, would see it too eventually. I never believed I could see it, but on those occasions when these former patients came in, I think I did.

Maybe it was just the praise they gave me and the glowing expressions on their faces, or maybe it was that aura that my grandmother said was there in some people, but there was something noticeably different about them that apparently only I saw, since my assistants and nurses never commented on it. It wasn't very many patients—a handful at best—but I do remember it because it happened so rarely. I was so pleased to see that the patients had recovered that I didn't go back to see what they were being treated for in the first place. I was just happy that they survived whatever it was they were originally diagnosed with. I knew that many seemed to be cured almost instantly, and that was why when I couldn't reproduce the formula, I asked my grandmother what to do. But even so, confirming that some were still alive after all these years further convinced me that the tea was indeed mystical.

As a researcher, I was now distressed that I hadn't been more careful in how I decided who to treat and why I didn't keep better records than I did. I was at least smart enough to keep their files in a separate folder I called my tea file for the tea treatment I gave them.

Again I wished I had been nicer to Joe Gilbert when he called. I should have gone over and seen him, to see if he had the aura too. Maybe when I went to Ann Arbor in September I'd call him and be more considerate than I was to him a couple of weeks ago.

*　　*　　*

I also decided to reexamine the process by which the nausea remedy was formulated, to see if there was some way to reproduce the mixture. But I soon realized, once again, that the combinatorial analysis I did thirteen years ago, when I found out that my tech had unintentionally mixed an entirely new compound, was still valid—it couldn't be done. My research question, "Were the leaves' cures based on sound pharmacological underpinnings?" was impossible to test from any data I had now or would ever have in the future.

I was left with only one conclusion: modern science could not help me find the answer to the leaves' powers. And if present-day science didn't do it, then the only other choices were mystical or science that we still didn't know about. In other words, there was something in the makeup or structure of the mixture such that independently no one herb could have been responsible for the cure, but all the leaves working under some unknown pharmacological principal (or other power) did the trick. What that unknown power was I would probably never know. The only person in the world who might have known what that answer could be was my grandmother, and she was gone. So I had to leave my conjecture at that plateau—hanging there unanswered. It was more rational to accept that I would never have an answer to a complex question rather than drive myself crazy, thinking that I must know. Most religions essentially called that faith.

After talking with Joe earlier in the month, I wondered about the other people around Ann Arbor that received the treatment—how were their lives changed by the leaves? Had they faced any other life-altering experiences that were in any way dealt with from their response to receiving the leaves? Maybe I would find that out when I went to my reunion. After all, it was life's many mysteries that made my job more interesting and rewarding than most. *I am so glad to be a doctor, able to reduce suffering and keep people around a little longer to enjoy the one life we have here on earth*, I thought as I put away my tea file.

CHAPTER 22

Nando Garcia

We had just returned from Maundy Thursday mass. It was still light at 7:30 p.m., although very cloudy, since daylight savings time started earlier now. We hadn't eaten yet, and we were hungry, especially Maria Elena—she was always hungry.

"Mami, what's for dinner?" she asked.

"Something light, baby. Tomorrow's your birthday, the big two one! I'll make you something special, your favorite dinner. I'm planning on cooking pescado the Veracruz way—you know, my own recipe—and we'll have white wine with dinner now that you'll be old enough to drink wine at the table. Is that okay?" Maribel said.

Easter is a special holiday for Mexicans, especially for people like us from Veracruz. And Good Friday was our special day, a day of much pageantry and celebration, frequently ending with a fish dinner, or I should say, a feast. But Maria Elena had grown very heavy. She was around two hundred pounds, and for someone a little more than five feet tall, she was very round. Many of the people from our part of Mexico, people of Afro-Cuban ancestry, were a little on the heavy side, but Maria Elena was beyond a little heavy.

"With all the food Mami is making for tomorrow, maybe we shouldn't eat anything tonight. What do you say we fast?" I said jokingly, but also a little seriously.

"No way! I'm hungry," Maria Elena said.

"When aren't you hungry?" I asked.

"Okay, that's enough, Nando," Maribel said. "Stop picking on her. She's trying very hard to loose weight. She does what her therapist tells her, and that's okay with me. So stop ragging on her!"

193

"I'm not ragging on her. I just think she needs to try a little harder. It's not healthy for her to carry around that much weight. It's bad for her heart."

"Papi, stop talking like I'm not here. I know all those things. Don't you think I'm trying my best to cut back to a normal diet? Don't you think . . . ah, fuck it!" said Maria Elena. She started to cry and ran into her room.

"See what you've done? You've made it worse and on such a holy day. Why don't you just leave her alone?" Maribel said.

"Oh, for Christ's sake, it's always me, isn't it? I'm the bad guy for just trying to help her out of a bad situation. She needs more help than that damn so-called therapist is doing with his charts and writing things down and weekly weigh-ins. She needs some good old-fashioned Veracruz style medicine, that's what she needs!" I shouted.

Hearing my rant Maria Elena slammed her bedroom door. She didn't come out for dinner or even a late snack. But I knew she had candy and other unhealthy things in her room, even though Maribel claimed she'd never seen any snacks hidden in there.

"What are we going to do with her?" I asked Maribel later when we were in bed.

"*We* are going to continue to support her efforts with her therapist. *We* are not going to yell at her or make her feel even more unwanted and undesirable than she already feels. *We* are going to continue to love her and—"

"I know, I know, but you know and I know that her therapist is for shit and a real waste of money. I'm going to look into some other more traditional therapies, some Veracruz therapies. Her problems go much deeper than eating. Having the baby was just the beginning; we should have started working with someone then, but—"

"So who are you going to get? Some quack from Catemaco, a *brujos* from the streets promising all kinds of cures for anything?"

"Stop it!" I said, "Just stop it. You know I wouldn't do that. But there are curanderos—honest healers—around who practice our type of folk medicine. I think I should talk to one, and see if they could help. Will you support me?"

"And what choice do I have?" Maribel answered. After reflecting a bit, she said, "You are right; she needs more help than we can give her. Too bad you returned that Greek incense—how long has it been, thirteen years? Maybe it would have worked for her again."

"That's funny you should mention that because that's exactly what started me thinking about curanderos. We'll just have to put our faith into his hands and hope for the best. I no longer know what to do, and I'm tired of seeking help from *gringos* who just don't understand our culture," I said with impatience. After thinking about what I said, I followed up with, "You know I don't mean any offense by that, but it's true, and as much as I love this country, these people just don't know anything about our world, our habits, or our religious beliefs, even though we are all supposedly Christians."

"Nando, don't lecture me. On that issue I agree with you 100 percent. I'm tired, and we have a busy weekend coming up, so let me sleep." With that Maribel turned to one side and closed her eyes.

*　　*　　*

I made contact with a curandera, a female shaman, who went by the name of Teresita, a name famous in my part of Mexico for someone who healed by using a variety of herbs, prayers, and incantations. She said she might be able to treat Maria Elena for her ailments and asked me to drop by, alone, for a consultation first. It was Tuesday, April 6, when I walked into her office on West Michigan Avenue above some older stores, typical for that part of the city. It was still raining, as it had been for most of the week.

"Senora Teresita?" I said.

"Please, just Teresita," she said as she motioned for me to sit down on a large couch in her office. It was just one room, sparsely furnished with a large closet I could see off to the back and a door I suspected that led to a bathroom. It was in an old building, like a number of buildings in downtown Ypsi, and the wood had not been modernized at all—dark walnut. I thought it might be a bit dreary for her practice, but if it worked for her, I couldn't complain.

"So let's start from the beginning. You said your daughter, Maria Elena, was having problems; what kind of problems?" Teresita was a tall, not very dark woman in her late forties or early fifties. She didn't look like someone from Veracruz, but I had no reason to doubt her when she told me she was from my part of Mexico.

I started to tell her about Maria Elena. "She was diagnosed with Duchene's muscular dystrophy when she was an infant, but she's been in remission for many years now." I related what had happened to her, how she became out of control as a teenager, and how it carried through until after graduation.

"In December 2007 she insisted on getting married. Her high school boyfriend for all of one year wanted to marry her and couldn't wait. We were against it, of course, but finally, as she knew we would, we let her marry him. And as soon as she got pregnant in the spring, he took off."

"Are they still married? Is the father involved with the baby?" Teresita asked.

"No, no, we never saw him again, and with counseling from our priest, we had the child placed for adoption immediately after he was born. That was in January last year. She—that is, Maria Elena—never got over it. She wanted to keep the baby, but there was no way." I hesitated after that, and then began again. "She changed; she let herself go, getting very overweigh. She just turned twenty-one, and she weighs almost two hundred pounds now. She sits around the house all day watching TV or reading."

"How does your wife feel about her behavior?" the curandera asked.

"Maribel, my wife, is always defending her, even after she had the baby last year. She said it was our fault that Maria Elena got pregnant. We let her do pretty much anything she wanted to do, including getting married, so what did we expect."

"Do you agree with her?"

"I guess in some sense she's right. After she was cured, or I should say went into remission from MD, we spoiled her half to death; anything she wanted she got. We tried to make up for all the years of pain and her lost childhood by letting her have or do just about anything she asked for. But she was such a good little girl that I did not think there was any way we could have spoiled her. I guess now I was wrong about that."

The curandera just listened; she didn't take any notes or write anything down, not even my name or address or anything about us.

"Do you think that she would come here, by herself, and spend some time with me, say about an hour or two a week at first, and then we'll see how that works out?"

"I don't see why not," I said. "I'll ask her tonight. When should she come in?"

After agreeing on a date and time, I left her office. I felt a little uneasy going back to work at West Middle School, like maybe I was making a mistake to trust my daughter to a complete stranger. I had only gotten the curandera's name a week or so ago from someone I hardly knew at church, but he had seemed pretty confident about her credentials when he recommended her.

After work I went home, anxious to tell Maribel about Teresita and how she felt that she could help Maria Elena.

"I made an appointment for her for next Monday at eleven. If she'll go, will you drive her?" I asked Maribel.

"If she'll go, of course I will. But let's see if you can get her to go. I have enough trouble getting her to the dietician, but if she'll go to your curandera, I'll drive," Maribel promised.

I went into Maria Elena's room; she was lying on her bed reading. "Hi, sweetheart, and how's my girl today?"

"Hi, Papi, I'm fine. I'm reading this great book about a Mexican hero. Emiliano Zapata was his name. Have you heard of him?" she asked me.

"Of course I have! Had you been raised in Veracruz, you would have heard of him from the very first day you went to school."

"Then why didn't you ever tell me about him, Papi? You schooled me from my first day of school, and I don't remember you ever saying anything about Zapata."

"I guess I was trying so hard to teach you about this country and subjects that the other children your age were taking that I forgot to tell you about our own culture," I explained. "I'm sorry, sweetheart, and I see now that was a big mistake." I waited for a minute and then I said, "In fact, that is exactly what I want to talk to you about."

"Learning more about our heritage?" she asked.

"In a way, yes, you see there is this woman who knows all about how in our culture we deal with all kinds of problems, and she told me she would be delighted to meet with you and explain the ways of our people. Would you like to meet her?"

"What kind of problems are we talking about, Papi?" she asked me warily.

"Problems like living a life of independence and understanding what is best for oneself—even like Zapata himself, knowing when one must be a revolutionary in his or her own home. And also like Zapata, being brave enough to accept life's challenges. Are you interested?" I asked.

"Sounds like something I would be interested in. When do I go?" she said with a smile on her face like she had when she was a little girl.

* * *

On Monday, April 12, Maria Elena was dropped off at the curandera's office at 11:00 a.m. sharp. Maribel told her that I'd be waiting for her out in front from 11:45 a.m. on, and depending on how Maria Elena felt, we might go out for lunch after her appointment. At around noon Maria Elena walked out of the office and got into my car.

"You feel like having some lunch?" I asked.

"Don't you want to know what happened in there first?" Maria Elena answered.

"Of course I want to know. I just thought that we could talk about it over lunch, that's all."

"I think I just want to go home. Maybe I'll have some fruit and read the materials Teresita gave me. There's tons of it," she said as she lifted a handful of pamphlets, loose-leaf pages, and articles. "She also gave me this." Maria Elena held up a small plastic bag of herbs and explained, "She said I should store these in the freezer. I should make a cup of tea with them every morning. She made me some in the office and added some honey. Do we have any honey at home?" she asked me.

"I don't know, sweetheart, but we can pick some up on the way home," I said. My voice was a little subdued because I was surprised that Maria Elena had passed up an opportunity to eat out. But even more important, Maria Elena wasn't ranting about having to go to some idiot who didn't understand her problems, and that was a first.

When we got home, Maria Elena went right to her room.

Maribel asked me, "How did it go? Did she seem all right about the curandera?"

I told her it seemed to have gone just fine.

After a quick sandwich I went back to work. Later in the day when I got home I asked Maribel how Maria Elena was.

"Go see for yourself. She's in her room."

I gently knocked on her door and then walked in. "Hi there, sweetheart. You didn't tell me earlier, but what did you think of Teresita? She's a striking woman, isn't she?"

"Papi, hi! Yes, she is striking, and I think we really hit it off just great. We talked for almost the whole hour, and you saw the tons of things she gave me to read—that's what I've been doing all afternoon—and I loved the way she massaged my neck and back. And all the time she massaged me she was humming and singing in a Spanish dialect that I've never heard before. She said it was NA-watya. Have you ever heard of that?

"Nahuatl, she was singing in Nahuatl? I didn't think she looked like a Nahuan woman. That's a native Mexican of Aztec descent, honey. Hey, but you can't tell everyone by just looking at them, right? And what else did you do?"

"I don't know. We drank tea and talked about me, what I wanted, how I felt about myself, what my plans were, if I went to church—she wanted to get to know me, that's all. She told me that she was Catholic too, but she knew other religions that she believed in as well—ancient ones. I think that's cool. Just like you said to me when you asked if I would go—understanding what is best for me, Maria Elena, not everyone else. That's what we did, that's what we talked about."

"That's great, honey. I'm assuming you have other appointments with her, right?"

"Yeah, I have to go back again on Wednesday after I've read all this stuff, and then probably just once a week as I see the need—it's my choice," she said with a firm and determined voice. "Just like Zapata, I can choose what is right for me and not have somebody else choosing for me!"

"You mean like me?" I asked with a smile on my face.

"I know you love me, Papi, but just this time let me make the decision, okay?"

"Whatever you say, honey, whatever you say," I said with a sigh of relief that we were off to a good start with Teresita.

I couldn't help but think about the incense that cured Maria Elena's MD, and how that, too, was probably based on ancient beliefs and practices that came from some country having primitive religions like the Aztecs. I only hoped it was true and that maybe once again we would see a miracle transformation for Maria Elena. But I was also prepared to be disappointed, because I wasn't sure that we—specifically, our little family—were deserving of two miracles in one lifetime.

I didn't ask Maria Elena if they talked about her weight problem or how she was coping with having to give up her baby, but I assumed that since I told Teresita those things, she probably covered that too. I was so pleased to see Maria Elena take such an interest that I wasn't about to jump in with all kinds of advice. I had also noted out of the corner of my eye that the readings she got seemed to be mostly about nutrition and health, so I didn't push it or ask her to tell me about them. After all, she was twenty-one now, not a child; she should be making her own decisions.

"Oh, and Mami said I could take her car to our meetings so I wouldn't need her to drive me there. That was nice of her, wasn't it, Papi?"

She called them meetings not sessions—that was refreshing. And she was willing to drive herself, something she hadn't done for some time. She'd take the car to the store or to visit a friend, but she never drove herself to any of the various therapy sessions that we had arranged for her over the last year. I thought we were finally on to something.

*   *   *

On Monday I got word from the adoption agency to come in and discuss some personal matters about Maria Elena's son. He was born in January 2009, and his prearranged adoption was with a family from the Detroit area. It was not an open arrangement, so we knew nothing about the adoptive parents.

"You wanted to talk with us about Maria Elena's baby, Mr. Baldacci?" Mr. Antonio Baldacci was the agency's director. He looked very nervous and upset.

"Yes, yes, thank you so much for coming in. I don't see Maria Elena with you. Is she all right? Is she back with her husband?" he asked.

"She's fine, and no, as far as we're concerned her husband deserted her for good. We've had the marriage officially annulled by the church. She's not here because she has a standing appointment at this time, and without knowing what this was all about, I thought it best that I come in alone."

"Of course. Do you recognize this?" he asked me as I sat down in the chair in front of his desk. He handed me the pre-adoption information sheets that we had filled out before the final papers were signed.

I looked at the forms and said, "I recognize the forms, but these are not the ones we filled out. They're missing lots of information, and that's not my handwriting—I clearly remember since I was the one who had filled it out for Maria Elena. She was having a lot of trouble dealing with the whole episode so I thought it best."

"Yes, yes, I was afraid of that. Let me get right to the point. It seems that Maria Elena's son has been diagnosed with muscular dystrophy, and the parents are beside themselves. They—or I should say their lawyer—wants to know if we knew that the child was possibly predisposed to MD when they adopted him, since that information was not listed on the child's health history." Mr. Baldacci rubbed his eyes and sat back in his chair and continued. "I also remember you and your daughter and how hard it was for her to give him up. And I do remember her telling me that she had MD as a child but was in remission," Baldacci said. "I think what happened here is that the original papers you gave us either got lost or were put in someone else's folder. You know that we're a small, privately run Catholic group and depend heavily on volunteers." He looked emotionally sapped while he explained. "No matter, their lawyer wants to sue us. Either we agree to pay for the child's medical care for the rest of his life or we must take the child back. We're at a loss. Our legal advisor told me to contact you and see how you feel about the whole thing."

I was in shock. I didn't quite understand why he would contact me; I thought we were done with the matter when the adoption was final.

"Why would any parent of any child, no matter how sick the child was, want to give their baby up?" I realized what I had said and explained. "I guess, that is, unless they were in the same circumstances as we were with Maria Elena's baby." I waited a minute and then asked, "What is it you expect of us? Do you want us to sign new papers or what?"

"No, no . . . we were just thinking that maybe now after more than a year, Maria Elena—she's twenty-one now, right?" he said, looking at the file on his desk. "She might want to reconsider the adoption. If we take him back here at our orphanage, it would be almost impossible for him to be readopted. We simply can't afford to pay his expenses outside our facility, so we would have to care for him here. We just thought that . . ." Again he sat back, looked at the ceiling, rubbed his eyes, and then shook his head back and forth.

I wanted to vomit. I felt sick to my stomach. The thought that my grandson was being made parentless over some ridiculous legal issue really bothered me.

"What are you asking of us, Mr. Baldacci? That decision to put him up for adoption was the most horrific thing we as a Catholic family had to go through—almost as horrific as having an abortion. And now you want us to go through with that again? What are you asking?" I pleaded.

"Please, call me Tony," he said, not looking me in the eye and still shaking his head. "I guess I'm asking you, or I should say, we're asking Maria Elena if she would like to care for her son—be his mother again, only this time forever." He waited before quickly adding, "I know . . . I know how unfair that may seem to you, but believe me I'm only doing it for her son's sake. We will of course take him back, but raising a child in this place, especially one that will have serious medical needs as he grows older, is not a desirable outcome. I just thought that your family should have the choice, that's all. I will not think any less of you or Maria Elena if you walk out the door and don't look back. I promise never to bother you again, but . . ."

"I see what you're asking." I felt numb, unable to move for a few minutes. "Let me talk it over with Maribel and Maria Elena. After all, it's really their decision more than it is mine. It will be Maribel who will have to do much of the work, so she should decide. How soon do we have to tell you our decision?" I felt like I was right in thinking that the curandera's power to heal was too much to ask for. We would not see another miracle cure for Maria Elena's problems or our suffering through them.

"Actually, there's no real rush. We've already started proceedings to take the child back, and he'll be here within the month," Baldacci said. "Once that's done, and if Maria Elena decides to take him home, we can finalize the papers in very short order for her to take full legal custody once again."

*   *   *

"So what do you think Maribel?" I asked that night after telling her and Maria Elena about my meeting with Baldacci.

"Why are you asking, Mami? It's my decision . . . mine alone to make, and I want my son. I want my Juan Carlos. I want my little prince back," Marie Elena said, sobbing so heavily that she could hardly breathe.

Maribel and I just stared at each other. "Juan Carlos? When did you name him Juan Carlos?" I asked Maria Elena, but she was crying so hard now she could not talk. We waited until she could speak.

"If you only knew how hard I've prayed . . . how much I've wanted him. If you only knew," she said, and she started sobbing so hard again that she could hardly catch her breath.

"It's okay, honey, it's okay," Maribel said as she put her arms around Maria Elena. "I understand, I really do. I know how you feel." Maribel started to cry too.

I sat there watching the two of them hugging each other and crying. I didn't know what to say. Maybe this was something only women knew about. I knew it would be a tough decision, but now I wasn't sure what was happening, so I kept my mouth shut. Then all of sudden Maria Elena started talking, spewing her words out in short, sharp thoughts like an erupting volcano.

"Teresita said today this would happen—she knew it, she knew it. We were preparing for it. It was all planned out. We prayed to so many gods. We sang together . . . oh my God, she knew it, she knew it," Maria Elena said.

"Knew what? That your baby was coming back to you! How could she know that?" I asked excitedly.

"No, no . . . not exactly, but she knew that my life was changing, that a new challenge was coming that I had to prepare for, a challenge so strong I could no longer just think of myself . . . think of killing myself, a new beginning, a new—"

"Killing yourself? You were thinking of killing yourself?" I said in total disbelief.

"Oh, Mami . . . Papi, I know you both love me, but I also know how much pain I'm causing you. I could think of no other solution, but then you sent me to Teresita—my savior! I don't know, maybe it was Zapata; maybe it was what you said, Papi, about why I should see her. But when we started to meet, first with the tea and the singing and the massages, and her telling me about parking the car so I would have to walk to the office . . ."

Maria Elena was all over the place, and I had trouble keeping up with her. "Hold it, wait a minute, but when did she know about your Juan Carlos and that he'd be coming home?"

"It wasn't like that . . . oh, you'll never understand, will he, Mami?" she said looking to Maribel for support.

"It's okay, honey, I understand . . . it's okay. So we're saying that Juan Carlos—you'll call him John, right?—is coming home for us to love and take care of no matter what. Is that right?" Maribel said.

"I always knew that God gave me MD so that I would understand what it's like and then be able to care for someone with MD, I always knew that. And Teresita knew that too. I was destined for that challenge, and she was preparing me for it. And I will work very hard to get myself back in shape, to get a job so that I can support my baby and take good care of him. I know I can do it . . . just like Zapata . . . just like my Papi. Right, Mr. T?" she said with a knowing smile.

*   *   *

Nothing more had to be said that night. Juan Carlos was coming home, and the three of us would care for him until such a time that Maria Elena could care for him alone or, God willing, with her own family someday. Somehow it all seemed to work out after all. For a time over the last few years I had almost wished that Maria Elena was not cured of MD—that she had stayed dependent on us, and that way she would not have been so wild and married so young and become so unhealthy. But that was not to be, and now things seemed to be coming around—normalizing, you might say. But what got me the most was her calling me Mr. T—how did she know about that? Was she saying that she knew it was the incense that cured her? Maybe someday I'd ask her.

Episode 5

LATE SUMMER 2010

CHAPTER 23

Father Pavlos

It had been five years since I'd talked to anyone about the leaves, and I felt the need to check in again with them. I was going on fifty-one, and the thought of getting a bishopric was still possible if I was deemed worthy. I had said that I would let nature take its course and I would just assume that the individuals were all leading normal lives, but I couldn't let it go at that. I was recently contacted by Dr. Kahn and asked if I would like to meet with him and Dr. Setiawan in September when the Indonesian doctor would be coming into town for his medical school reunion. I was so surprised that they would want to meet with me about the leaves that I, of course, wholeheartedly accepted his invitation. I also felt that this meeting was just the excuse I needed to talk with all of the leaf recipients again.

I had seen Mitch on occasion—in fact earlier this year he spoke at one of our ecumenical meetings—but none of the other recipients. Mitch always told me, without me even asking, that he and Gerry were doing fine, which to me was his way of saying the leaves were still working.

A week or so after Mitch's talk at the church meeting, he called and told me that he had recently gotten engaged to the police officer stationed in the high school. He said he had worked with her on occasion and wanted to know if I would attend the wedding, and naturally I said I would.

Mitch went on to tell me a most interesting story of how they finally got together and what happened to her and how she almost lost her life after an altercation with a violent student. He said that for a while there he was so upset that he felt that he was angry enough to do great physical harm to the person who attacked his fiancée. But after he caught the student who beat her, he maintained his professional demeanor and did her no harm. He said that he came away from the incident certain in the knowledge that if that didn't make him become violent again, then nothing would. Finding Cheryl was the fulfillment of his life's dreams, he said, and when he thought that he might lose her, it was the most devastated he had ever felt. But he also believed that his exposure to the leaves had not only prepared him for the worst life had to offer, but also for the best that life had in store for him.

I told him how pleased I was for him and his fiancée and that I was even more pleased to know that his faith in God and the leaves was not breached. Even after being faced with such a life-altering experience, his healing had survived and he was better off for having faced it and come away healthy.

After talking with Mitch, I contacted the others to see what—if anything—had happened in their lives that might have changed their outlook on their faith in the leaves.

I called Connie Sarbanes and asked how he was and if anything in his life had happened that might have affected him or his family in any way out of the ordinary. Needless to say, I was quite upset to find out that with less than one year of work left before he was eligible to retire, Connie—along with a number of other TSA agents—had been forced out of the agency. He had been made to take early retirement, for which he only received half of his full retirement benefits. If he hadn't accepted that, he would have been placed on indefinite layoff with little, if any, chance of coming back.

Just prior to learning about his forced retirement, Connie had found out that he had been accepted into the certificate program in human services at the community college. He had anticipated going into a new and, for him, more satisfying career after retirement. But after learning about his new financial status, he felt he couldn't afford to go back to school and even entertained thoughts of suicide. However, with the help and understanding of his wife Sally, he realized that he would still be able to go to school, with only minor adjustments to their lifestyle. They knew that in less than two years he would be able to enter into a new profession—although a lower-paying one—where he would be helping others.

I had never heard Connie sound happier and more excited about the direction his life was taking. He continued to credit his exposure to the leaves and the Holy Spirit with his being able to see again. Now he felt that the leaves and his faith gave him the ability to go back to school and enter a whole new career in a field he felt certain he was always meant to be part of.

And it was the same with the Gilberts and Garcias. Both families had gone through life-altering experiences and came out of them better off emotionally and spiritually, if not necessarily better off financially.

There had to be a lesson in all this that I hoped to be able to grasp when I finally met with Dr. Kahn and Dr. Setiawan in September. I dug up my old T file and started to read it in order to refresh my memory about all the years I'd been living with the leaves. It was like reading it for the first time. Once again I felt our Lord had chosen them—and maybe me—for something special. I guessed my role in the saga might merely have been helping them to find our Lord in the healing. And that wasn't such a minor role after all, was it? I looked forward with some anticipation to meeting the doctors and hopefully settling the mystery once and for all.

Chapter 24

Wayan Setiawan

My old friend and colleague Dr. William Kahn was waiting for me at the baggage exit from the United Airlines terminal at Detroit Metro. He spotted me coming out of the secured area.

"I can't believe you're here," Bill said when he saw me. "What is it now, almost twenty years? Has it been that long? So glad to see you. How was your flight?"

We walked out of the building with our arms around each other's shoulders on that beautiful sunshiny day in mid September.

"Long! The flight seemed much longer than I remember—even traveling business class; Denpasar to Singapore to Chicago and then here," I said, shaking my head as if exhausted—which I was. "It's going to be so great to be in Ann Arbor again, though. How are you? How's Lenore? I bet she looks just great, doesn't she? And you—you still look like a young stud."

We were both smiling broadly as we got into the waiting Lexus hybrid van with Lenore Kahn in the driver's seat.

"You can see for yourself. She insisted on driving out here to welcome you," Bill said.

Lenore greeted me. "Hi there, stranger. So good to see you again. I'm your chauffer," she said as the three of us drove off toward the expressway back to Ann Arbor.

Bill started to tell me all about the reunion. He was very excited.

"Our twenty-fifth reunion should be fun—if it's anything like my twenty-fifth high school reunion was. I know that everyone will be looking like a bunch of fat old farts." He paused while looking out the car window and beaming, before saying, "I'm really looking forward to seeing some of those old farts. And I know they're looking forward to seeing you."

"And as if you don't look like an old fart," Lenore proclaimed.

"No, he doesn't," I said. "And you . . . wow! You're looking great, Lenore."

"You better watch him, honey—he goes wild away from the island," Bill teased.

And so the good-natured banter continued as we drove back to Ann Arbor during rush hour traffic. When we got to the Kahn residence and I settled in, we sat down for a drink and to simply reacquaint ourselves with each other. Seeing someone face to face after a number of years can be a strange experience for old friends, even if they'd been in frequent contact over the years by phone and e-mail. This was the first time we were all together in some time. After about an hour of mostly small talk, Bill asked about something that had obviously been on his mind for a long time.

"You know, it's been—what?—thirteen years since we talked at length about anything serious. Our annual news letters tell us about our families, our practices, our vacations, but not about what's going on in our lives. I know I've asked you before, but now that I can look at you . . . well, I've always wondered what ever happened with those herbs that you concocted—the ones I sent back to you in '97. You never did fill me in on their disposition. I asked you a couple of times in e-mails and then dropped it when you didn't respond. But this time I want to hear all about it."

I was a little stunned that the leaves discussion was brought up so soon, and I was unprepared, unwilling even, to discuss it right now. I, too, had questions about them that had been building up over the years, but I didn't feel I could broach the topic all at once like that.

"You mean to tell me that's been on your mind for thirteen years? I'd of thought you would have forgotten about that by now," I said, hoping I could change the subject, which I did. "Okay, yes, but first, what's our schedule for the reunion? What have you got me signed up for?"

Bill sighed, giving me the benefit of the doubt and not wanting to make me any more uncomfortable than he already seemed to have done by raising the subject of the leaves so soon after my arrival. He told me about our agenda.

"There's a general reception tomorrow night, some presentations Friday morning—that I don't want to go to—then Saturday there's the football game in the afternoon, and dinner that evening for the twenty-five-year reunion folks. That's probably where we'll see all our old classmates. The rest of the time it's just you and me, so I've taken the liberty of setting up a meeting with someone Friday morning that you and I still need to talk about."

211

"What kind of a meeting is that?" I asked.

"It's about those leaves. Will you go?" he asked me with a pleading look in his eyes.

I was quiet for a while, and I knew I had a distant look on my face that I might have frightened Bill. I was trying to gather my thoughts from earlier that summer about this inevitable conversation.

Finally I said, "You're right, it's time I told you what happened with those cursed—or blessed—tea leaves, but not right now, okay?"

We left it at that and went to bed early. I was feeling the effects of jet lag and needed to rest before getting into anything as heavy as the tea leaf discussion.

*   *   *

Lenore had errands to run on Thursday, so she left the two of us alone to do what we wanted for the entire day. I still didn't want to talk about the leaves that morning, so I asked if we could go on a brief tour of the campus. I hadn't been back in years and was anxious to see what changes had taken place in Ann Arbor. I wanted to believe, like most alumni, that Ann Arbor would never change. But change was as inevitable as that discussion I would soon have with Bill.

After breakfast at Angelo's we walked down Ann Street to the new Med Sci buildings.

"Unbelievable!" I said. "What was here before all these new buildings went up? I can't picture it. And the new stadium—is that a monstrosity or what?"

"Lots of changes since you were here last, but it's still the same Ann Arbor. How do you like the new hospital complex? It's a lot bigger now than when we did our residencies," Bill said.

"Hey, look over there," I said, pointing up the street to the observatory. "I'm glad the old Detroit observatory is still around. Do they still use it?"

"I doubt it. It's probably just a museum now or a storage facility," Bill said.

We were smiling broadly as old alums are wont to do, coming back for their reunions. We walked toward the diag and checked out the stores on State Street. All we could talk about was the old days in the eighties when we were students and what we did at this place or that place. For lunch we headed over to Dominick's for tuna subs in the garden, only to find out the garden area was closed to the general public. So we took our sandwiches and went over to the Bus Ad school plaza to eat outside and finally talk about my tea leaves.

"Are the sandwiches as good as you remember?" Bill asked me.

"Not really, but then again, nothing is as good as you remember it, is it?" I said philosophically.

We sat and ate in silence; we were talked out about everything small and everything fun. I finally felt composed enough to tell my story about the tea.

"I'm not sure where to start. I guess the best place is back in Denpasar when I got that call from your patient, Joe Gilbert. In fact, I did talk with him earlier this year, but that's another story."

Bill gave me a startled look when I told him I had spoken with Joe Gilbert recently. I filled him in about the call and told him what had happened. I then continued my story.

"When Joe called thirteen years ago, I remembered that I was very busy, and from what he told me, I thought he might need something for nausea caused by his cancer and the pain pills you prescribed." I then explained to Bill how I asked my tech to put together a mixture of some relatively standard herbs that we used for the treatment of cancer-related nausea. I was surprised later when my tech handed me such a large bag—we usually didn't give out that much at one time because they should be freshly prepared. I told Bill how I went over personally to give Joe the leaves because I wanted to hear about you, and I was a little disappointed when I found out that he really didn't know you. Bill smiled over that last comment, and when I said, "But he and his wife were pleasant, and it's always nice talking to people from Ann Arbor," he nodded while still smiling.

I then hesitated, concentrating very hard on how to continue. I thought Bill saw how serious I looked and became a little concerned, but he didn't say anything. I looked right at him and said, "I was surprised to hear from you about a month later—I think it was around a month or so—telling me you were sending the leaves back to me. You told me that the tea we mixed somehow caused a bunch of people to be cured from various incurable ailments. I thought you were nuts." I was smiling again, and Bill relaxed.

"You thought I was nuts? Wait till you meet this guy tomorrow, and then you can tell me who's nuts," Bill said.

"No, no . . . I know that you weren't nuts, because the day I got them back I was on my way to one of my village clinics, and there was an older man, who also happened to be diagnosed with pancreatic cancer, that I was going to visit. I planned on treating his pain and discomfort as much as I possibly could. After you told me about Joe's remission and the other supposedly cured patients, I took some of those tea leaves with me on that visit. I didn't expect much from them because they weren't very fresh, but I gave some to the old man anyway. I also treated him with some standard medications for his general pain and instructed his family on how to care for him."

"Did he respond to the tea leaves?" Bill asked.

"When I went back the following week, I couldn't believe it—he was jaundice free and said he felt great. I took blood samples back, and as far as we could tell, he was cancer free. Of course we didn't do any CT scans on him, but when he died at around age ninety-seven about three years ago, it wasn't from cancer. But he was just the start of it." Again I stopped briefly to think about what I wanted to tell my friend. Bill sat there, quietly waiting to hear the rest of the story.

"I can't tell you how many others I treated—maybe it was as many as two dozen—and watched as they almost instantaneously got well. One cup of tea and that was it. Even stranger in some sense, the leaves still seemed fresh. They didn't feel dried out like they should have been after that long. I felt I had to replicate the mixture. I was certain that I found the cure for most, if not all, of mankind's illnesses." Here again I waited, looking into my friends eyes, and then said, "Can you imagine how I, as a doctor, would feel if that was true, Bill?"

"I really can't imagine, Seti, but go on. What happened after that?" he said, referring to me by my old college nickname.

"The bag was getting depleted, because I would always leave some with the patients' families when they left the clinic. I called my herbal tech in and asked him if he could look up what mixture he had prepared. I thought he would pull out his log book for that date and just tell me what mixture he had assembled from all the variations we have for nausea in our formulary. But instead he told me that he blew it. He was in a rush that day, got started on one mixture, got called away, and lost his place. So he started over with another mixture we used for essentially the same symptoms, and that's what he gave me. That's why the bag was so big—it was almost a whole pound of product. He had no way of knowing which herbs finally ended up in the bag, or in what proportions they were mixed. He knew that he hadn't prepared anything harmful since he was familiar with all the herbs we kept.

He was all apologetic about it and was certain the double mixture would work. I told him not to worry but asked him to try and replicate it for me if he could."

"Did you try to analyze them? You had a mass spec setup back then, didn't you?" Bill asked.

"Yes, of course we did, but you know that for organic substances mass spec analysis is not very specific—especially thirteen years ago. The computers were not nearly as sophisticated as they are today. Today we have a library of literally hundreds of thousands of organic compounds to compare with, but not back then. All I found out was that some general non-alkaloids were present. In herbs we know that it's not just the so-called active elements that lead to successful treatment, but the inactive ones as well."

"So you're saying you didn't know exactly what was in there?" Bill said.

"That's right. We keep around three hundred various plant leaves, roots, and stems, and any one formula can have upward of twelve different substances in various proportions mixed together. The odds of us figuring out exactly which twelve—or probably even more—plants we used and in what proportions were astronomical. It was then that I realized what I had to do." I stopped talking, looked right into my friend's eyes, and said, "I had to destroy the rest of the package." I felt a little strange not saying that my grandmother told me to do that, but I knew if I did, Bill would not understand why I would listen to some superstitious old lady rather than continue using them until they were all gone.

"You destroyed them?!" Bill said. "But you could have saved more lives. Why would you do that?" It was that comment that convinced me I could never tell Bill why I incinerated the leaves.

"Stop right there . . . just stop. Don't you think I've asked myself that question a million times or more?" I was looking up to the sky, shaken by my recollection of how I disposed of the leaves. "Basically, I did not want to play God. I did not want to have to choose who should live and who should die. Can't you understand that?" I said, feeling emotionally racked over the incident.

I didn't feel the need to explain any more to him. I didn't want to tell him that that was why I never filled him in on the final outcome. I knew he would have difficulty understanding anything I would try to explain over e-mail or over the telephone, so I just ignored his inquiries. We left it at that and didn't discuss the leaves anymore the rest of the day.

*   *   *

The conversations at the general reception that night were informal and lighthearted, as would be expected in that kind of setting. The reception was one of those champagne-and-hors d'oeuvres affairs held in the new Museum of Art, and the place was so packed that we had difficulty finding any of our other classmates. There were ten different reunion years represented there, plus the reunion group of fifty or more years was also in attendance. It was one of those mass gatherings where there seems to be lots of hugging, general greetings, and "I'll see you at the dinner" or "See you at the game" remarks. We did see a few from our class, and it was fun talking with them. They all looked so prosperous and elegantly dressed, as I expected them to be. We got home late and didn't talk about anything of substance that night.

The next morning Bill reminded me about our meeting and asked if I was still willing to go.

"You say this guy is a Greek Orthodox priest, and he was the one who gave you the leaves. How did he get them . . . wait! Is his name Pavlos or something like that?" I asked.

"As a matter of fact, it is! How do you know him?" Bill asked.

I then told him about the priest's call to me shortly after I destroyed the leaves. Bill said that he hadn't known that I talked with him and was a bit surprised to find that out.

I told Bill, "I was still pretty upset when this priest called me asking for the recipe. I couldn't help but think what a nervy person he was. Is this the priest you want me to see?"

"Yes, it is, but I think you should hear him out now. You didn't answer me—are you still willing to meet with him?" Bill asked me.

"Yeah, why not, let's do this. I very much want to meet him and ask him how he got the nerve to ask me for the recipe for the elixir of life," I said with a pompous smile on my face.

As a matter of fact, I was indeed anxious to talk with the priest. I wanted to know how his patients—or I guess you might say charges—in the United States were doing. What other life experiences had they had? Were their diseases still in check? And most important, did they have auras about them that only he could see? I wasn't sure how I'd bring up that last topic; I planned on just playing it by ear.

CHAPTER 25

Father Pavlos

It was around 11:00 a.m. when the two doctors walked into my office at Saint Demetrios. I was now the senior priest, and I have a large, nicely appointed office in this relatively small but magnificent old church.

"Can I get you something to drink, some coffee or tea?" I asked them. They shook their heads.

"And how are you, Dr. Kahn? So nice finally meeting you in person. And this must be Dr. Setiawan. So nice to finally meet you too," I said as I motioned for them to sit at the conference table with me. "I recall talking with your patient, Mr. Gilbert, when he said that you would return the leaves to Dr. Setiawan," I told Dr. Kahn. "I'm so glad you did, and I can't wait to hear what happened to them." I was talking to both of them, but then I turned and looked right at Dr. Setiawan. "I don't know if you recall, but I did call you to inquire about getting some of the leaves. Do you remember? Were you able to make more packages of the mixture? Did they have any, er . . . mystical characteristics?" I couldn't wait any longer to find out about the herbs.

Setiawan then told me the story he had related to Dr. Kahn the day before, even the part about why he destroyed the leaves.

"And what about the other users who had them here in the States?" Setiawan asked me. "All I know is that they were cured of supposedly incurable illnesses too. Is that true?"

I related all the stories, referring briefly at times to my T file that I had left opened in front of me. They seemed surprised that I followed up over the years after my initial meetings with all the individuals involved. I even told them the part about how had I misremembered one of the recipient's names in a criminal investigation, and how the wrong name turned out to be the real criminal's name. I said how I felt there must have been more to the leaves than just medicine—something supernatural.

217

"Let me see if I have this straight. The first person treated was Joe Gilbert, and we know that he actually made tea with them just like I prescribed. The second person smoked the leaves like marijuana; the third breathed their fumes thinking they were incense; and the fourth and fifth contacts merely touched them, and one of them merely put them on his bandaged chest. Is that right, Father Pavlos?" Setiawan asked.

"Well, yes, now that you mention it. I guess I never really thought about the method by which they were administered," I said. "Do you think that's important?"

"In order for a medicine to be effective it has to enter the body's circulatory system in some form. Injection or ingestion are the most common forms, but inhalation also works—not always as effective, but it will work," Setiawan explained to me. "However, coming in contact through touching is probably the least effective way, unless, of course, it's a cream or other topical agent that the body can absorb through the skin. But I know of no medicine, especially in raw herbal form, that is effective in all four ways of entering the body. I just find that curious. In Indonesia I always administered the herbs as tea."

There was silence while we all considered Setiawan's observation, and then he added, "It would seem to me that such a material is unlike any medicinal agent I have ever seen. It makes me think that the healing was caused by something that was not based on known pharmaceutical principles. And what that other process might be, I can only wonder."

I knew he was thinking that the other process had to be unearthly.

We were again quiet for a while, and then I said, "I never told anyone this, but the weekend before I gave Mr. Gilbert the leaves to return to you, Dr. Kahn, I put some in the censer during the church service on Sunday. And like you, Dr. Setiawan, I realized that in some way I, too, was playing God. I never found out—nor did I really try to—if anyone was impacted by that selfish act of mine. So, like you, I destroyed them, or rather sent them to you to do what you saw fit."

I told Dr. Setiawan how, after I found out that they were returned, my ambition began to get the best of me. That was when I called him asking for the formula. I apologized to him for being so presumptuous that he would just send me the recipe, not even knowing who I was or what I had intended to do with the leaves.

"I'm glad you destroyed them," I told him. "It was the morally right thing to do, don't you think?"

Dr. Setiawan wholeheartedly agreed with me that destroying them had been the appropriate way to go. Then he asked me if I had noticed anything different about the recipients. He explained that the few patients he had seen later in their lives had had an aura about them; he wanted to know if I had seen that too. I assumed he didn't necessarily mean a physical aura but more of a sense of serenity and peace with themselves, and I told him I did notice that. He seemed pleased to hear that and to know that the leaves' initial response was still active after only one administration more than thirteen years ago.

After a little more talk of a relatively lighter nature, and since we had exhausted the question about what was the morally right thing to do with the leaves, the conversation more or less ended. There was a general feeling of incompleteness when the two doctors left the church. I sat there for a long time after they left, thinking about what had just happened, and was as confounded as ever over exactly what the leaves were and why I had received them to minister as I saw fit. I hadn't asked Dr. Setiawan if the people he treated were in some sense special—as a doctor, I doubt if he would understand what I was asking. But there was no doubt in my mind now that the leaves were heaven-sent—for what purpose, I was still not sure. But I was just as certain that someday, maybe not in this lifetime, my Lord would tell me.

CHAPTER 26

Wayan Setiawan

Bill and I left the church well after noon, but we weren't hungry yet, and I declined getting something to eat. At first we were quiet in Bill's car on the way back to Ann Arbor, but then I broke the silence.

"You don't think that's right, do you, Bill?" I asked.

"What?" he asked, although he knew exactly what I was asking.

"Destroying the leaves—you don't think I should have done that, do you?"

"I don't know what to think. When Joe Gilbert asked me to get them back to you, he just sketched out what Father Pavlos told us today in detail. I had never had the full story before. If I had really known their full power, I don't know what I would have done. I know one thing—I would have pressed you harder on filling me in as to their disposition than I did."

"But you would still have sent them back to me, you're saying?"

"Of course—why, do you think I would have kept them?" Bill asked with some indignation.

"We're both healers—you may practice surgical oncology and I may practice general medicine, but we're both healers. Why wouldn't you have kept them if you knew they would heal?"

"I don't know . . . I don't know. I'm confused by all this morality business. I'm not a religious man, you know that, but I do believe I'm a moral man. This whole incident had me puzzled from the beginning, and I guess I was hoping that you could resolve it for me—that your sense of righteousness, which I always admired, would tell you the right thing to do. What I guessed, and didn't expect, was for you to tell me that you destroyed them once you knew their efficacy. But now after hearing the priest, I don't know."

After we got back to Ann Arbor, Bill said, "Remember that little bar on Liberty? Why don't we stop there for a drink?"

"The one on the other side of Main Street? Sure, let's do it." I was pleased to drop the subject and continue to enjoy my Ann Arbor visit, but the thought of drinking on an empty stomach was not exactly what I had envisioned, even though I had passed up the chance for lunch earlier.

Bill parked the car in a lot, and we walked over to the bar.

"I don't remember this area looking so upscale," I said.

"Yeah, some things do change, and Ann Arbor's downtown is one of them."

We sat at a booth. The bar wasn't that crowded in the early afternoon on a Friday. We were quiet for a while and just making small talk about the changes in Ann Arbor, but we couldn't help getting back to the topic of the leaves.

"What do you think it's all about?" I said.

Bill shook his head and then asked me to briefly repeat the part about my tech and how he mixed up the formulas. He was still curious as to why we couldn't replicate the mixture.

I retold Bill the story, adding, "As I've said, trying to repeat the exact mix would have been impossible. I weighed the package, and it was exactly four hundred grams. We usually give out somewhere between two hundred and two fifty grams—"

"Four hundred—that's tav, the Hebrew equivalent of T. It has a numerical value of four hundred, the highest value of all the Hebrew letters. It's also the last letter in the Hebrew alphabet," Bill said to me in sort of a daydreamy fashion.

I looked at him, a little surprised. "And that's supposed to mean what?" I asked.

"I don't know, I'm just mumbling. I guess I'm also looking for something mystical in the leaves, so I'm grasping at straws; and when you said four hundred, my ancient Hebrew School lessons popped in my head." After a brief period of silence, he said, "I just recalled the fact that the Kabbalists read all kinds of things into letters and numbers, so tav, or T—and didn't the priest mention tau and other forms of the letter T in his so-called T file—who knows . . ."

Bill was quiet and stopped talking about mysticism and got back to science. I had noticed the priest's T file, too, and thought of my own Tea file. I couldn't help but think that it must be more than coincidence, but I didn't comment on it. I knew Bill was in science mode now, and I didn't want to mess with his line of reasoning, so I remained silent on the matter.

I was explaining how statistically impossible it would be for me to reformulate the mixture again, when Bill once again became wistful. "You know I was a physics major as an undergrad and learned that the only Hebrew letter used universally in scientific notation was aleph, the first letter of the Hebrew alphabet."

"Yes, that's right, aleph-null and all the other aleph orders of infinity," I added.

"But later I had heard that some Israeli scientists were using tav as the symbol for stasis, or steady state—that place of equilibrium, where all forces are balanced against each other, essentially keeping things from drastically going haywire."

"And your point now is?" I said.

"I'm not sure if I have a point," Bill said in an exasperated manner. "But do you think that the universe is in some sense at a steady state? I mean, given all the massive violent forces of biblical proportions at work—black holes, dark matter, and other cosmic events—don't you still get a sense of underlying stability that the whole thing won't just blow up. But by the same token there's always a chance that some singularity, some strange and unlikely event, could occur that would change everything forever."

"You mean like us discovering the secret of immortality—or simply the fruit from the tree of life?" I answered almost jokingly.

"Yes, exactly something like that. Wouldn't that completely and unalterably change the dynamics of the universe? Can you imagine how that would impact the world? Or essentially having the knowledge that we could make ourselves immortal, or at least disease free—would that be enough to change the world?"

"If I'm getting your gist, then you do think that Father Pavlos was right when he said that destroying the leaves was the morally right thing to do?" I asked.

"You know we doctors get blamed enough for playing God. Had you kept those leaves and found the secret formula, well that would have settled it once and for all. I guess destroying them was the right thing to do, because after all, we are not gods."

We ordered more drinks and some sandwiches to help absorb the alcohol and continued our talk along religious—or mystical—rather than a scientific path.

"In Bali most of us who were born there are not members of any Western-styled organized religion. Yes, many of us call ourselves Christians or Muslims, but most of us are Hindi, and many of us follow the teachings of Buddha who was not a god, and he didn't accept the concept of one god. It also makes it easy when someone asks me my religion. I say I'm a Buddhist, but my ancestors made offerings to many gods. When I began to study Judeo-Christian practices, I couldn't help but notice the multi-god theme in your Old Testament."

"What are you talking about? Judaism has always been a monotheistic religion. What multi-god theme are you alluding to?" Bill asked.

"C'mon, you must have read Exodus? What's the first commandment? Isn't it about placing no other gods before me?"

Bill was about to jump in with an explanation, but I cut him short, saying, "No, it's not just referring to golden calves and other such idols. It's an admission that other gods exist, or at least existed at one time. And that famous part in Exodus that both Jews and Christians love to quote for different reasons, about the Jews being the chosen people—if I read it right, it seems to me that God said to Moses something like, 'Since you've chosen me to be your God, then I choose you to spread my word to all nations.' Chosen me? From what draft pool did your ancestors choose your God from? Enough, let's be honest most, if not all, religions initially believed in many gods."

"And what's your point?" Bill said. Both of us were a little high by now and were actually enjoying the discussion, like we had so many times before when we were in school. All the cross-cultural dialogues we had were coming back now.

"My point is that the so-called singularity you were referring to may not be God driven but the result of other deities playing out their hand. That's my point," I said, feeling quite self-satisfied with myself.

"Well, then I guess you did the right thing after all by destroying the devil's cursed potion," Bill said sarcastically as he finished his drink.

"Maybe I just chopped down the beanstalk like Jack did," I said with a smile. The story about Jack was actually an allegory about someone who received some magic beans that grew a stairway to heaven for him. He was able to go up there and come away richer for the experience, but also fearful of its full consequences. He had to give up his chance for immortality by destroying the passageway. I then chided my friend, saying, "'Devil's cursed potion—don't be so dramatic, doctor."

*   *   *

The dinner at a nice restaurant on Saturday night after the game was very pleasant. There were only about eighty alumni and their guests there, so it wasn't an unmanageable group. We got to see lots of old colleagues, talk medicine, and recall famous discussions with ancient faculty, many of whom were no longer around. I, in some sense, felt that maybe I was the center of attention. That was probably because I came from the farthest place, or maybe Americans still thought that Indonesia was some exotic paradise. But I enjoyed all the attention.

"Not too many fat old farts here, except for you and Bill," Lenore said to me.

"They look great. They do really look good. I'm glad I came, but I look forward to going home—though I dread that damn long flight back. I miss my wife and kids, and even though it's only been a very long weekend, I miss my practice. You know I practice seven days a week," I told them, "and I miss not seeing my patients."

Bill looked at me and smiled. "I'm going to miss you, old friend, but with Skype, e-mail, and even 4G phones now, let's stay in closer contact this time. If that singularity happens again, I want to be in on it with you."

"What singularity are you boys talking about? Did I miss anything this weekend?" Lenore asked.

"Nothing important—just the chance for immortality, that's all," I said as I smiled lovingly at both of them. "But fortunately for the universe, the steady state prevailed."

*   *   *

I left Ann Arbor convinced that the ancient gods and spirits on Bali had somehow been embedded in those leaves, and it was those phantoms that had cured my patients and Father Pavlos's charges. I was also somewhat convinced that, even after all the talk of Hebrew mysticism that buttressed my arguments, my dear friend Bill Kahn thought all the cures were in the chemistry. He knew that new miracle drugs, like penicillin and insulin that cured diseases and prolonged life, were found all the time, but that did not make us immortal. I thought he felt that if we had the leaves today, we could reproduce them and get the same results. I also knew that Father Pavlos was certain that the leaves were healing vessels through the compassion of Christ.

Whatever they were and whoever was right, I felt truly blessed that they passed my way for a time and I was able to do some good before sending them back to their original home with the spirits in the sea. My grandmother would be very proud of me. I would never have disappointed her by trying to do something that neither one of us would have done—which would have been to take advantage of the spirits' accidental presence here on earth for a short period of time.

CHAPTER 27

Father Pavlos

I had just finished talking with my recipients of the leaves once again, touching base to wish them a reflective and peaceful Thanksgiving. They were all doing well in their expected new ventures: Joe's new company and Gabriella's orphanage project; Maria Elena's son; Connie's future college career in human services and grandchildren; and Mitch's new family life with Cheryl. Even Gerry's promotion and enormous new responsibilities seemed to fit the mold. I couldn't help but notice the thread of new life entering into all their lives and how grand that was. Yet any one of those ventures could easily have ended up being a major tragedy or life-ending disaster—especially for Maria Elena and Connie, who had both thought of committing suicide. Even Mitch had been faced with total devastation at the prospect of losing Cheryl. But it all worked out in the end, and it was a joy to know that their healing was not without purpose since they had all gone on to do, what I would call, the Lord's work.

When I met with Dr. Kahn later in November—at my request—he filled me in on the conversations he had had over the reunion weekend with Dr. Setiawan. I was fascinated by their take on the scientific elements of the leaves' position in the universe, as well as their various sacred, and not so sacred, interpretations of the healings.

In a sense I was bothered by all this, since I was certain that they—the leaves—were just another of our Lord's various manifestations over the centuries—the numerous recordings of his compassion for the physically and spiritually ill and his desire to heal the common people afflicted. But to some extent I was also disappointed to realize that I wasn't the only one who had been chosen to be the conduit for that healing. I think that also my ambition for a higher calling might have clouded my judgment, and I was truly repentant for that, just as I was for having thoughtlessly put some leaves in the censer so many years before.

I thought it best that I tried to remember the people who were healed or cured by something—pantheism, medical chemistry, or God's will. I recalled that at first I relied on scripture to guide me as I went looking for the clues as to why these people were selected by our Lord. Not really finding any, I had to accept the fact that this was another of His mysteries. And whether or not God shone his countenance on them and chose me to somehow get the leaves back to Indonesia (for whatever reason) was not, and maybe never be, for me to know. Could the Garden of Eden, as some scholars believed, have actually been in Bali, Indonesia? And if it was, was the tree of life still there? Speculation, all is speculation—so many interpretations, and who was to say which one was right.

And so that is where I am at now, accepting and believing. I have put away my T file once again, and if for some reason our Lord has nobler plans for my future, then I will accept that with grace. But in the long run I can only pray that I, too, will do no harm.

23331690R00141

Made in the USA
Lexington, KY
08 June 2013